FINDING JUSTICE

A STEALTH OPS NOVEL

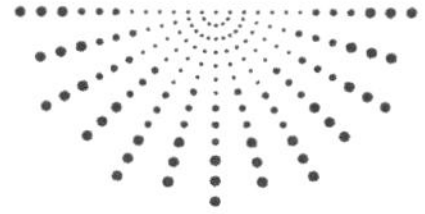

BRITTNEY SAHIN

EMKO MEDIA

Finding Justice

By: Brittney Sahin

Published by: EmKo Media, LLC

Editor: Carol, WordsRU.com

Editor: Anja, HourGlass Editing

Proofreader: Judy Zweifel, Judy's Proofreading

Cover Design: LJ, Mayhem Cover Creations

Paperback ISBN: 9781728922676

❀ Created with Vellum

To our veterans.

PROLOGUE: RECRUITMENT

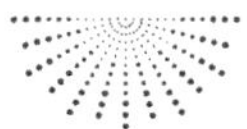

"IF YOU'RE HERE I MUST BE IN HEAVEN." OWEN SQUINTED, the harsh light too bright in his eyes as he observed his old SEAL friend Luke Scott standing alongside him. "But you're not dead, and so . . ."

A smile stretched Luke's mouth, and he left his side and killed the lights.

"Thanks," he mumbled, preferring the sunlight coming through the window to one of man's worst inventions—fluorescent bulbs. "What happened to me?"

Luke returned to his bedside. "Your helmet came off during the blast, and you got yourself a concussion. Doc says you'll be fine."

That explained the slightly shrill noise, like a ringtone buzzing in his ears. "A woman was on the porch when we went for the extraction . . . she was strapped with a vest, right?" After that, everything went black.

"Yeah. Sorry, man."

After losing his brother five years ago in the same damn city in Iraq, he couldn't believe he nearly died there, too. "My men? Are they okay?"

"CO said they're good."

Owen tried to sit, but Luke shook his head, and so, he relaxed onto the bed. "The HVT?"

"I can't confirm, but it doesn't look like he was ever inside the house."

"Knew it was a damn trap." Owen closed his eyes, his stomach shaky. "What are you doing here?"

"What? I can't visit a friend who got hurt?"

Owen opened his eyes and shot him a pointed look. "I heard whispers of your retirement, but since you're at a military hospital, I'm guessing those were rumors."

Luke had been on Team Three with him up until two years ago when he was pretty sure DEVGRU, or Team Six, had recruited him.

"He did retire. Well, sort of." It was a woman's voice.

He studied the gorgeous blonde sitting to his left. How had he not noticed her? He blinked and shook his head as if that would dispel the head-detached-from-body feeling he had going on right now.

He narrowed his eyes, catching her long legs cross, then dragged his gaze up to her face. "Aw, you brought me a gift."

"Watch it," Luke said. "She's my sister."

"Now I see why you never showed any of the guys on base her picture."

"Didn't want to have to kill anyone for—"

"Luke . . ." Even in Owen's foggy state, he could hear the clipped warning in Luke's sister's tone. "I'm Jessica."

"I'd say it's nice to meet you, but until I know why you're here . . ." He clasped his hands atop his chest and burrowed the back of his head deeper into the not-so-fluffy pillow.

His stomach tucked as a sudden wave of nausea hit him. *Damn concussion.*

Jessica looked at Luke. "Do you want to enlighten him as

to why we're here, or do you want me to?"

"Did someone die?" Owen nervously asked.

"No, no one died."

Luke's words afforded Owen the chance to take a breath, and a pinch of lucidity flowed through his mind. "How'd you get her in here, by the way?"

Luke folded his arms, his biceps still the size of tanks. "She's government." There was a definite bite to his voice.

"Guessing this is news to you?" Owen pressed his palms alongside his body to sit. Sister or not, if Luke brought a government official with him, he was about to be leveled by something serious.

"Easy." She was on her feet and pressing a palm to his shoulder, urging him back down. He swerved his gaze up to her blue eyes and settled his head back onto the pillow.

"She dropped the bomb on me a few weeks ago about her place of employment."

"And what are you about to drop on me now?" Owen coughed into a closed fist, his stomach muscles tightening.

Luke scratched at the blond stubble on his jaw, his cheeks inflating a touch as if the tension in the room had been magnified.

What was he afraid to say, or ask?

"The suspense is killing me, man, and I can't afford to take any more hits. The suicide bomber nearly put me six feet under, so—"

"I'm here to recruit you," Luke cut him off, and it had Owen's clenched fists atop his abdomen relaxing.

"Say what?" Owen arched a brow and touched his forehead to find a bandage above his left eye.

Luke's Adam's apple became visible as he swallowed. "The president asked me to co-lead a covert team of SEALs with Jessica. I know this is shit timing, and I hadn't expected to find you laid up in bed when I got here, but the clock is sort of ticking. POTUS wants a team assembled as of yesterday."

Luke's words had Owen dropping his eyes to the white blanket covering most of his body. "Did I hear you correctly, or are the drugs screwing with my head?" Owen closed and opened his eyes to ensure he was actually awake.

"This is legit. You'll still technically be a SEAL, but for all intents and purposes it'll appear to the outside world as if you've retired," Luke explained.

"I'm leaving the CIA for this gig," Jessica noted.

CIA? Figures. "And what's different about this team opposed to what I'm already doing?" His gaze drifted lazily skyward.

"To put it plainly," Jessica started, "there are certain missions the president needs off-the-books."

"Aren't we already fairly off-the-books?"

"Redacted documents still leave a trail," Jessica answered. "We wouldn't even exist in the government system."

"So, if shit gets hairy we'll be up the creek without a paddle." A quick smile met Owen's lips.

"Pretty much," Luke commented. "But you're always the guy up for an adventure." He rounded the bed and stood next to his sister. Maybe he finally realized the back and forth head movements weren't great for a guy waking up after an explosion. "The thing is, I need you to be comfortable with lying to everyone about what we do."

"We do that now." Owen shrugged, but lifting his shoulders was a bad idea. Pain flowed down his spine and into his damn tailbone.

"Yeah, but we'll be operating everywhere around the globe, even in the U.S.," Jessica said. "We'll be working under an alias—Scott & Scott Securities, so if we stumble across the press or Feds—we'll have some type of rationale for our work, so we don't expose the truth."

"Man, and here I thought you'd call it Scott & York." He slipped a quick grin to his face. "So, anything else I should know?"

"You can keep the tavern your family turned over to you in Charleston, that's no issue. It actually might help with the cover story." She glanced at her brother out of her peripheral view. "We'll have to take some legit jobs for our alias to keep up appearances, as well. This means you'll work with some retired SEALs. They can't know the truth, though, and that can be a hard pill to swallow."

He didn't like lying, but he said, "I understand. I might need some time to think about this." He didn't want to leave his platoon, but he also liked a challenge.

"We could really use a man like you on the team." Luke tucked his hands into his jeans pockets.

This shit is real, isn't it? "Sounds like you assume I'd say *yes,* or you wouldn't be so candid."

Luke half-shrugged. "I hate stealing our best people from the Teams, but, thankfully, I only need to steal nine. You're one of those nine. Plus, you saved my ass big-time three years ago, and it'd be nice to work with you again."

"I almost forgot about that." Jessica folded her arms across her silky blue blouse. "You guys lost both your pilots on an op, and you flew the team out, right?"

Owen nodded.

She dropped her head a little as if pained by the memory. "It was CIA intel that sent you guys on that op. ISR didn't detect the mujs hiding there. Sorry."

"Lead-lined bunkers, so it wasn't anyone's fault." He was quiet for a moment. "But, damn, woman, you really were deep in our shit, and *you*"—he pointed to Luke—"didn't know this?"

Luke rolled his eyes. "Don't remind me."

"Well, your experience as a Naval pilot before being a Teamguy could come in handy. You trained with both jets and helos, huh?" She released a soft breath. "Why'd you switch from being a pilot to a SEAL?"

The memory of his loss fastened tight around his heart. "My brother." But he had a feeling she knew that, and maybe she wanted to bring up the topic to see if it was an issue for him. Maybe this was also an interview . . .

Silence punctuated the room for a few minutes before she cleared her throat. "If you accept this role, you won't be able to go after his killer."

"It's not like I'm allowed to here, either." A taste of anger at that fact rolled around the back of his throat, and he tried to swallow it and move on. Well, move on for the moment, at least.

"Command has concerns about your past interfering with this new role." She was direct and to the point, he'd give her that.

"Jessica," Luke hissed.

"He should know the truth."

"And I disagree with Command on that. *And* I'll fight like hell to include Owen on every op, regardless of the target."

Owen sat upright, to hell with the drugs and pain. "You saying there's a chance we might be able to find my brother's killer?" His eyes darted back and forth between the two of them.

"I promise I'll do whatever I can to bring him to justice." Luke's jaw became hard-set, and his blue eyes thinned. "You have my word."

"Then I'm in."

CHAPTER ONE

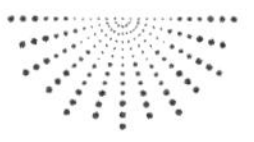

New York City
Five and a Half Years Later

Owen snapped his gloves together, eying Asher in the boxing ring.

Asher lowered his fists and winked. "Come on, princess. Is that all you got?"

Owen raised his leg in the air and brought it down, straight like an axe, onto Asher's leg and then shifted on the ball of his foot upon landing and caught him across the jaw with a right hook.

Asher shook it off and grinned. "Better." He motioned for him to come at him again.

Owen attacked with jabs and uppercuts, but Asher deftly blocked each one of his moves and then wrapped his arms around him in a cinch position.

"Aww, are you boys hugging?" Jess rested her wrists on the rope that circled their makeshift fighting area and flashed a smile.

"You want to swap with him? I'd be happy to teach you a few moves." Asher released his hold on Owen, but Owen caught him with an elbow to the chin in the process. "Fucker." Asher half-laughed.

Owen ducked Asher's next swing and swiped his leg to bring him down.

Asher's body smacked the ground with a heavy thud, and another smirk found his lips. "Finally got the drop on me, man. Won't happen again."

Owen may have been a decent fighter, but Asher was practically a pro.

"So, Peaches, you want me to teach you, or what?" Asher shoved upright, his attention focused on Jess.

"I don't need lessons from a caveman like you. I'm capable of defending myself, but thanks."

"Sure, honey. You keep telling yourself that." He directed his gaze back to Owen and raised his guard.

Owen was ready to let loose again, to alleviate some of his stress, but before he could swing, he caught Jess tilting her head to the side, her quiet way of saying *we need to talk.* "Give me a minute."

He lifted the rope, ducked under, and started after her while removing his gloves.

"Can we chat in my office?" She stopped in front of the private elevator and faced him.

He tossed his gloves on a nearby chair. "You want me up in your swanky office like this?" He thought about their admin who always sat coyly behind her desk whenever the guys were in the office.

A grin teased her lips as she observed his sweaty and bare chest. "Tyra would have a heart attack."

He propped a hand on the wall over her shoulder and angled his head. "You okay?" His eyes thinned as he studied the woman who had become like a sister to him over the years.

Her blues traveled over his shoulder, and he followed her gaze to where Asher banged out burpees in the middle of the fighting ring.

Owen cleared his throat and fought a smile. "You two should get it out of your systems, and soon, it'd be better for all of us."

The muted red of her shirt now matched her cheeks. "Are you nuts? He drives me crazy."

"And your brother would kill him if he touched you, but why let that stop you?" He dropped his hand from the wall when the elevator doors opened.

"I don't want . . ." She shook her head. "Can we just talk upstairs?"

"With or without the shirt?"

She rolled her eyes and *tsked.* "Get cleaned up first."

He waited for her to disappear behind the closed elevator doors before heading back to Asher. "I'm being summoned. We'll have to pick this up later."

"I wonder if she'll ever get that stick removed from her ass."

I'm sure you'd like to be the one to do it. Owen bit back his thought, though. He wondered if Luke purposefully ignored the tension that pounded the room whenever his sis and Asher were together. They really were going to either kill each other one day—or tear each other's clothes off.

"So, what does Boss Lady want with you?" He shoved a hand through his dark hair before reaching for his gloves on the floor.

"I don't know, but it can't be about an op."

"She requested both of us to fly in yesterday, so what else

could it be about?" Asher crossed his tatted arms and eyed him. "Luke's still on vacation with Eva, right?"

Owen nodded. He still couldn't believe his boss had fallen in love. He broke the rule of *no commitments allowed* Luke himself had made mandatory after their only married teammate died on an op.

Guess the rule was null and void now.

"Maybe she needs us on one of her school-boy missions," Asher said as they went into the men's locker room. The entire gym was for their team and only their team. No one in the Manhattan sky rise was aware of its existence.

"'School-boy missions.' Is that what you're calling them these days?" Owen turned on the shower.

The cases they took on under the Scott & Scott Securities alias could still get dangerous, but maybe Asher was right—compared to what they did on the DL for the president those ops were like a walk in the park. A dark park with shadowy motherfuckers hiding, but still.

"Well, she didn't request your ass up in her office. So, maybe she just brought you in to release some tension?"

Asher's dark brown eyes caught Owen's in the reflection of the mirror as he braced against the vanity counter. "Fuck you."

"Pretty sure it's not me you want to screw. Well, it'd sure as hell better not be."

"You want to get back in the ring so I can show you how easy I've been taking it on you?"

"Right. You're as old as me. Those days are almost over."

Asher shook his head. "Speak for yourself. Thirty-seven is looking to be my best year yet. I'm getting better with age."

"Sure, buddy." Owen cracked his neck and shook off the tension that wrapped up his arms and bit into his biceps.

After cleaning up, he punched in the code inside the elevator and ascended the fifty stories to Jess's office.

When the doors opened, he greeted Jess's admin. "How's it going, Tyra?"

She tucked her short dark hair behind her ears and smiled. The woman had no idea whom she really worked for—she thought she was answering calls for a cybersecurity and PI firm. The less she knew, the better.

"I'm hanging in there." She smiled. "Miss Scott is expecting you."

"Thanks." He went to Jess's office and found her leaning back in her leather chair with closed eyes.

"What's up?" He shut the door and dropped down in front of her desk. He caught a whiff of vanilla and musk with a hint of cinnamon. "You change perfumes?"

Her eyes opened, and she laughed. "You and your hound's nose."

He held his palms open and up. "What can I say? My mom's influence." His smile dissolved, though, when he remembered the memorial slash celebration-of-life party his folks would be throwing this weekend for his brother.

Was it really ten years on Saturday since he'd been gone? He pressed his palms onto his jeaned thighs. "So, you didn't answer me."

"I did change perfumes. Do you like it?"

"He'll still call you *Peaches*, you know." Owen shrugged. "Changing perfumes won't get Asher to leave you alone. Well, maybe he'll switch to calling you *Cinnamon*. Whatever will piss you off."

She rolled her eyes. "Anyway, I asked you here because we need to talk."

He arched a brow. "We are talking."

An exaggerated sigh slipped from her lips. "I'm worried about you."

He straightened his slouched position. "What are you talking about?"

"It's almost the ten-year anniversary."

He stabbed a finger at his chest and stood. "Do you think I don't know that?" He strode to the floor-to-ceiling windows, stealing a glimpse of the Brooklyn Bridge in the distance.

"I know how you get every September . . . but ten years is—"

"How I get?" He scoffed. "It's the same way we all get every November around the time Marcus died. We haven't avenged our own teammate's death, and it burns us all—not just in November, but year-fucking-round." He stiffened and took a breath before facing her. "So, if anyone understands how I feel it's you. And you hate talking about feelings as much as the rest of us."

"Jason was your brother. It's different."

"Luke. Asher." He tightened a fist and tapped it at his lips. "All the guys on the team—they're blood to me."

"I didn't mean that, but it still doesn't change the fact that you were ready to kill Asher downstairs in that ring. You're on edge, so I can't help but assume it's because it's ten—"

"Stop." An iciness curved around his spine and splintered out, like an infection, into the rest of his body. "I don't want to talk about this. I can't fucking talk about this."

The military's mandatory shrink sessions after Jason's death had driven him nuts. And when his team had lost Marcus—they all had to sit with a therapist, without divulging classified details, and discuss their "feelings."

Jumping from a plane without a chute was the more reasonable thing to do.

After all, the odds were in his favor he'd still land on his feet. He'd been lucky over the years. And some days, he wondered if he was invincible.

She stood in front of him now and pressed a hand to his shoulder. "I won't stop because I care about you."

He stepped away, and her arm fell to her side. She tried to pose as a heartless and icy woman, but deep down he knew the truth about her. He knew she wore a mask—just like him. "Why'd you have us fly in? You need us for a job? That's all I care to talk about."

"I do have somewhere I need both you and Asher." She returned to her desk, grabbed a folder, and handed it to him.

"Why isn't he up here with me, then? You wanted to have this heart-to-heart first?" A sharp breath left his lips.

When she didn't say anything, he knew he was right.

"Where are you sending us? Is this for Uncle Sam or one of our school-boy missions?" He had decided he liked Asher's terminology.

"Neither."

He opened the folder. "Los Cabos? Why am I going to a resort in Mexico?"

"You're going on vacation, and I want someone with you to make sure you actually go . . . and stay out of trouble."

He laughed. "You think Asher will keep me out of trouble?" *More like get me into it.* The two of them together —they'd probably end up in a Mexican prison, and she'd have to send the team to bust them out. "I'm good, but thanks." He tried to hand it back to her, but she wouldn't take it.

"This is a direct order. I want you to get away for a week to clear your head. To take some time to just, you know, breathe."

"I don't need time. I need justice," he said, louder than he'd meant to.

"Jason's killer may not even be alive. It's been a long time. He may have been wiped out during the war." She pinched the bridge of her nose and dropped her gaze to the floor. "I'm sorry, but we just can't be sure."

He shook his head. "Shahid Ismail's on the list of terror suspects at large."

"That doesn't mean he's still alive."

"Yeah, our government said the same about Osama—and then we found the motherfucker."

"If he's alive we'll find him. But right now, I want you to take a break. We're between jobs, it's the perfect time."

"Luke's out of town. It wouldn't make sense for us both to be gone."

"He'll be back in two days. Besides, this was his idea. He noticed how tense you've been lately. If your head isn't in the game it could compromise the team."

"I'd never put the team at risk."

She carefully edged closer and reached for his forearm. "Do this for me. Please."

God, she was going to guilt trip him into a damn vacation.

"Fine."

Maybe he could use some time off.

She let go of him and went back to her desk. "Do me a favor?"

"Yeah?"

"If Asher gets thrown in jail for whatever reason . . . leave him there."

He fought back a laugh. "Sure, and lose one of our best trackers."

She huffed out an exasperated breath. "Fine. Have fun." She smiled. "Not *too* much fun, though."

"You have my word."

CHAPTER TWO

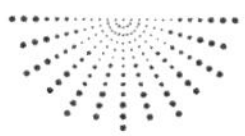

"We're one signature away from pushing this through the House and Senate, sir. We'd really appreciate your support." Sam squeezed her eyes closed, waiting for an answer.

"I'm sorry. I like you and your father, but I just think this will stir up too much trouble."

She could imagine Senator Drake standing in his office, with his belly flopping over his belt and his tail between his legs.

"With all due respect, sir, if you're scared about some Russian plot to attack anyone on board with this proposal, well, you don't need to worry. The days of KGB spies in the U.S. are over." Well, she hoped they were, at least.

"You were at the Summit in Brussels in July. You saw how tense things were between Ukraine and Russia. The timing of this—"

"The timing is necessary." Her fists touched the desk, and she pushed upright to stand, irritation scuttling up her spine. If Drake was out, that only left her with one more option, and she couldn't imagine the amount of smooth-talking and ass-kissing she'd have to do to get Senator Abrams's vote tonight. "Reconsider coming to the benefit next week, then. You'll see we do have some Russian support for this. There will be a lot of heads of state there, even former President Jones is on board."

"And why isn't President Rydell attending?" He paused for only a second. "I'll tell you why—he knows it's a bad idea to be stirring up trouble over there."

She inwardly groaned, stifling her frustration the best she could. "Please, can you just hear me out?"

There was a pause, which gave her a pebble of hope. "Senator—"

"My family has gotten threats, Samantha," he said in a low voice.

She took a moment to consider his words. "Senator Drake, we all get threats. This is D.C., but we can't succumb to manipulation."

"I'm sorry. Please tell your father my answer is *no*. Good day."

The call ended, and she dropped back onto the worn leather chair. "Threats," she mumbled. How many threats did she get on a weekly basis? She'd never be able to do her job if she let anonymous messages scare her out of leaving her house.

A soft hiss of irritation left her lips and she tossed her phone on the desk. "Shit." She reached for the framed photo her cell had knocked over.

A familiar lump gathered quickly in her throat as she stared at the picture of her and Brad.

Promise me we'll die old and gray together, she'd asked of him before he'd left for deployment.

It's unlucky to make promises about coming back. Brad had leveled her with his words.

"Miss McCarthy?"

Sam dropped the photo as if she'd been caught tampering with evidence in a case or conspiring against the U.S.

It was a photo, she reminded herself. But it was a photo she'd clung to, always keeping it visible as if someday Brad would come back to her.

"Sorry, I didn't mean to startle you."

Sam did her best to shrug away the memories as if that were even possible. Of course, for years, she'd buried herself in work so she wouldn't continue down the "rabbit hole," as her father liked to call it, of trying to find the terrorist who'd killed Brad and his best friend during a SEAL operation.

"I'm fine." She cleared her throat and positioned the photo back in its normal spot before peeling her focus up to her admin, Liz. "Are you ever going to give in and call me *Sam*?"

Liz's light green eyes creased at the edges. "Best I can do is Miss Samantha."

"After all these years?" Sam chuckled lightly. "I guess I'll take it, though." She clasped her hands on the desk and angled her head. "So, is everything okay?"

"No. Senator Abrams called, and he had to cancel dinner tonight."

Damn it. "Did he say why, or when he can reschedule?"

Liz's lips puckered as if she didn't want to tell her the news.

"What is it?" She pressed back in her seat and gripped the arms of her chair.

"He found out your father's in Russia and that he wouldn't be in attendance tonight. He didn't want to meet with only you, I guess."

She needed to be able to share the good news at the benefit in Russia next week—that they had enough support from Congress to push forward with her proposal. With Drake out, and Abrams unwilling to meet today, she might be screwed.

"You're the daughter of the chairman for the Intelligence Committee, you'd think Abrams would be a little more respectful toward you."

"Abrams thinks women are good for only one thing." *Sex.*

"I'm guessing your call with Senator Drake didn't go well, then?"

She drummed her fingers atop her smartphone. "Drake is a coward." Plus a few other words, but she'd keep them to herself. "I'll reach out to my father and see if he can get Abrams on the phone. Dad will have to work some magic from Moscow."

"He's pretty great at brokering deals. I'm sure it'll be fine."

"Let's hope so, or else, everything could fall apart."

"You really think it'll be a deal-breaker at the Sven Group Benefit without announcing you'll have the backing of Congress?"

"You know how lucky we are to get the support of a Russian billion-dollar defense company to support our efforts?" Her cheeks filled with air before she let her breath go. "We can't show up empty-handed."

"Well, if anyone can make it happen, you and your father can." Liz smiled. "I have everything set up and confirmed for your trip Tuesday. Do you need anything else before I head out on vacation?"

"No, but thank you." She glanced in the direction of the door. "Hopefully, the interns can hold down the fort while we're all gone."

Liz lightly shook her head. "I don't know about that." She smiled, but then her lips slanted into a frown when her attention veered to the lone framed photo on Sam's desk. "Are you sure you'll be okay with me leaving?"

"Of course. You and your husband deserve to have some cocktails on a beach now that your kids are off at college. Go and relax."

"Okay," she said before a heavy sigh followed. "I just hate thinking about you here all alone with Saturday being the ten-year-anniversary . . . maybe I should've picked a different week to be gone?"

Sam forced her signature fake D.C. smile, which she only reserved for politicians or situations like these. "I'll be good. Promise." She'd do her best not to allow sadness to bait her into its bear trap, at least.

"Okay, then." Liz's blues softened. "Well, I have to catch a flight to Fiji. Good luck next week. And stay safe. Rostov-on-Don is so close to the Ukrainian border—"

"I know, I know," she said.

Sam's mom frequently went on trips with her father, but in this case, her dad didn't want her anywhere near the benefit in case there were separatist protests—and, if any of the threats they'd received actually did come to fruition.

Her dad couldn't stop Sam from going, though. Hell, this was really her baby, not his.

"The goal is to alleviate the tension in the border zone," Sam noted. "I can't exactly show up in an armored vehicle flanked by Secret Service. No one will believe it can ever be safe and peaceful over there then."

Liz squinted one eye. "If your dad has your mom being guarded at their house in Arlington, thousands of miles away from the event, surely, you'll have some protection, too?"

She blew out an exhausted breath. "Of course, but I don't want to make a show of it."

"Well, I don't know how you do it, but the world's lucky to have someone like you." She winked a blue eye.

"Now, go have some fun!" Sam shooed her away with her hand and waited for her to leave before looking back at the photo on her desk. The sinking feeling in the pit of her stomach returned, and she leaned forward and reached for the frame.

Brad was on one knee in the picture, with her hand between his palms.

Her best friend, Emily, had been hiding at the tavern, in position to capture the engagement.

Three weeks later, he'd been killed on an operation in Iraq.

Ten years. Ten damn years on Saturday since Brad had been stolen from her.

Life wasn't fair.

"Miss McCarthy?"

Sam looked up to see the office's newest intern, Phillip, standing in the doorframe, and it had her drawing in a quick breath to get her mind focused back on work, yet again.

Phillip's inexperience gave him a deer-in-the-headlights look whenever he entered her room. He was wide-eyed and impressionable, not yet tainted by Washington; she hoped she could keep him from turning to what she'd dubbed over the years as *the D.C. Dark Side*.

"Um, a deliveryman dropped off an envelope for you." His brown eyes met hers.

"You can just set it on my desk. Thanks." She smiled, hoping to weaken some of his nervous energy.

He slowly entered the room, but there was something off.

"What's wrong?"

"Well, it's sort of weird, ma'am."

She straightened in her seat and reached for the mailer,

and his gaze traveled to the ink that peeked out from her sleeve as she took it from him. "Weird how?"

He pointed to the front of the envelope. "It just has your last name on it."

"You didn't ask Shawn who it was from?"

"Shawn didn't deliver it. It was someone else, and the guy just insisted you have it ASAP, and that I give it to you personally."

"So, a man you didn't recognize handed you an envelope, and you just took it?" If she weren't a professional, she would've rolled her eyes and planted a palm to her forehead.

"He couldn't get by security without showing some form of identification, right?" He lifted his shoulders, and red fanned across his cheeks. "Before I realized the envelope didn't look official, he'd already left my desk."

She dropped the mailer on her desk. "Get security. I want him tracked down."

"Why? I-I don't—"

"Just do it."

He hurried out of the office, and she crossed her arms, tucking her thumbnail between her teeth as she warily eyed the envelope.

Ideas ran through her head for the next few minutes until Phillip returned.

With his hands pressed to his knees, he took a moment to gather a few quick breaths. "Sorry. I tried to catch him myself. I thought I'd have a better chance since I knew what he looked like."

"And?" But she knew the answer.

"He didn't go out the front door, and by the time I caught sight of him at the back exit of the building, he'd already disappeared into a black SUV."

"Plate number? Make and model?"

“Range Rover, I think.” He shook his head. “But, uh, there wasn’t a plate.”

The envelope was paper-light; it couldn’t contain an explosive, but something sure as hell felt off about it. “Security,” she sputtered in a rush. “Get them here right now.”

CHAPTER THREE

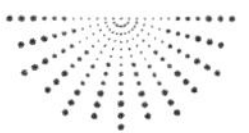

OWEN GLANCED AT ASHER ON APPROACH. "YOU'RE LATE. It's already ten."

Asher slipped onto the lounge chair by him at the infinity pool and stretched out. "Can't a guy get a little shut-eye while on vacation?"

"Sure, like you did much sleeping with that brunette from last night."

"Nah, man." He shrugged. "Went to bed alone. She wasn't my type."

A lazy yawn left Owen's mouth before he said, "Well, we missed the boat. No fishing, I guess."

"Did we really come to Mexico to fish?" Asher rolled his head to the side and lifted his shades to catch Owen's eyes. "I don't think so." He rested his head back down. "You need to get laid. It's our second day here, and you haven't hooked up with anyone. Nothing like a good lay to take the edge off."

"Must be why you're so damn edgy all the time since the only woman you want is Je—"

"Hell no. I'm just taking a brief vow of celibacy."

Owen sat upright, doing his best not to laugh his ass off. "Right. You're a monk now?"

Asher cursed under his breath. "Yeah, yeah, yeah. So, what's it going to be? You want me to be your wingman and help you find a woman here, or what?"

"A woman isn't going to fix my problems." He'd hoped parasailing and bungee jumping yesterday would've taken off some of the edge, but nothing seemed to alleviate the hard throb in his chest.

Tonight, he'd try whiskey, he supposed. A lot of it.

"Well, women never actually fix problems. They only complicate shit. But sex, that's a different story. I wasn't talking about you falling in love."

"Says the monk." He chuckled lightly.

Asher's legs fell to each side of the lounger. "But, uh, if you need to talk about your feelings or some shit like that . . ."

"Yeah, I'll just pencil that talk in for February thirtieth."

Asher whistled out a breath as he pressed a hand to his chest. "Whew, you had me scared for a second."

"Yeah, and what would you have done if I had said *yes*?" Owen dropped his legs to the side of the lounger and patted his side pocket, realizing he'd forgotten his room key.

"Gone to the ocean to practice drown-proofing, like the good ol' days at BUD/S."

Owen thought back to BUD/S when he'd nearly missed the age cutoff. It'd been rough, but his anger over the loss of his brother had pushed him through. "I gotta grab a new key. I left mine upstairs. Stay out of trouble while I'm gone. I promised Jess I'd keep you out of jail."

A massive grin stretched his face. "She just can't help but worry about me."

Monk my ass, he thought as he started for the hotel.

The smell of the ocean wafted to his nose as he walked the path to the side entrance. Jessica had done a decent job in her choice of vacation, but clearly, the resort had done nothing to minimize his pent-up anger.

Once inside the lobby, he tucked his shades in his pocket, but stopped short of the desk and closed his eyes for a brief moment, his hands bunching at his sides.

He needed a moment to calm down before he faced the concierge like a replica of the Hulk.

At the feel of something, or someone, bumping into him, he instinctively reached out. A soft gasp hit his ears, and he opened his eyes to find his hands still touching something . . . a woman's ass. "Shit. Sorry."

The woman spun to face him and lowered to her knees.

He crouched for an assist, to help pick up the strewn items from her purse, but instead, he found himself eying her as if in a trance.

Short black hair to her chin, long dark lashes, a straight nose, and high cheekbones. Her beautiful lips were pressed into a tight line.

"Sorry again," he said under his breath.

"No, it was probably my fault." She stood with her purse.

Once they were both upright, he noted the red rose tattooed to the inside of her wrist as she swept a lock of hair behind her ear.

Her light brown eyes found his, and he sucked in a sharp breath, catching a whiff of her perfume: lavender. Clean and uncomplicated. He liked it.

Her beautiful browns narrowed for a brief moment as her tongue teased her bottom lip. A strange pull of familiarity grabbed hold of him, then his gaze flicked to the suitcase and computer bag at her side. He caught sight of her first name on the airline tag still attached to the luggage handle. "Are you here for work, Samantha?" Her mouth rounded in surprise. "Saw it on the bag."

"Oh. Um, vacation." A touch of pink that matched her lips swept up her cheeks. "And you can call me Sam."

He checked her ring finger, and his lips crooked into a slight smile. "Well, perhaps I'll see you around the resort."

Her eyes remained on his as if she were waiting for him to say more, but then she said, "I'd like that."

Her voice had the sexy, just-woke-up huskiness to it that had the immediate effect of making his cock get excited.

"Your name?"

Right. "Owen."

Her fingers splayed across her collarbone, and her dark brows drew together. "Well, I hope to see you soon."

He tipped his head goodbye and approached the concierge to grab his key. He stole a glimpse of her from over his shoulder as he drummed his fingers on the desk while waiting for his card.

He almost laughed as he watched her shake her head and mumble something to herself while lifting her bags.

He studied the pair of long, shapely legs she had on her. And when she turned toward the elevators, he clamped his teeth down on his bottom lip, wishing he was sinking his teeth into the delicious curve of her ass. Damn, those white shorts left just enough to the imagination to have a guy wondering.

His body tensed with the idea of having those legs wrapped around him later.

Asher was a damn genius—maybe he did need to get laid.

When he returned to the pool, he found Asher at the bar talking to a woman in a string bikini paired with ridiculously high heels. He wondered if her heels doubled as a weapon.

He'd had to use one to stab a guy in the jugular before, so it wasn't that crazy of an idea.

Asher popped to his feet when he caught Owen's eye. "There he is. This is Liza." He turned away from her and mouthed, "She's a model." He raised his brows a few times, his silent way of inviting Owen to make a move.

Owen feigned interest with a quick smile, but for some damn reason, he wasn't the least bit interested. All he could think about was the woman from the lobby.

"If you boys wanna come to my photo shoot tomorrow, you're more than welcome to join."

"Maybe," Owen said, even though he had no intention of showing up.

"Here's my digits." Liza scribbled her number on a bar napkin. "Later."

"That was fast," Owen said once the woman was out of sight. "How the hell did you manage that?"

"She thought I was some actor. Forgot who. And hell, I just went with it. I told her you're like the real version of Tom Cruise from *Top Gun.*"

"You're such an asshole."

"Yeah, well, this asshole just got you a date with a model."

"You can have her." Owen started to hand him the napkin but then retracted his hand. "But no . . . you're celibate right now. Forgot." He chucked the napkin into the closest trash can before they started down the path for the beach.

"Anyway." Asher slapped his palms together. "The bartender says there's a poolside party tonight. DJ is supposed to be decent. We should go."

"Sure." Owen grabbed his sunglasses from his pocket and slipped them on. "Was it your idea or Jessica's to distract me with mindless entertainment?"

"You're the one who wanted to fish today. Isn't that like the definition of 'mindless entertainment'?" he asked while using air quotes.

"True." To be honest, he didn't even know how to fish. He loved being on a boat, though, so it seemed like a natural choice. "Fine. We'll go to this party tonight."

"Promise me you'll have some fun."

"I always have fun." He stopped walking and crossed his arms, staring off at the Pacific, catching sight of two people parasailing off in the distance.

"Yeah, but not this time of year. This time of year, you're a pain in the ass." Asher raised his palms in the air.

"Do you blame me?" he asked, his voice dropping low.

Owen thought about reminding Asher how pissed off and moody he became whenever Marcus's name was brought up, the teammate he'd replaced.

Asher swiped a hand over his brownish-black beard and tipped his head skyward, remaining quiet, and he had to assume his mind had swirled to darker thoughts as well.

"You're right, though. Maybe I do need to loosen up." He remembered the woman from the lobby whom he'd love to sink his teeth into. He hadn't had such a below-the-belt reaction since his early teenage years when he hadn't even known the meaning of *rubbing one out*.

Asher rested an elbow atop Owen's shoulder and looked off at the ocean. "She's a thing of beauty, ain't she?"

The glittering water held his eye, and he sucked in a sharp breath at the memory that tugged at his mind.

I'm gonna join the SEALs, bro. You wait and see, his brother had said before tossing the football to Owen on the beach the summer before Jason had gone off to college. *I heard they use live ammunition and train in what they call "kill houses."*

You crazy? Those guys are way too hardcore for you. Owen had caught the ball and flung it back at Jason. *Don't stress Mom and Pops out.*

His brother had laughed. *Right, you already do that enough for the both of us. But, seriously—I'm gonna make it happen.*

"Too bad I never met Jason." Asher's words took him by surprise and pulled him back to the present.

"You would've driven my brother nuts."

"Shit, that's what I seem to do best."

His throat grew thick, he dropped his eyes and listened to the sound of the water lapping the shore. And then the sound of laughter from children nearby stirred something deep inside.

Jason had wanted kids. A lot of them. Owen had never been interested.

Now, he wasn't so sure.

But the idea of kids, of a family, was a topic he'd have to shelve until justice was served for his brother. And not a damn minute sooner.

"CHEERS." ASHER TOUCHED HIS CORONA TO OWEN'S BOTTLE before looking toward the outdoor dance area, which was partially surrounded by stacked stone and tiki lights. "Hottie at your nine o'clock. She's eye-fucking the shit out of you."

Owen casually sipped the gold liquid and glanced over his shoulder, and his eyes thinned at the beautiful woman in his line of sight. "Sam."

"You know that chick?"

As soon as she met Owen's gaze, Sam's lashes dropped, stealing her browns from view. She stared down at the cocktail in front of her and ran her fingers through her short mass of slightly wavy black hair.

She was in a white V-neck tee that accentuated her curves and had him taking a breath.

"I feel like I do," he said in a bit of a daze then blinked away his thoughts. "But, uh, we collided in the lobby earlier today."

"Well, it looks like she needs loosening up as much as you. Although, I have a feeling that one is wild beneath the surface."

Owen polished off the rest of his drink to try and steel his nerves.

It'd been too long since he'd approached a woman. In fact, he'd never had to do much of the chasing the past few years. Word had gotten around he used to be a pilot, and for some reason, that made women's panties soak.

He swore women were dirtier than men; they just didn't admit it. Guys, on the other hand, were pretty candid about their appetite for sex.

"Go. I know how to stay out of trouble."

"You sure about that?"

Asher rolled his eyes and flicked his wrist, dismissing him.

"Fine." Owen tossed some money on the bar and then strode around to where she was sitting.

A slight breeze moved some of her short locks in front of her face, and she tucked them behind her ears, catching his eyes in the process.

He motioned for the bartender and slid onto the empty seat at her side. "Hi. Sam, right?"

She squeezed one eye closed as if trying to remember his name. She was better at playing it cool than he was, so it seemed. “Oliver?” A sweet smile created a dimple in her right cheek as she tapped at her lip. “No. Owen?”

He chuckled lightly and fully faced her, noting the way her fingers dropped to her lap.

Red linen pants, and he was anxious for her to stand, so he could catch sight of her perfect tight ass again.

Her fingertips bit into her thighs, and when he looked back at her face, her smile dissolved and was replaced by a tight line. “You okay?”

She took a long breath, her chest rising slowly before she expelled it. “Yeah, I’m just exhausted. Long trip here.” She polished off the rest of her drink.

“Where’d you fly in from?”

“D.C.”

“Oh, okay. Are you a lawyer or something?” he asked while directing his focus to the bartender. He flicked his finger toward her drink, his silent request to order her another round.

“Another Corona?” the bartender asked him.

Owen nodded at the man before his attention met her eyes, which were wrapped in a dark liner, making the light brown pop even more.

“I’m not a practicing lawyer. But, um, let’s talk about you. I don’t really want to think about work, to be honest.”

God, the damn way she talked. Had he ever been so aroused at the sound of a woman’s voice? “I don’t want to talk about work, either. Vacation and all.”

“Ditto, but, what do people talk about if they don’t talk about work?”

Since he never talked about his job, he’d become a pro at small talk.

The bartender delivered their drinks, and she took a quick

swallow of hers and winced. “I think he put more tequila in it this time.” She set it down and looked at him again.

“How about some rapid-fire questions to get to know each other faster, so that way when I ask you to dance, I won’t be some stranger grinding up against you.”

She tipped her head back and laughed. “What makes you think grinding will be involved?”

“Is there any other way to dance?” He edged a little closer, and he noticed she’d changed perfumes. Earthy with smoky undertones and a hint of leather. *Interesting.*

Red crawled up her neck and to her cheeks. She grabbed her drink again, this time, sucking through the straw, and he couldn’t help but envision those lips wrapped around his cock.

He drank more of his beer. “So, what do you say?”

She braced her thighs and nodded. “Shoot.”

He released his hold on the Corona. “Hm. Steak or sushi?”

“Gotta have my food cooked. So, steak.”

He nodded in agreement. “Dog or cat?”

Her lips curved at the edges. “That’s tough.”

“This is very important. If we differ on this answer, I just might have to walk away.”

“Okay. Good point.” She cut her hand through the air. “Dog.”

“Thank God.”

“Do you have a favorite kind?” she asked.

“Siberian Husky. If I’m ever not traveling so much, I’d love to get one.”

“A beautiful breed.”

“You have one?”

“What happened to rapid-fire?” She raised a brow.

“You messed it up.” He smiled.

"True." She shook her head. "I'm too busy for an animal right now. I travel a lot, too."

He was tempted to ask her what she did and why she globe-trotted, but he remembered the conversation was off-limits, and so he asked, "Mountains or ocean?"

"I have to go with both. I can't budge on that." She gave an innocent lift of her shoulders.

My kind of woman. "Ski or snowboard?"

"Neither."

"We'll have to work on that." He rubbed his palms together. "Winter or summer?"

"Winter. The summer is . . ." She waved a hand in the air. "Next question."

"Swim or sunbathe?"

"Swim."

Hopefully, he'd see her already sun-kissed body beneath the tropical rays while on vacation. The idea of this woman in a bikini had his pulse ramping up. "Treadmill or trail?"

"You assume I work out, huh?"

He angled his head and dragged his attention from her red pants to her face. "Unless you did something to really win God over, I'm thinking that body is hard-earned."

She smiled. "Spin class and yoga. You?"

"Oh yeah, give me a downward dog any day." He winked, and she swatted his chest before drawing her fingers back as if surprised by her action.

He allowed the moment to sit between them for a second, for the music to fade into the background. He wasn't sure what was going on between them, but he didn't want to question it, either. "Beer or wine?" he asked after clearing his mind.

"I hate the taste of beer, but wine gives me a headache."

"Hard liquor, then. Noted." He glanced in the direction of the dance floor. "Sing or dance?"

"You'd never want to hear me belt out a tune. But I'm a decent dancer. I mean, I took ten years of dance lessons growing up."

"Tutu or tap?"

"Both."

He brought the rim of the beer to his lips, allowing it to hover there as a thought crossed his mind. "Lights on or off?"

"For when?" A small smile touched the edges of her mouth.

He took a sip of his Corona. "Open for interpretation."

Her tongue peeked between her lips like a delicious tease. "Definitely on, then."

The bottle began to perspire beneath his palm as he held it, and he stole a second to gather his thoughts by taking another hard swallow. "Boxers or briefs?"

"For me?" She chuckled, but her focus dropped to his crotch, and it had him instantly stirring beneath her stare. "I'd have to assess the package to make such a determination." Her long fingers covered her mouth as if embarrassed by her slip of the truth.

She was probably a polished D.C. woman, and he'd managed to pull her fairly fast out of her comfort zone.

"Okay. Fair enough," he finally answered. "Country music or ED—"

"Electronic dance music."

He grabbed her hand and held it between his palms. "The fact that you know that—marry me?"

She laughed, and he rested his hand over her wrist, feeling the climb of her pulse beneath his thumb.

"My turn," she said, her voice whisper-light like a kiss of air across his skin.

He retracted his hand and finished his drink, trying to brush away the thoughts of familiarity that tried to cling to him. "Bring it on."

Her white teeth flashed as she smiled. "Ink?"

His gaze touched upon her tattoo for a second, which had her pressing a palm to her chest to conceal it.

"I'm terrified of needles, so I don't have any."

She jerked her head back a touch, her eyes creasing at the edges. "You're lying."

"Honest to God."

"I have a hard time believing you'd be afraid of anything."

"Really? I give off a certain impression, do I? Well, I'd take jumping out of a plane over a needle any day."

"Oh, you jump out of planes a lot, huh?"

Little do you know. "On occasion."

"Occupational hazard?"

His hand slid to her knee. Only her knee. He'd need permission before it skirted any higher. "Next question, ma'am."

"Mm." She took a long sip of her drink. "Another round, please," she requested from the bartender. "Okay, let's see." She tapped a red nail against her lip. "So, does that mean you prefer to fly? Or do you hate it so much that you get the strange compulsion to jump out?"

"Definitely fly. Nothing beats being in the air." His shoulders arched back, and he straightened his spine. "Well, I half-lied. I love being in the water, too."

"Yeah, well, I can handle the water. The air—not so much. I gripped the guy's arm next to me the entire flight here. Thank God I have short nails, or he'd be sporting marks on his skin for a week." A nervous laugh met his ears this time. That feminine huskiness she had rushed beneath his skin, and he'd swear it kicked up his internal temperature ten degrees.

"Lucky guy," he said, a little deeper than he'd meant to.

"I think he'd disagree." She smiled and thanked the bartender when he slid her a new drink. "Siblings or only child?"

A sudden unease blew across her face, mirroring how he felt on the inside from her question. Why'd she ask if it made her uncomfortable?

"Brother," he finally said and cleared his throat. "You?"

She was quiet, which had him focusing his eyes back on hers. A somberness met him, and he wondered what that was all about. Had she suffered a loss like him? He'd seen that look before, because whenever he observed his own reflection, he saw it: pain.

"Only child." She rubbed her hands up and down her thighs a few times. "How long are you staying here?"

"Another five days."

"And where do you go after? I mean, where do you live?" she asked.

"I have a place in Charleston, but I'm in D.C. and New York a lot, too."

"Oh. So, you're familiar with my stomping ground?"

He nodded, his eyes falling to the bar counter where someone had keyed the initials R.M.H into the wood.

She must have followed his gaze because her index finger smoothed over the letters. "Ride me hard, maybe?"

He laughed and looked up at her. "If you'd like to."

"Funny." She smiled. "The initials."

"Really? That was the first thing that popped into your mind? Not—Rose Marie Hanson?"

"Rose? You have a grab bag of women's names in your head?"

"I prefer the way you think, actually."

Some of the smile she'd lost came back, and her dimple almost reappeared when she looked at him. He'd do anything to get those generous lips to stretch again.

"Well, I feel like I know you. Covered all the bases, right? What do you say?" He stood and held a palm out. "Ready to dance?"

"I might need a shot to loosen up first." She smiled. "Maybe even more than one."

"Really?" He quirked a brow. "You seem fairly loose to me."

She bit her lip as if fighting a grin. "I do, do I?"

His palm met his face as he grumbled, "Didn't mean it like that."

She pinched his bicep. "Kidding."

He dropped his hand, and she stood.

"Two shots of tequila." He faced her and found her eyes, the brown color softening as she stared at him.

He hoped to salvage the moment, but when she leaned into him, pressing a palm to his chest, he realized he didn't have to. The moment never left. Hell, he was pretty sure their banter had heated things up a few notches.

Memories of his past, of his loss, tried to scrape into his mind, but he didn't want to give in to the pain.

He just wanted this woman. Right damn now.

Her eyes lowered to her hand on his chest. Maybe she could feel the racing of his heart? "You as nervous as me?"

Her whispered words chucked every last thought he'd been harboring out the window—all he was thinking about was her. Only her.

"Honey, I'm only nervous I might step on your toes on that dance floor."

"I can lead."

"Not on my watch." He listened to the sounds of the tropical house music with rich drum beats and a hard bass in the background—anxious to dance with her, to feel her body against his.

"Your shots," the bartender said, and they both dropped their hands as if caught joining the mile-high club. Not that he could ever have sex in a bathroom with a woman like her—hell no.

"You ready?" he asked as he handed her the first shot.

She wet her lips, and he'd swear he could see the pulse at her neck heightening. She *was* nervous.

"Guess we'll find out," she said then downed the shot.

Two more rounds later, they found themselves on the deck, joining the rest of the dancers.

The alcohol probably caught up with her because she was the definition of laid-back now. Her fingertips traveled up his chest before she hung her arms loosely around his neck and danced with him.

Her pelvis touched his body in circular movements, creating a permanent hard-on, as he held on to her trim waist.

"It's beautiful here," she whispered as he seized her eyes, noting the hungry look in her browns.

"You're beautiful," he answered instead and edged his face closer to hers, dying to see how she tasted.

"You're . . . unexpected." Her eyes narrowed as if a question hung in her mind she couldn't bring herself to ask. And then, she inched up higher, so their faces were nearly touching, like an invitation to kiss her.

And, hell, he took it.

His mouth came down over hers. Soft at first. Slowly kissing her. Nipping her bottom lip.

But when she pushed her tongue into his mouth and

threaded her fingers through his hair, he groaned against her lips, and the blood rushed south.

His hands slid down to the curve of her ass as she continued to dance, her body moving in perfect time with the beat—driving him damn wild.

Her ass was as tight as he'd imagined, and he couldn't wait to touch the rest of her.

"My room," she cried against his mouth.

She held his hand while they broke into a sprint to head back to the hotel.

Was she drunk?

Shit, was he drunk?

"Hurry," she begged, as he worked her key into the card reader once they were outside her room.

She looped her arms around his hips and pressed her mouth close to his ear as she fumbled with his belt buckle. "You're killing my focus."

"Come on, you can be stealthier than that."

He almost laughed as he finally got the door open.

She maneuvered around him in one quick moment, and he allowed the door to shut behind them.

She faced him with a smile and began walking backward toward the sliding doors, slowly removing her clothes.

Heels.

Top.

Pants.

He'd groaned during her striptease when she'd kept her lip between her teeth and her eyes pinned to his. He'd remained locked in position in front of the door, unable to do anything other than watch the stunning woman as she'd undressed, and his length had throbbed against the confines of his jeans.

Now, he braced a palm on the wall and kicked off his

shoes, noting the swell of her full breasts in the nude-colored bra.

She turned, unsnapped her bra, and tossed it over her shoulder before opening the glass doors.

With her back to him, he spotted a second tattoo on her right shoulder blade: rosary beads. He was going to commit all kinds of sins with this woman tonight.

She slowly faced him. "I want to feel the breeze on my skin while we fuc—"

"Sam," he nearly growled her name as their eyes met, which had her dropping her words.

She flicked her finger in a come-hither motion. "Well, you going to come and get me, or what?"

CHAPTER FOUR

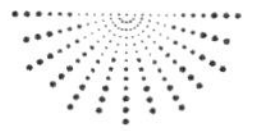

SHE PRESSED THE HEEL OF HER PALM TO HER FOREHEAD. THE sharp throb in her temples was too much.

After forcing her eyes open, she clutched the sheet to her chest and rolled to her side. “What the hell?” A glass of tomato juice with two red pills at her bedside table had her sitting upright.

It was then that she noticed the sound of running water from the en-suite. “No.” She rushed her free hand over her mouth and gasped.

Did I . . .? She scrambled to remember the night, but the last thing that came to mind was dancing with Owen.

She lifted the sheet and confirmed her nakedness.

“Uh, hello?” It hurt too much to talk. To think.

She was in hangover hell.

And then it dawned on her.

Her fade-to-black night was a result of the emergency prescription of Valium she used to calm her nerves while flying. Ironically, she’d managed to skip it on the flight, but when she’d arrived at the hotel and bumped into Owen, she’d freaked out and popped one in her room before heading down to the bar.

But, oh God.

Would he forgive her when he discovered she'd kept her identity from him last night? How would he react when she showed him the photo from the envelope?

The photo. God, it's why I'm here, and now . . .

She tried to capture her memories, but it was like trying to snatch puffs of smoke in the air—everything after their bar chat slipped through her fingers.

Jason's brother. No. She pressed her closed hands to her eyes.

The water stopped a moment later, and the sound of steps had her heart in her throat.

"You're awake. How'd you sleep?"

His voice. Had it been this sexy last night? Low and deep?

No wonder she'd lost her senses and slept with him. Tequila and a hot guy were never a good mix.

Maybe it was a good thing she didn't remember.

She forced her eyes on him, finding him standing with a towel wrapped around his hips as he rubbed another smaller one against his hair to dry his longish blond locks.

She vaguely remembered his hair being closely cropped when they'd met ten years ago. Last night, she was pretty sure it had nearly brushed the collar of his shirt.

He'd packed on more muscles, too. Where he'd been leaner in the past, his V-shaped physique, hard chest, and six-pack were like heaven in a bottle now.

Why him? Anyone but him.

She was there for answers, for help. Not for a one-night stand with the brother of Brad's best friend. *No. No. No!*

She hadn't talked yet, and now, he was approaching her with a beautiful smirk on his face.

"That's a Bloody Mary." He tipped his chin toward the bedside table. "Drink it with the two ibuprofens; it should help with the hangover I'm sure you've got."

"That was my old remedy during my party days." The party days she had to hide from her overbearing parents, as well as from the rest of the watchful eye of D.C. politicians and the press.

She reached for the Bloody Mary but kept one arm over her chest to hold the sheet in place.

He cocked his head and observed her with a smile in his eyes. His face was more angular than square, but his jaw was definitely chiseled. Strength just poured from every fiber of the man, even from his mouth.

"I hope you don't mind me taking a shower here," he said. "I didn't want to be one of those guys to leave you waking in bed alone, especially if you didn't feel good."

And, of course, he had to be a nice guy. But would he still be charming after he discovered who she was? "Thanks."

She took a sip of the drink and forced her eyes back onto his. A swirl of colors danced within his irises, making for an incredible and unique shade, a shade she could get lost in.

This wasn't like her. Drunken one-night stands had happened. Sure. But lusting after the guy the next morning? Nope. She was normally the one to disappear before sun-up.

Owen York. How can this be happening? At thirty-two, she was an accomplished and sophisticated woman, but right now, she felt like she was fourteen, in braces, with her awkward, long legs that didn't match the rest of her body yet.

"You okay?" He sat next to her, which had her scooting over, still hanging on to the sheet in a desperate attempt to reclaim the sense of modesty a McCarthy was supposed to have. Of course, she'd never been the poster child for the McCarthy "brand" as her mother liked to call it, especially after she'd broken down after Brad's death.

She lowered her brows in thought, observing his hazel eyes. How could she have ever forgotten that color?

A memory of their brief conversation ten years ago at the funeral found its way into her mind.

I'll have someone check in on you. Look after you. I promise, Owen had said, and his stunning eyes had appeared haunted at the time.

"Um. The thing is, I don't remember sleeping with you." Her forehead creased, the pain in her skull intensifying.

Owen pressed a palm to his cheek and eyed her with a dash of amusement in his eyes. "I was worried about that." His nose wrinkled a little. "So, uh, we didn't end up having sex."

"But I'm naked, and you're naked. Well, beneath that towel, anyway."

"I realized how drunk you were at the last second, and somehow, I managed to come to my senses, even though I was fairly shit-faced, too."

She pointed at his naked chest. His oh, so gorgeous naked chest. "That doesn't explain the nudity."

"Well, I was still drunk, and so we kind of passed out next to each other before we had a chance to get dressed."

A major sigh of relief fell from her lips. "Thank you." She shook her head. "Not every guy would've done the same."

"I'm not gonna lie. I really wanted to. I mean, turning you down while you were naked and begging me . . ."

Her eyes widened to the point of pain. "What? I begged?"

He chuckled and held his index finger and thumb close to his face to showcase an inch. "A little, yeah."

She felt the heat rise in her cheeks, but at least she'd forgotten about the pain in her skull. "I'm so embarrassed."

"Don't be. I wouldn't be able to live with myself if we'd hooked up, and you hadn't been in the right state of mind at the time." He stood. "I mean, the first time we're together, I want you to remember every detail."

The first time? But she didn't have it in her to tell him there could never be any time.

She needed to tell him the truth, but it didn't feel like the time or place.

"I called down to the desk, and they said I could get a sailboat for the day. There was a cancelation, and so I was wondering if you'd like to sail with me?"

"Oh." She could tell him there, couldn't she? "Yeah, okay. What time?"

"Will an hour be enough time to get ready?"

"I'm not a girl who takes that long." She smiled. "But the hangover cure might."

He grinned. "Sounds good. Meet you in the lobby at eleven." He grabbed his strewn clothes off the floor and went to change in the bathroom.

She fell back onto the pillow and stared at the ceiling. When her best friend heard about this, she'd have a field day over it.

A flash from the night before popped into her head, and a memory of the kiss on the dance floor tore through her mind at lightning speed.

Her fingers brushed over her mouth, and her thighs squeezed.

Owen was one hell of a kisser. Maybe even the king of it.

"Well, I'll let you get situated," he said, once back in the room in his jeans and tee.

She sat back up and focused on his denim, and one of the

questions from the previous night came to mind. "Boxers or briefs?" She arched a brow.

"Guess you'll have to wait and find out."

* * *

"Is your new boyfriend at your place right now?" Sam asked her best friend, Emily, over FaceTime on her phone.

"No, Blane went to grab us coffee. You have the all clear to talk."

She propped her phone up against the tissue box on the vanity then rushed out, "Owen and I slept naked in bed together last night." She took a step back, twisting her lips to the side as she waited for her friend to comprehend her words.

Emily pulled the phone closer to her face, her brown eyes widening. "What do you mean by you *slept in bed naked together*?"

"Naked but no sex. I don't remember most of the night, though."

Emily's brows lifted. "Are you sure you believe nothing happened then?"

"Trust me, I'd know. I'd probably be sore if we had. It's been forever since anything other than my vibrator has gone near me. Hell, I'm probably collecting dust."

"And that's your fault." She pointed a finger at the screen. "Well, how much do you remember?"

"Almost everything before I began heavily drinking, but I definitely came across as a stranger, which will—"

"Piss him off when he discovers the truth." Emily shook her head. "Surprised he didn't recognize you."

"I'm not. It's been ten years, and he could barely look at me at the funeral. He spoke to me for all of thirty seconds and then was out of sight." She tensed. "I should've told him who I am last night. I never meant for things to go down like they did. I didn't expect he'd be so . . ."

"'So' what?"

"Funny. Sweet. Sexy."

"Shit, Sam. Why'd I tell you where to find him?"

She thought back to Emily's lecture before she'd booked the flight. "Yeah, well, this wasn't on that long list you made of things that could go wrong."

"Well, I guess I should've considered this when trying to talk you off the ledge of jetting to Mexico to find him."

Sam tipped her head heavenward, trying to gather her thoughts. Ever since she opened the envelope on Wednesday, her mind had been spinning nonstop with possibilities as to why she was given the picture. "You're normally such a stickler for protocol. Surprised you helped me."

"I may work for the AG, but look at your own job. If someone finds out . . ."

"I know, I know. But how could I not track Owen down?" She pinched her cheeks, realizing she needed some color to distract from her partially bloodshot eyes.

"You still have no idea if he can help you, or if he'll even want you to help when he learns the truth."

The truth . . . The truth was such a messy thing.

She slumped her shoulders as she grappled with her regrets over the night.

"How are you going to reclaim his trust? He's a military guy. I don't see this ending well," Emily said while Sam swiped rose blush on her cheekbones.

"I can be persuasive." She was her father's daughter, after all. She'd managed to get nearly half of D.C. to agree to her proposal—still one man short, though.

And maybe she shouldn't have been in Mexico when she

needed to be on a plane to Russia Tuesday, but her father promised her he'd handle Senator Abrams, and so . . . she needed to handle this situation.

Of course, if her dad knew where she was right now, and more importantly *why* she was there, he'd have a heart attack.

She grabbed the phone and left the en-suite and went out on the terrace off the bedroom. She stared at the cabanas dotting the white sand; the waves slowly rolled in and receded. "We're going sailing today. I'm going to talk to Owen on the boat."

"What are you wearing?" Emily cocked her head. "Hold the phone out."

"Why does it matter?"

"You need to look hot, or he might just toss your ass overboard when he learns the truth."

"Funny." She huffed but lifted her pink halter to show a black eyelet bikini top.

She nodded. "Sexy enough."

"Glad you approve. Anyway, I gotta go, or I'll be late. Say hi to Blane." She waved goodbye and ended the call before her best friend could give her any more grief.

She grabbed her belongings and then headed to the lobby, her nerves twisting as she played in her head what she'd say to him and how she'd lay the truth out between them.

I can do this, she thought when she caught sight of him talking to some guy who was maybe two inches taller than Owen's already tall frame.

Owen looked casually sexy in a white tee, navy blue swim trunks, and wide-strapped flip-flops. It was obvious he still kept up his SEAL exercise routine to some extent based on the rippled tone of his flesh.

She inwardly groaned at her thoughts. She needed to focus.

But when Owen pivoted, catching her gaze, his eyes narrowed, and his lips became tight. There was something there, something between them entirely too strong she wasn't sure how she'd ignore. She'd have to find a way, though.

"Who's this beauty?" Owen's friend asked when noticing her.

"Sam." She smiled and shook the guy's hand.

"I'm Asher."

"Are you sure you don't want to join us?" Owen asked, and Asher dropped his hold of her palm.

"Nah, man. Maybe we'll meet up in San Lucas tonight, though?" He slapped him on the shoulder. "You two have fun." Asher winked at Sam then walked off.

"He's a bit—"

"Of a pain in the ass."

"I was going to go with intimidating looking."

"Nah, he's a teddy bear; just don't tell him I said that." He reached for her bag like a gentleman.

The sweet gesture made her feel even worse. How could she tell him: *I knew your brother*? "I'm excited about the boat."

"Good. How's the headache?"

She touched her temple and shrugged. "Already forgot about it. Thank you."

He nodded. "So, you ready to go?"

As ready as I'll ever be. She slipped on her sunglasses once they were outside and nervously tucked her hands into her pockets as they walked away from the hotel and to the marina nearby.

"Do you remember anything else from last night?" He tossed the strap of her beach bag over his shoulder without the least bit of shame at carrying a woman's pink bag.

"Nothing after the dance floor." She didn't feel like

mentioning their first kiss had played on repeat for the last hour.

"I think this is our ride," he said once they were in front of a sailboat. "Sixty-five-footer." The mast and two sails were fairly calm, only flapping a little in the gentle breeze. "Let me check with the captain."

The way he said *captain* rolled off his tongue like a form of respect. His words were firm and a little hard around the edges.

Military, she reminded herself. She'd been around generals and other distinguished servicemen in her line of work, but she'd never again dated anyone who'd donned the uniform. She couldn't bring herself to do it after having lost Brad.

She turned and observed the hotel behind them. The desert served as a backdrop to the resort that was tucked into craggy cliffs along the Baja Peninsula, nestled by the Sea of Cortez and the coastline of the Pacific.

Why haven't I been here before? Most places she'd visited in the last five years had been war-torn areas related to her work.

"You ready?" At the sound of his voice, she faced him. He'd dropped her bag on the boat deck and was holding his hand out for her.

Once on board, his palms landed on her hips, and she lifted her chin. Her lips parted, and she was thankful they were both masking their eyes with glasses.

She'd prefer to hide her emotions for as long as possible.

"Are you folks ready?" The captain was American and probably in his late fifties. He tipped his hat in greeting and then started toward the dock, probably to untie the boat.

"So, are you thinking about letting me go at some point?"

He smiled and released his hold, but then reached for her hand and guided her to a seating area.

"I'm probably not going to drink champagne right now," she said while eying the uncorked bottle on ice. "But the cheese and crackers look perfect."

"Yeah, I'm in the same boat," he deadpanned, and it had her cracking another broad smile as he helped her take a seat.

"Do you know much about boats?" She dropped her head back to feel the rays of the sun pour over her, hoping it'd cleanse her of her sins.

"A little."

Why'd I ask that? She couldn't keep up the act of being ignorant about who he was for much longer, and any more questions like that would only make it worse. She also couldn't bring herself to spill the truth. Not yet, at least.

But—she was running out of time. Someone had sent her that photo for a reason, and she wouldn't be able to move on until she got to the bottom of it.

She sat upright as he removed his tee. He crossed his arms and leaned back as if he wanted to bake in the sun as well.

Of course, the sight of him was much more distracting than the scenery, even if she wasn't supposed to let her mind wander to thoughts of his body.

Her fingers skated across her collarbone as she guiltily continued to observe him, noticing the strength of his forearms and the overall hardness of every inch of him.

"Do you have a swimsuit on under your top?" He interrupted her thoughts, and she jerked her attention back to the ocean and away from his golden body.

"Um, yeah." She lifted the hem of her halter and peeled it off. He'd already seen her naked, so what was the big deal about a bikini top?

"So, tell me the craziest thing you've ever done."

"Sleep naked with you," she blurted, which had him looking her way. "But I'm betting my crazy is like a standard day for you."

He laughed. "Favorite childhood memory?"

"Are we playing rapid questions again?"

"I'm trying to learn more about you."

"Well, whatever perception you already have of me is probably pretty off base. I wasn't exactly myself last night."

"So, who are you really, then?"

Good question. But the words dried up in her throat, and she reached for a bottle of water from the cooler at her feet to buy time. "I'm the daughter of a senator. I work with my dad."

"Hm. And this means what, exactly?"

She wished she could see his eyes, but then again, she'd probably simply get lost in the color. "It means I have a certain reputation I'm supposed to maintain."

"And getting drunk and naked with a stranger isn't on the list of things to do, huh?" His arm fell between them, and his fingers drummed the faded blue material of the seat.

"Not exactly." *Lying again. Great.* "But my dad acts like I have to carry the weight of the world on my shoulders."

"And do you?" His lips became a line as if he were considering her admission.

She thought about the benefit next week, and how damn important it was. And yet, here she was . . . "I guess I try." She half-shrugged and then felt the need to lighten the mood, so she joked, "But I think it's giving me serious spine problems. Probably should see a chiropractor."

He was quiet for a moment, before he asked in a deeper voice, "Do you ever wish you were someone else?"

"No, I don't think so." She gulped. "But I wish I could

change the past." She had to tell him the truth. She owed it to not only him, but Brad. "Listen, I—"

The feel of his hand atop hers cut her off. And the way he caressed her skin with the pad of his thumb had her swallowing back every possible word that would kill the moment, a moment she couldn't possibly have.

He reached for her glasses with his free hand and removed them. "There's something in your eyes that tells me you know how I . . ."

Oh, God. Do you remember? Why didn't he finish his line of thought?

He heaved out a deep breath and placed her glasses back on before standing. He moved over to the railing and braced against it, his hair catching in the wind as they sailed, and she stood alongside him.

She found herself whispering, "I lost someone I cared about when I was younger." Her stomach roiled as she'd dropped her words into the ocean air. "I still have trouble allowing myself to be happy sometimes."

She had wanted to see a therapist back when times had been the toughest, but her father had concerns about it getting leaked to the press—had to maintain the McCarthy image, he'd said.

"I've lost a lot of people in my life." His mouth tightened as if pain spiraled around every one of his limbs, and he recalled a play-by-play of when someone died.

Tomorrow was the anniversary of Brad's and Jason's deaths. They shared the miserable day, and he didn't even know it.

Two hard knocks on the door.

A man in dress blues.

A letter in hand.

A dark, haunted look on his face.

He'd been the man to deliver her the harshest blow of her life.

She knew what she'd gotten herself into when falling in love with a man in uniform, though. Well, she thought she had; she'd only been twenty-one when she'd met Brad on a girls' trip to Charleston with Emily.

God, her life had turned upside down inside that bar—a bar the guy next to her owned.

"I was in the military, so . . ." His admission had her turning toward him, her heart heavy for his loss. He'd endured losing a blood brother and brothers in arms.

She touched his bicep and skirted her fingers north to his shoulder before he pivoted to face her, capturing her wrist and pressing her palm to his own cheek. "There's something about you."

She kept her hand cupping his cheek with his resting atop hers, and she seized a lungful of air so deep she grew dizzy. "Owen, I . . ." *Tell him.* And for some reason, the words remained stuck in her throat, weighed down and sludgy. "I'm, uh, starving." Her glasses hid an exasperated eye roll, and she forced herself to pull away and left his side to sit back down.

He assumed his previous spot next to her, and they shifted into casual conversation fairly quickly. It shouldn't have been so easy to talk to him, especially while she kept the truth about why she was there hidden from him—but it was.

He caught her by surprise when he paused their conversation about sailing and touched her cheek with the back of his hand. He closed his eyes and took in a breath. "You smell different every time we're together. I never know what I'm going to get with you." His eyelids lifted. "Jasmine?"

She smiled. "And how do you know so much about fragrances?"

"I'll tell you if you tell me why you wear so many different ones." The pad of his thumb brushed over her lips, slightly pulling her bottom one down, which had her breath catching.

"I, um." She blinked, searching for the words. "Some people have mood rings. I have mood fragrances."

"And what is your mood today?"

"Confused," she whispered and brought her face closer to his.

He lifted his brow and smiled. "Not sure that's a mood."

She pulled away and lost his touch. She'd fallen back into the spell of Owen York, yet again. "So, do you have a special nose that affords you the ability to detect types of perfume?"

"It's a secret skill."

"You have to tell me." She poked him in the ribs, hating that she wanted to do much more than that.

He raised his palms in surrender. "My mom used to have a little shop in our town. She'd create her own special perfumes and sell them there." He tipped his head in the direction of the sun. "She had a lab, which of course, seemed badass to me."

"Oh my God, that's precious."

He shrugged. "She used to test me on the fragrances. I can basically identify every smell by nose. It's like second nature to me now, but I bet you could do it, too."

"I doubt that."

His hand met her thigh. "Try it. Shut your eyes. Tell me what you think."

There was so much she needed to tell him, but . . . Her eyes dropped closed, and she gathered in a deep breath, trying to focus. "Hm." She scooted closer to him and rested a hand on his shoulder, sitting taller to get closer to his neck. "Woodsy. Like freshly sanded floors." She laughed a little.

"No, no." She opened her eyes. "Sandalwood. Maybe cedar wood?"

He nodded. "Not bad."

She wet her lips and took in another whiff. "Simple, not too strong." She swallowed. "Raw."

His hand dove through her hair, and he cupped the back of her head as she tipped up her chin.

"We're here," the captain announced.

"Wow." She stood, catching sight of El Arco. "It's beautiful." They slowed near the famous arch, a distinct rock formation. The towering gray rocks had been created by wind and water as if touched by the hand of God. "Majestic." Her fingertips went to her lips, and when she looked at Owen, he was observing her instead of the arch.

She swallowed the desire swirling inside and glanced over at the captain who was motioning their way. "Waters are too dangerous to swim in, but there's a great sea lion colony up ahead. Taking you now," the captain said.

"Will you come with me into the city tonight?" Owen's question pulled her focus back to him as he stood alongside her now. "If you don't want to dance, we could grab dinner."

And for a beat, it was as if she felt a little less fractured than normal, as if his presence somehow could help crush her pain. "I'd like to come, but first, I need to—"

He bent his head and kissed her, stealing the truth from her lips, allowing the lie to live.

And she gave in.

He gathered her into his arms and held her like they'd been kissing like this their entire lives.

He felt like home, but how was that possible?

She'd lost her sense of home the day Brad died.

He threaded his fingers through her hair, tugging at it to

guide her even closer to him as their tongues twined between quick, hungry kisses.

His fingers trailed down her spine, and a rush of excitement had her knees buckling. "Sam," he murmured and tipped her head back to kiss her neck.

She wanted to cry when his hand slipped beneath her bikini top, and he pinched her nipple. "Where's the captain?"

"Hopefully steering." His warm breath at her ear had her mewling.

Hot lust crept beneath her lids, and the thought of being tangled with this man beneath the sheets had her biting her fingertips into his biceps, and she clutched him as if he were a lifeline and she was about to go overboard.

"What if the," she asked between kisses, "captain's watching us?"

He pinched her again, and she wanted to cry as desire swelled inside of her.

"Then, I guess he's gonna get a massive hard-on."

She smiled against his mouth, and for some reason being wrapped in the arms of this man, off the coast of Los Cabos, had her feeling free. Free of the chains that had claimed her for years. Self-imposed, but confining nevertheless.

"I—" A frustrated groan touched her lips, and he pulled back, which was like a knife of reason to the heart. "Sorry. My work phone's vibrating."

She stared at him in surprise. "You have great reception."

"Unfortunately," he said with a lift of his shoulders after he'd stepped back and retrieved his phone. "Give me a sec."

"Sure." She glanced at the captain from over her shoulder, and he had an easy and knowing smile on his face. Of course, he'd probably witnessed much more sinful acts on his boat than a kiss.

But it wasn't an innocent kiss.

It was an unforgivable one—one that she couldn't blame on alcohol.

She looked over at Owen, his face drawn tight. Hard. Resolute.

He started for the captain, swirling a finger in a circular motion in the air.

"Everything okay?" she asked while putting her halter top back on after he'd ended the call.

Owen stood before her and rubbed his thumb in a circle over her cheek. "I have to go."

"Oh."

"It's a work thing." His hand fell to his side, and he averted his gaze to the water for a brief moment as the boat made a U-turn. "I'm heading to D.C., though. Maybe I'll run into you while I'm there?"

Hope flickered in her chest and warmed her cheeks. She'd have a second chance to tell him the truth—to ask him for help. She'd nearly forgotten why she'd come, and she had to get her head back into the game.

"I'd like that." She nodded. "I'm, uh, heading back tomorrow morning."

"Short trip."

"Yeah, it was a last-minute decision to come here." She didn't want to add fuel to the fire of her lie, so she kept her words short. "And I leave for Russia Tuesday."

"Why are you going to Russia?"

"I, uh—it's an event to encourage bilateral talks between heads of state about the current situation on the border zone between Russia and Ukraine," she rushed out the mouthful.

"Wow." He grinned. "You sound important."

She almost laughed. "We're hoping to ease tension over there, and if the region is stable enough then maybe Ukraine can join NATO."

"Hm." He turned to grab his tee. "Isn't Russia against having NATO so close to its border?"

She nodded, even though he couldn't see her with his back to her. "Uh, yeah. But, when I was at the NATO Summit in July, I managed to garner the support of a huge Russian defense company, and they're actually the ones hosting the event next week."

He faced her once his shirt was on. "You keep on impressing me. But I can see why you didn't want to talk work last night." He chuckled. "Pretty intense stuff."

His lips parted like he wanted to say something else, but no sound came out. His eyes thinned, and he angled his head, assessing her. As if remembering her.

She clutched her stomach with one hand, her fingertips biting into the material as she fished around in her head for what to say.

"Listen, I'm not normally, um, the kind of guy to . . ." He scratched at the back of his head and dropped his eyes to the floor. "What I mean is that I don't get involved . . ."

She almost smiled at how he stumbled through letting her know he didn't do relationships. "I don't either." She hoped to diffuse the awkwardness.

"You don't what?" He tipped her chin up with a closed hand.

She chewed on the inside of her cheek for a second. "Relationships. No time. You know"—she innocently lifted her shoulders—"saving the world and all." Then she added, "But I'd like to see you while you're in D.C., maybe before I leave on Tuesday?"

Not to have sex, of course, which was what he probably assumed.

The idea of him hating her when the truth was laid out between them nearly shredded her. But what choice did she have? She couldn't sputter out a quick version of honesty right now.

No, she needed more time.

He smiled, his teeth a bright white with the afternoon sun hitting his tan skin. "I'd like that, Sam. A lot." He bent his head down, and she realized he was going to kiss her again.

And for some stupid reason, she couldn't get herself to turn her cheek.

She let him kiss her goodbye, hoping to hell he'd forgive her the next time he saw her.

CHAPTER FIVE

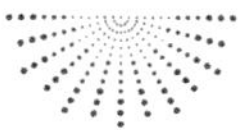

"HOW THE HELL DID YOU MAKE TIME TO GET YOUR HAIR CUT today?" Asher asked when meeting Owen outside their hotel on the street.

Owen swiped a hand over his much shorter locks. "We're meeting face-to-face with"—he looked around to see if anyone was in earshot—"the secretary of defense. I can't show up looking grungy. Haven't seen the man since he nearly vetoed my membership on the team way back when."

"Aw, you gotta look pretty for him, then, huh?" Asher knocked him in the bicep before they began down Virginia Avenue, leaving the Washington Monument farther behind them with each passing step. "Looks like you couldn't lose the facial hair, though."

"It's trimmed." He slipped on his shades and hid an eye roll. "Apparently, you don't care how you look."

"POTUS could call me into the Oval Office for all I care, and I wouldn't give a damn if I were in my Sunday best or my briefs, let alone worry about my hair."

Owen cracked a smile. "Like you have any 'Sunday best' digs, anyway."

Asher mumbled something under his breath then said, "Too bad vacay was cut short. You were finally starting to have some fun."

Owen peered up at the jet trails in the sky. He needed to remember to clock in some flying hours. "I might call Sam later, though. She said she was coming home today, and since she lives here—"

"You're going to see her again?"

Owen stopped walking and moved off to the side of the foot traffic. "What, you think I shouldn't?"

Asher leaned against the exterior of an office building. "I've just never known you to see a woman twice."

"You talking about me? Or yourself?" Owen flicked his gaze to the reflection in the window, noting a dark Suburban rolling up to the curb behind them. "I think that ride is for us."

As much as he hadn't wanted to leave Sam yesterday, it was always good to be on an op. It helped take his mind off heavy thoughts. He was more than happy to have a reason to dodge his mother's constant requests to attend Jason's celebration-of-life party today.

Jess opened the passenger side door. "Are you guys going to get in, or what?"

"We could've walked," Asher said. "Slide over, Peaches."

Jess ignored him and looked to Owen. "Why don't you sit in the middle?" She held a palm up, requesting Asher to remain standing, and Owen sidestepped him to scoot inside.

"Good to have you back," Owen said when eying Luke in the front passenger seat, alongside Liam, who was behind the wheel. "How's Eva feeling? Are you going to have one of those gender-reveal-party things to share the sex of the baby?"

"How do you even know about those?" Asher laughed, elbowing him in the ribs once the door was closed.

Luke shifted to face the three of them, wearing a smirk. "She wants to be surprised and wait until the baby is here, but—"

"But you want to have everything planned ahead of time." Owen smiled, knowing his hard-ass boss wouldn't be able to handle the not-knowing.

"It'll be a boy, though. It has to be." Luke closed his eyes for a moment, and Owen knew exactly what he was thinking. A daughter would be dangerous—for any boyfriend who dated her, at least.

"Girl," Liam sputtered from behind the wheel with a chuckle.

"Anyway." Luke pivoted back to face the front window. "How was your time in the sun?"

Mexico had been better than he'd expected. Sam was a hell of a woman. Maybe Asher was right, and he didn't usually make the time to see people again, because he hated keeping up the lie of who he was, but this felt different. He'd felt a connection with her he didn't remember ever experiencing, and that had to mean something.

"It was good," Owen finally said when he felt the soft touch of Jess's fingers on his tense forearm.

"You okay?" she asked in a near-whisper as if she didn't want the rest of the crew to know she had a sensitive side—a side he wondered if only he knew about. She was all hard angles with almost everyone, even sometimes with Luke. Although, ever since Luke had "found love," as Jess liked to call it, she'd softened a touch toward her brother.

But Owen also knew Jess had concerns that love might make Luke weak. That's what she'd confided to Owen, at least.

Walls all around her, and he knew a thing or two about walls. Most of his team did, too.

“I’m good.” Owen added a nod when it looked like she didn’t believe him.

“Sorry again about cutting your trip short.” She removed her fingers from his arm. “Knox is rendezvousing at the meet.”

“Echo’s not being brought in?” Asher asked.

“Half of them are on a job for the company, and Handlin only requested a five-man team.”

He was surprised they were all meeting with Handlin. The secretary of defense never met with anyone other than Luke or Jess. He preferred to maintain his distance from the team to prevent any suspicious eyebrows from catching everyone together.

“Well, he’s actually getting five guys and a chick.” Asher rested his elbows on his knees and leaned forward, and it had Owen flipping his eyes to the ceiling, wishing he could remove himself from the center of their hate-slash-want-to-screw sandwich.

“‘Chick’?” Jess bit out. “I had hoped Mexico would’ve gotten rid of some of your testosterone. Guess I was wrong.”

Clearly, the vacation had done nothing to break the tension between them.

Asher edged even more forward as the SUV moved into the flow of traffic. “You love how I am, Peaches.” He kissed the air and winked.

She mumbled something beneath her breath and averted her blues out the tinted side window.

“You two.” Luke shook his head.

“Any clue what this job is about?” Owen asked.

“Only that Handlin red-flagged this meeting as critical, and he needed our asses in D.C. ASAP,” Luke said, and a couple of minutes later, he pointed to a two-story brick building not far from the State Department. "We're here. Handlin said to park around back."

"A law office?" Owen asked.

"It's a front for an off-the-books meeting site," Jess explained as she reached for the door handle.

Once outside, Owen started to walk to the building, spotting Knox waiting near the side door.

Luke motioned for the team to go in, but he turned to face Owen, stopping him in his tracks. "Can we talk?"

Owen's hands disappeared into his pockets when Luke's gaze dropped to the asphalt. "Uh, sure. What's up?"

"Are you sure you're good to go on an op right now? With Jason's—"

"It's exactly what I need. And I don't need a reminder of what today is. Believe me, I know."

"You're sure?" Luke found his eyes again. "I need you at the top of your game, so you don't get hurt."

"Have I ever let you down?"

Luke's mouth tightened before he gave a curt nod and headed for the building.

Owen swept his hands to his face and dragged his palms down to collect himself before following after the team.

Once inside, Knox met up with him in the hall and bumped a fist into Owen's shoulder. "How was México?" he asked, adding a Spanish accent to his tone. "Lots of fine women there." He flashed his classic broad smile.

"It was"—he let his words hang in the air for a moment while he'd thought about what Sam had said to him on the dance floor two nights back—"unexpected."

"You want to tell me what that means?"

"I'll let you fill in the blanks." Owen grinned, his

thoughts circling back to Sam. Had a woman ever gotten into his head like this?

The team filtered into a room, and Jess motioned for them to take a seat at a long oval conference table. The room looked to be a place where boring business meetings were held—not a place for highly secretive government briefings.

He dropped into a seat as if gravity were sucking him down with more force than normal today.

"We're all clear," Liam announced once he finished sweeping the room for bugs.

When Secretary Handlin stalked into the room with his glossy polished shoes and expensive suit, Owen's gaze snapped up, and any lingering thoughts in his mind vaporized.

"Thank you for coming on such short notice."

"Of course." Luke remained standing off to the side of the table that took up most of the space.

Handlin's eyes narrowed when his gaze fell upon Owen. "I thought I requested Echo Team." He lifted a brow and looked over at Luke.

"Yeah, but I have two guys from Echo on another job for our private security company right now. I couldn't pull them in time to meet you today," Luke explained. "So, you got your five-man team here."

Owen was pretty sure everyone in the room was wondering the same damn thing: *why not Bravo?*

"I can't have York on this mission. I didn't want to be so blunt over the phone, but that's the truth." Handlin coughed into a closed fist a few times and scanned the room, as if expecting a reaction from the team, but they all remained silent, waiting for him to continue.

Jess looked over at Owen, worry crossing her face before she redirected her eyes to the secretary of defense.

Luke's jaw tightened for a moment before he finally spoke, cutting the palpable tension in the room. "We're a team. If you want me, you get all of us. No exceptions."

Handlin circled the table as if the movement would help him collect his thoughts. Owen caught a whiff of rubbing alcohol from him, or the kind of antibiotic soap surgeons use in the OR.

"I was afraid you'd say that." Handlin gestured toward the door. "Luke. Jessica. Outside, please." And he left the room without another word.

"What the hell was that all about?" Knox stretched back, his gaze narrowing on Owen.

"I'm about to go find out." Luke left the room, and Jess gave an apologetic glance Owen's way and followed him out.

"Why the hell wouldn't he want me on an op?"

"I can only think of one reason." Asher's facial muscles went taut as he gave Owen a quick nod as if to say *we've got your back.*

"Luke and Jess will handle it," Liam said a beat later. "Don't worry, mate." His Aussie accent swept through his words, and he tapped a closed fist against the table a couple of times.

Hope stirred inside as he latched on to the idea that he'd finally get vengeance for his brother.

Maybe he was grasping at straws, but if it were true, there was no way he could sit on the sidelines.

He tipped his head back as he waited for what felt like hours for them to return, even though it was a matter of minutes.

"Welcome back," Asher said with a mock of sarcasm in his tone once Luke, Handlin, and Jess returned.

Jess took the empty seat next to Owen and Luke assumed his previous stance of leaning against the wall with crossed arms. A dark look of worry clouded Luke's blue eyes.

"Let's get started." Handlin eyed Owen one last time before announcing, "I'm going to cut straight to the point. Two Navy SEALs have been taken."

Handlin's words had Owen's spine straightening and the hairs on his arms pricking to attention.

Dropped curses from his teammates filled the room.

"Hank Shaw retired ten years ago, and Aaron Robins, who is still active duty, was on leave."

The name Shaw didn't spark recognition, but Robins—he'd been at Jason's funeral. He'd given his condolences while holding his baby tucked in the crook of his arm with his wife alongside him.

Your brother was a good man. An honorable man. I'm sorry for your loss, Robins had said.

"Robins has a daughter," Owen rushed out. "She'd be eleven now. Is she okay? Is his wife okay?"

A SEAL wouldn't cave under pressure, but if their loved ones were on the line . . . Luke had never wanted any of them to have a family while active duty to prevent something like this from happening. Then he went and fell in love and blew that idea to pieces.

"Shaw's wife is at a safe house, as well as Robins's wife and daughter," Handlin said, and thank God for something.

"What the hell happened, sir? I'm assuming these were targeted hits?" Asher's palms flattened onto the table, a grim twist to his lips.

"Shaw was on a fishing trip in Montana, and Robins was on his way home from the VA outside Dam Neck. When Shaw didn't check in with his wife, she got nervous, and troopers went to his rental cabin, and they found signs of a fight." Handlin cleared his throat. "Robins's car was found abandoned off the side of the road, and there was blood in the driver's seat."

"You thinking he was shot?" Owen asked, his stomach tucking in at the thought.

"Probably resisted," Asher commented. "That's what any one of us would've done."

"Must have been outnumbered," Liam said.

"Shaw and Robins were Tier One operatives," Handlin said, catching everyone off guard.

The government had never officially admitted a "Team Six" even existed, despite the press and Hollywood hoopla about the covert group. But if two Tier One operatives were truly now in the hands of someone, especially a terrorist, Owen couldn't begin to imagine the blowback that'd result in.

"There's more I have to tell you." He paused. "As of zero eight hundred hours yesterday, we learned Roger Canton's also missing. Based on our calculations, we think all three men were taken simultaneously, we just didn't know about it at the time. A well-coordinated hit."

"And who's Canton?" Asher asked.

"A former CIA officer," Jess whispered, and her eyes fell to the table.

"You know him?" Asher's gaze winged straight to her.

She softly nodded but kept her eyes lowered. "He was one of my teachers at the Farm. Sort of a mentor."

The room grew silent, as if giving Jess a moment to process—to grieve what could be a possible loss if they didn't find him before it was too late.

Owen's hands became white-knuckled on the table before him, and he finally broke the quiet and asked, "And what does Canton have to do with Shaw and Robins? What's the connection?" He paused. "Because I'm assuming there has to be a connection, right?"

Handlin's gaze journeyed the room, eying the team. "Canton worked an op with Shaw and Robins." He held up his index finger. "Only one time. One mission ten years ago." He coughed into his fist a few times and cleared his throat. "Only a handful of people alive today are even privy to that op, so it wasn't until I heard of all three abductions did I put two and two together."

Ten years. The number was like a blow to the side of his skull, and Owen's mind raced with thoughts about his brother again.

"As you know, NCIS handles cases with military personnel, but given the nature of this situation, the FBI is also getting involved. But, under orders by the president, we're not able to share intel from the op ten years ago with any federal agent. It's above their security clearance."

"And the personnel connected to that op, where are they now? Are they being watched in case someone comes for them?" Luke asked, possibly recommending a bait-and-trap play.

"The names linked to the op in question have been alerted. Most of those men already have security detail given their line of work, but we've amped it up—without drawing too much attention."

"They're okay with using themselves as bait?" Knox asked, surprise in his tone.

"Washington can't up and fall apart over this—over something that may or may not have to do with that op. The wheels of the nation need to keep running, and these are powerful men we're talking about. They don't *want* to go into hiding."

Handlin referred to the brass being safe, but what about

the men who'd worn the uniform? "And the other SEALs from that op? Are they being protected?"

Handlin's eyes became pinned to Owen's, and he said in a steady tone, "No other SEAL from that particular operation is alive."

His words were like a right hook to the jaw leading to a KO—a knockout, and a flurry of ideas crossed through his mind.

Jason? Brad? Was this the connection? Was this the op that took them out?

But no, they weren't DEVGRU. It wasn't possible.

"President Rydell doesn't want to create a crisis or draw international attention from the media about this. We can't let people think it's okay to abduct three of our men. Or have journalists digging into the connection between the three men, either . . ." His voice trailed off as he began hacking into his closed hand again.

"We've got to get our men back." Asher's fist met the table, and Owen could feel the angry vibrations beneath his palms.

Jess grabbed a bottle of Evian from her work bag and brought it over to Handlin. "You okay, sir?"

Handlin nodded while gulping down some of the water.

"Sir, why were there only four operatives working with Canton? Since when do we send in a four-man team?" Owen's mind whirled, his heart still pumping blood up and into his ears.

Handlin lowered the bottle to the table. "It was only meant to be a recon and surveillance op, and we needed to keep a low profile." He filled his chest with air and released it like a balloon losing helium.

"Guessing the op didn't go as planned." Asher shook his head.

"I can't tell you more right now, I'm afraid," Handlin said.

"Why not?" Luke stepped closer to the table.

"I need to get the final go-ahead from the president. He still has concerns about sharing the operational file with anyone without knowing for sure if the abductions relate to that mission."

Luke's jaw tightened at the news. "We don't have time to sit on this."

Handlin patted the air with both hands as if to say calm down. "And we have every agent scouring the country for them, believe me."

"Hard to do without setting off the media alarm bells," Knox grumbled. He knew a thing or two about the media having grown up in the political spotlight of his father.

"They're doing their best," Handlin said.

Knox stood, his palms landing on the table. "Their best is not our best. We need to get started."

"I'll give you an answer by tomorrow. We're waiting for one more piece of information to determine if you get the greenlight." Handlin swung his gaze over to his shoulder and gave a quick nod to Luke. "Okay?"

"You wouldn't have called us here if you didn't already think you needed us," Asher said, joining Knox on his feet. And hell, everyone was standing now. How could they sit given what they'd learned?

"Why are you against me working this case?" Owen couldn't help but ask, and his question had Handlin looking over at him.

Handlin took another sip of water as if buying himself time, and then he said, "Your brother was on the operation with Shaw and Robins—the op that took his life."

Owen braced the table, so he didn't fall. "No." He shook his head, his brows darting together.

"Jason was DEVGRU," Luke said.

His words had Owen's attention floating back to Luke as if time stood still for a beat.

Had Luke always known the truth? Or had Handlin just informed him in the hall before the meeting?

The way Luke's gaze dropped to the floor had Owen's heart rate kicking up even higher.

His stomach squeezed.

Luke had known . . . After all these years, how could he not tell him Jason had been DEVGRU?

"Don't blame him," Handlin said. "Luke was under direct orders not to tell you about who Jason worked for. And no, he wasn't privy to the details about the op that took your brother's life."

Owen pulled at the skin of his throat, trying to maintain his composure, so he didn't lose a shot at being part of the mission.

Handlin's leathery skin tightened around his eyes. "I can't tell you more right now. I'm sorry."

"Then what can you tell me?" He cleared his throat. "Tell *us,* I mean."

"I need you to understand this case can't be about finding justice for your brother." He paused and his nostrils flared.

Justice? Justice meant Jason's killer was still alive . . .

"THIS CRYPTIC BULLSHIT WE CONSTANTLY DEAL WITH IS starting to get on my damn nerves." Asher eyed the Reflecting Pool, the light of the full moon casting a glow onto the water.

"Considering we do Command's bidding, you'd think we could get a little more honesty out of them." Owen looked over at the Washington Monument, American flags skirting the perimeter, and a harsh reminder of the loss of his brother resurfaced in his mind.

Of course, the memory never faded, but today, it was like his insides had been hacked by a machete.

He looked over at Asher, a question burning in his mind. Asher had been an elite operative for Charlie Team before taking Marcus's place nearly three years ago. "Did you know Jason was DEVGRU?"

Asher met his stare, his brows pinching briefly. "Nah, I joined after him." He pivoted to better face him. "Regardless of what Handlin said back there, we'll get our people back and fix whatever the hell he needs us to. But we'll also get revenge for Jason and Brad."

A knot fisted in his stomach, unease moving swiftly through him like a wildfire. "Brad didn't have any family after his grandmother died," he said after a minute. "Well, he had a fiancée." He let out a weary sigh. "And I promised her justice." He dropped his head forward, trying to remember his brief conversation with Brad's fiancée at the funeral. "I also told her I'd look after her, but I didn't have the balls to do it myself." *Hell, I could hardly look her in the eyes that day.*

Asher gripped his shoulder. "Well, we'll make shit right." He gave a hard nod.

"It's time I deliver on my promise."

Regret circled around his mind as he thought about his past, and then a wave of heat suddenly torched his chest and worked its way up his throat and into his face.

He clutched his stomach as Brad's fiancée's face came to mind. "Fuuuck."

CHAPTER SIX

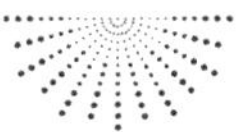

"ARE YOU SURE YOU AND MR. IVAN DRAGO ARE A MATCH made in heaven?" She handed Emily a glass of wine and sat next to her on the couch in Sam's living room.

"Is that what you're calling him?" Emily laughed. "And who is that, exactly?"

Her mouth went agape. "The Russian boxer from *Rocky IV*. How are we even friends if you don't know that?"

"You have Russia on the brain." Emily sipped her Riesling.

"Well, I don't like him."

"You just don't like his job." She lifted a brow.

Sam held her palms up and shrugged. "Blane's a D.C. fixer. What can I say?" Besides, she had to look out for her best friend, the same way she'd always looked out for Sam.

Emily set her glass on the coffee table. "He promotes positive messages about politicians. He's not Olivia Pope from that *Scandal* show."

Sam flicked her wrist. "I don't know. He rubs me the wrong way."

"And you only met him the one time before you had to

leave your own dinner party." She crossed her arms and eyed her best friend with her typical I-call-bullshit stare.

"Sorry again about that." Work never seemed to let up. Of course, in Mexico, she'd tasted what it'd be like to live a little —but with the wrong guy and at the wrong time.

She hung her head and rubbed the heel of her hand against her cheek.

"Well, 'Mr. Drago,'" she said while using air quotes, "is really good in bed, so I'll be staying with him for as long as the sex remains so deliciously hot."

"There's more to life than great sex."

"Says the woman who isn't getting any."

She crossed her arms and leaned back into the couch. "Give me a break. You're always in court, working a case. You're not one to talk."

"Lunch-break sex is where it's at." She chuckled.

"Well, like I said, I don't like the guy."

Emily edged closer with a smile on her lips. "That makes me want to hook up with him even more."

"Such a rebel," she teased. "But, in all seriousness, I don't want to see you get hurt again. After you and Mr. British Guy broke up—"

Emily silenced her with a palm. "Next topic."

Sam's phone buzzed, cutting off her thoughts, and she reached for it to view the text. "My dad."

"What does he want?"

She set the phone back down. "Just letting me know he still hasn't gotten Senator Abrams to agree to the proposal." She released a long-winded breath of frustration. "I should be focusing on getting Abrams on board instead of chasing down a photo. The benefit is Wednesday."

"And maybe this is exactly what they want."

"And by 'they' you mean whoever sent me the photo?"

Emily shrugged. "You and I are both smart enough to know it can't be a coincidence someone sent you a photo from Ukraine, given what you're working on right now."

"I don't know." Her thoughts were becoming too heavy, and she needed a second to just breathe. She snatched Emily's wine glass off the table and took a sip. "To hell with whatever headache it may give me."

"You never drink wine, and yet, your bar is packed full of it." Emily smiled.

Sam gathered more of the liquid into her mouth and gulped. "The bar is stashed with wine because my *best friend* loves the stuff."

"Such a good friend."

Sam finished the drink and grabbed the open bottle by the couch and refilled the glass before handing it over to Emily.

"So, I take it you still haven't told your dad about the photo."

Her shoulders shrank forward with the weight of guilt. "He'd freak out. You know how much he hated when I looked into Brad's death before—if he knew about the photo, he'd turn it over to the Feds, and I might lose my only shot at the truth."

Emily rolled her eyes. "And . . . we're back to that."

"It could be legit. Maybe from a whistleblower trying to expose a cover-up?" But what the hell was covered up? Shivers blew over her skin at the thought, and she stood. "And I think I need a stronger drink." She went over to her bar by the window. "Of course, I don't seem to make the best decisions when drunk." She thought back to her close call at sex with Owen the other night.

"Some things don't change. I'll never forget the first time you met Brad. Wet T-shirt contest coupled with loads of shots makes for a crazy combination."

Her words reminded her of a past that still felt like yesterday. "I did win the contest, though." She set the bottle of vodka back in its place, deciding against the drink.

"And Brad was your consolation prize. The guy couldn't keep his eyes off you that night."

"I thought he was faking being a SEAL just to win me over."

When she turned, she spied her old collection of CDs on the bottom shelf of her entertainment system from across the room, and she moved toward it like she was being mindlessly lulled into the past.

"Wouldn't be the first time a guy did that," Emily said as Sam crouched down to find a particular CD.

"What are you looking for, by the way?"

"The CD Brad gave me before his last deployment."

"The song he dedicated to you after he proposed?"

And sang to me over Skype two days before he was taken from me. But she couldn't get herself to voice the thought.

"*'Two Souls,'* right?"

"Yeah." She found the disc and then stood upright and popped it into the stereo she hadn't used in years. Her fingers smoothed over the rose tattoo on the inside of her wrist just as the musician's lyrics floated to her ears and burned a gaping hole in her heart—Brad had called Sam his rose, same as the musician to whatever woman he'd sung the song for.

"When was the last time you listened to this?"

"Not in a long time," she whispered.

Ten years had gone by, and it never truly got easier. Time minimized the pain, but it didn't extinguish it.

And every man she'd dated had been a pale comparison to Brad.

Strings of endless one-night dates and a few one-night stands.

She hadn't thought another man would ever be able to capture her heart, but then she'd met Owen, and as crazy as it sounded, meeting him had given her hope that someday she might fall in love again.

"You okay?" Emily stood and came behind her, resting a hand on her shoulder.

Sam closed her eyes and buried her emotions the best she could. She knew she wouldn't be able to fix on the painted smile she used for D.C. politicians—not with her best friend.

"Sam," she said softly. "I saw what happened to you after you lost Brad, and how looking into his death back then nearly destroyed you. And ever since you got that picture at the office, you've looked like a woman determined for revenge again." Emily whispered the word *revenge* like it was dirty, and it had Sam facing her with open eyes. "Is that what this is really about?" She lifted a brow. "Are you planning to go down that path again?"

"You sound like my father now," she bit back.

But was Emily right? Would chasing after the photo break her?

Would she crack into too many pieces and be unable to patch herself back up?

Of course, she wasn't really whole now, was she?

"I should have told Owen the truth on the boat," she said, finally getting her vocal cords to work.

"And why didn't you?"

She turned off the stereo, remembering now why she never played the song. It was too painful. "I couldn't lay the truth on him at the last minute like that."

"You shouldn't have left without telling him who you are," Emily said when Sam turned back around.

"We kissed again on the boat," she sputtered as quickly as she could. She hadn't been sure if she was going to tell Emily or not, but she felt like she needed absolution of her sins. Besides, Emily was the only one who could see through her walls, walls that, some days, were constructed with straw instead of brick. "I went there to ask him about the photo, not to get swept off my feet."

Shit. She clicked her tongue at the roof of her mouth.

"You're allowed to have feelings, Sam."

"Not with him."

Emily held her hands out, palms up. "Love tends to find us when we're not looking for it."

"He's Jason's brother. Even if I felt something for him, it doesn't matter. He's him. I'm me. There are rules about this kind of thing, right?"

She gripped her shoulders. "First of all, stop calling him that. He has a name. Second of all, Owen's *Jason's* brother, not Brad's. And Brad would want you to be happy."

"Owen will never forgive me. A man like him. I could see the pain in his eyes. I could see what loss has done to him. I went all the way to Mexico, only to come home with a pile of guilt and no answers." She turned back to the bar and braced the counter.

"Not true. You did discover something."

"Yeah? That I suck?" She faked a laugh.

"No, but if Owen was on vacation and kissing you, I highly doubt someone delivered him a creepy photo like the one you got, which means this is only about you."

"Unless Owen handles situations differently. Or, maybe no one needed to send him anything because he'd been a SEAL and knew the truth about what happened."

"You're *still* treating the photo you got like the gospel truth, which is absurd. And hell, maybe you should consider getting security like your father has. What if you're not safe?"

"It was a picture. If someone wanted to hurt me, they

wouldn't send a photo." Sam puffed out her cheeks, but she couldn't bring herself to turn around. "Did your brother ever ID the third guy in the image, by the way?"

Emily snorted. "Uh, I would've led with that when I came over."

"Right." She squeezed her eyes closed. "I'm not myself. Sor—" She cut herself off at the sound of her doorbell from the security system outside her building.

"A visitor this late?"

Sam hurried to the security intercom system to view the outdoor camera. "Shit." She jumped back as if he could see her. "It's Owen."

Emily came up next to her. "You gave him your address? You didn't tell me that."

"I only gave him my number. Hell, I didn't even give him my last name." Her brows slanted in surprise. "How'd he find me?"

"Only one way to find out. Let him up."

Sam peered at the security system, her nerves fraying by the second. "Hello."

"Hi, it's, uh, me." The low and sexy voice flitted straight to her ears. "Owen, I mean."

Anxiety bunched in her stomach and swept through her body.

"He *is* hot. Damn." Emily observed the security screen. "Did he look this good ten years ago?"

Sam's eyes widened. "Focus. What do I do?"

"Let him in." She patted her on the shoulder and then started for the door.

"Where are you going?"

"I'm leaving so you guys can have some privacy."

"Right. Okay." She closed her eyes and held down the button. "Hi," she said softly.

"Hey, sorry to drop in on you. I was hoping we could talk."

"He must know who I am," she said to Emily. She had hoped to reveal the truth on her own terms, though.

"I was surprised he didn't recognize you sooner." Emily lightly shrugged. "Just get this talk over with."

Different emotions stacked up inside of her like layers on a cake, but she wasn't ready to cut through them all yet. She needed more time to work up the nerve. But she whispered, "Okay." She pressed her finger back onto the talk button. "Come on up." She buzzed him in and shook her arms out at her sides to get rid of the sudden feeling of needles pricking her skin.

"Good luck." Emily patted her shoulder. "Maybe I'll get a sneak peek of him on my way out."

"I'll call you after he leaves."

Emily nodded and left.

A rap at the door a minute later had her tongue pinned to the top of her mouth. She secured her hand on the knob and released a lungful of air before opening it.

Owen stood with a palm braced against the exterior of the doorframe, and her lips twitched into a smile when she noticed he'd cut his hair.

His hair was now tapered at the sides, with his beard connecting up and to his hairline. The top of his hair was still a little longer and maybe purposefully spiky—that, or he'd been running his fingers through it as if something was wrong.

He looked dangerously hot, and it had her stomach physically hurting at the sight of him, especially if he now knew the truth.

"Hi." He looked over her shoulder and into her home, his eyes tracking the visible area from left to right. "You alone?"

She forced herself to step back and find her voice. "Yeah. Come in."

He remained standing, though, with his eyes now positioned back on hers. It was like every ounce of his energy pinged off him, hitting her like a punch to the gut.

He tucked his hands in his pockets, jingling change or a set of keys. "You're not wearing perfume."

Even from that far he could tell? *Wow.*

She found herself smiling, but it faded quickly at the continued harsh look in his eyes and the tight line of his lips. *He knows. He knows!* Everything inside of her screamed like a child throwing a tantrum, and it was all her fault. The lie had been like silk, smoothly slipping from her tongue the moment they'd collided in Mexico. Now, she'd have to grate out an explanation that made sense.

"I, uh, just got out of the shower," she said and blinked away her thoughts. Her wet locks threaded between her fingers when she remembered she was makeup free and only in pajama shorts and a tee.

Emily had shown up right after she'd showered, forcing her to talk about what had happened on her trip.

Jason's brother. She shuddered at the thought and turned away, expecting him to follow. But when she peered back at him, he remained standing in the hall.

He stared down at the change from the wood floors in the hall to the carpet in her home, as if there was some sort of red line he couldn't bring himself to cross.

"Do you know who I am?"

She fully faced him, her arms dead at her sides.

"Do you remember me?" He finally stepped over the line and nudged the door shut behind him.

"I—" The rest of the words jammed up in her throat, and she couldn't seem to free them.

He closed the gap between them in one stride, which had her pulse doubling. "Do you know I'm Jason York's brother?"

Chills swept over her skin as he propped a palm on the wall in the mini foyer of her home.

She eyed his bicep, a few veins wrapping around the muscle like a rope. "Yes. Yes, I know." She dropped her gaze to the floor.

A deep sigh blew from his lips. "When did you realize? On the boat?" The deep sexiness of his normal tone had been replaced by a harsh grit that was cutting.

"I knew before then." She hugged her body and rubbed her arms, wondering if she should get dressed before baring the truth to him. "Maybe we could go for a walk?"

He took a moment to consider her words then nodded, and so, she hurried to her bedroom to get dressed before he changed his mind.

A minute later, she came back toward him like a nervous bride on her wedding day.

"Why didn't you tell me?" he asked once they were outside. "Why'd you let me believe we were strangers?"

She turned and faced him. "I, uh, tried so many times. I never meant to sleep with you. Or, whatever we did."

"You knew that soon?" His brows slanted inward, and his lips remained parted in surprise.

She nodded. "I didn't expect to feel . . ."

He shifted the weight of his stance as his gaze swerved up and over her shoulder. "Is there a reason why someone would be following you?"

"What?" She twisted around to find a guy standing on the other side of the four-lane road. He was in a dark sweatshirt and jeans, and the moment their eyes connected he lifted his hood and turned to go the other way down the street.

Owen reached for her arm and redirected her focus back to him. "I'd chase after him, but I'm not leaving you on the street alone. Not if he's a distraction and there's someone else nearby looking to grab you."

"'Grab' me? Why would you think that? And how do you even know he was looking at me?"

"In my line of work . . ." He allowed his voice to trail off, then he shook his head. "Come on, let's just get you off the street, okay?" He touched the small of her back and directed her toward the entrance.

Once they were back in her place, Owen locked up, sliding the chain in place. "You really have no idea who that was?"

"Who knows if he was even watching me?" *But* . . . She thought back to the description of the deliveryman Phillip had given her: tall, dark hair, dark eyes. He could be one in a million. "I don't know, maybe it could be him," she said as if he'd been following along with her line of thought.

"'Him' who?" A pair of hazel eyes were sharp on her.

She massaged her temples and took a few breaths before softly admitting, "I lied to you."

"Yeah, I already got that part. You didn't tell me who you are," he rasped.

When she couldn't find the words, he strode past her and approached the bookshelves that flanked her entertainment center. The muscles pinched in his back as he lifted a photo of her and Brad.

"You should've told me. You should never have let me goddamn touch you."

"I'm sorry." But would sorry ever be enough?

He handed her the photo and strode to the door, but instead of leaving, he placed his balled hands against it and hung his head. "Do you understand how wrong this is? How bad I feel now?" He tapped his head lightly against the wood before pushing back.

Her heart took a terrifying climb into her throat, and she inwardly groaned. "I-I'm so sorry. I was drunk, and I—"

He swiveled around. "And on the boat?" His jaw clenched as he asked through barely parted lips, "What were you then?"

"Stupid . . ."

He bowed his head as if he couldn't stomach the sight of her.

"There's something I have to show you to explain why I followed you to Mexico."

He looked up at her, and his brows rose in surprise.

Had she left that part out? *Shit.* Before he could say anything, she turned and went to her desk to retrieve the photo from the envelope.

Clutching it to her chest, she slowly ate up the space between them as if she were walking toward him with a grenade in hand.

"Here." She extended her arm and finally offered the photo, the reason why she went to Los Cabos.

His eyes narrowed as he examined it, bringing it close to his face the same way she had done the first time she'd seen it. "Where the hell did you get this?" An edge of darkness, of pain, wrapped tight around his words.

"A delivery guy dropped it off at my office and then took off. I didn't see him, but it's possible the guy outside . . ." She rubbed her forehead, trying to collect her thoughts and make sense of everything. "I haven't been able to authenticate whether it's real or not. Anyone with Photoshop could fake this—but if they did, they went to a hell of a lot of trouble to do so."

He remained quiet, his eyes pinned to the image.

"This picture is a copy, though. I gave the original to my friend at the FBI." She curled her fingertips into her palms. "After Brad died, I did my best to look into what happened. I couldn't handle that he was just gone, and that the terrorist responsible hadn't been captured."

Her last few words were like an echo in the room, and it had him looking straight at her. He lowered the photo to his side with a grim twist to his lips.

"This picture doesn't make sense, right?" she asked. "It shows Brad, Jason, and some other guy in Kiev instead of Ramadi, the day they died."

"How do you know they're in Ukraine?"

She came around next to him and touched the picture, her finger falling upon the large dome and five green cupolas, which served as the backdrop of the photo. "That's St. Andrew's Cathedral in the background. I was just in Kiev in July with my father." When he kept quiet, she continued, "You were a SEAL, right? You must know more than me about what happened to them."

"How do you know that about me? Hell, how'd you know where to find me?"

She owed him the truth, but she hoped she wouldn't get her friends in trouble. "My best friend's brother used to work for the FBI. He works in the private sector now, but he pulled a few strings and looked you up for me."

Had she made a mistake in finding him, in reaching out to him?

She took small breaths and backed away. "Shahid Ismail was responsible for the attack against Brad and Jason in Iraq, right? They died trying to rescue that scientist from al-Qaeda?"

He didn't say anything. His jaw remained locked tight,

the muscle clenching so hard she could see it beneath his closely trimmed beard.

"The photo was delivered on Wednesday," she continued since he remained quiet. "I had security check it for anthrax first—can't be too certain with what I do—then I looked inside once I got the all clear." She lifted her shoulders. "If this is real, I'm thinking someone wanted to expose a cover-up; that, or they wanted to make me think there was a cover-up. Who knows in Washington these days? We get all kinds of crazy mail at the office, but this was the first time it didn't come with a postage stamp." She swallowed. "And the first time it hit so close to home."

He set the image on her coffee table and gripped his temples with his forefinger and thumb. "The timing of this . . ."

There was something he knew, something in his eyes, which told her he was keeping a secret. Maybe her instincts to find him had been right, after all.

He didn't owe her anything, especially after she'd lied. But she hadn't gone to Cabo expecting him to be so amazing, for him to knock her off her focus with a quick smile and a few charming rapid-fire questions.

"Didn't you say you were going to Russia next week to discuss Ukrainian-Russian relations or something like that?"

She nodded. Maybe he was drawing the same conclusions as Emily, and probably rightfully so.

"If that photo is legit, whoever took it was on overwatch."

"What's 'overwatch'?"

"It's when someone's at a high vantage point, and they're either there to surveil or protect. Brad, Jason, and this third guy were in the crosshairs of a scope. Well, if this photo hasn't been photoshopped."

Her heart leaped into her throat. "You think this is real?"

"I didn't say that."

"Then what are you saying?"

"I honestly don't know what to think."

"You don't recognize the third guy in the picture, do you?" She retrieved the image from the table and rolled her lips inward in thought.

"No." He scratched at the nape of his neck. "You need protection."

Maybe he was right, especially if the guy outside was, in fact, watching her. "I can stay at my folks' place. They live in Arlington. My dad isn't home, but my mom is, and she's heavily guarded. It's probably as secure as the White House."

"Why the heavy security?" He raised a questioning brow.

"My dad's a bit overprotective." Her lips curved down at the thought. "But he has good reason. Let's just say it can be dangerous being in the public eye, especially if people disagree with your political positions."

"And this"—he circled a finger in the air—"is what you call secure?"

"I get a few threats here and there, but most people seem to target my dad. They only see me as a woman behind a man, I suppose."

"Looks like someone is targeting you now." He rubbed his forehead. "There's a good chance this is somehow linked to . . ."

And again, the dropped words.

What was he hiding?

"Linked to what?" She had to ask. She had to know. If he could somehow help her, she'd prod and poke for answers, even if she didn't deserve them.

"It's classified. I'm sorry."

Classified? Didn't he retire?

Silence seized hold of the room, and it was as if he were contemplating what to do, assessing options and risks.

"I have a picture of the deliveryman. I had security look through the footage. The guy did a good job at keeping his face away from the cameras, so I barely got a partial profile." She grabbed the image from the top drawer of her desk. "Hard to tell if it's the man from outside tonight."

"We probably can't get any hits off of this, but I'll see what I can do." He found her eyes. "I think you should stay with me tonight, though."

"With *you*?" The idea had her heart thumping even harder.

"I'm at a hotel nearby. I'll make sure we're not being followed. Besides, no one will come busting down my door, and if they do—good luck with that. But we should meet up with your Fed friend tomorrow and get the original back. I'd rather have my people look at it."

At his words, heat crawled up her throat to her face, and her stomach muscles tightened.

"I work for a private security company. Keeping people safe is basically my job."

"I don't want to screw up your schedule. Aren't you here for work?"

"It's fine. Don't worry." His forehead creased, concern there. "But if you're being targeted, do you really want to be near your mom?"

"Good point. Should I give my folk's a heads-up, though, especially if this is about the event on Wednesday?"

"Let me sort through a few things tonight, then we'll decide what to say."

She nodded her *okay*.

"I have a call to make." He produced his phone from his pocket. "Why don't you pack?" Without giving her a chance to answer, he stepped out of her apartment, leaving her alone to allow her mind to spin.

This was his job, she reminded herself. He was a SEAL, and now he worked for a security company. If anyone could help keep her safe, it was him.

After going to her room and packing a couple of things, she snapped out a quick text to Emily.

Sam: *Staying with Owen at his hotel tonight. And no, it's not what you think.*

Em: *What do you mean, it's not what I think?*

Sam: *Something has come up. I'll fill you in later.*

Em: *I want answers. Call me as soon as you can. Drumming nails while I wait . . . P.S.—saw him in the stairwell. He's ridiculously hot.*

"You ready?"

She flinched and dropped her cell and looked over at Owen in the doorframe.

He scanned the room, his eyes falling upon the bed before looking at her. "Got what you need?"

"Yeah." She nodded. "Are you sure you want to help me, though? I don't want to endanger you."

"I can handle myself, but I did promise to keep an eye out for you ten years ago, didn't I?"

He didn't recognize her in Mexico, but that, he recalled? "You remember?"

"I remember everything now."

She released a soft sigh and approached him standing so damn rigid in her doorway. Their kiss brushed across the front of her mind. "How come you never checked in on me yourself?"

"Because I don't like to talk about what happened," he said, his voice sharp, his honesty almost surprising.

"So you never think about it? You never used your government clearance to try and find who killed them?"

His jaw tightened as his eyes dropped to her parted lips.

"How could you not go after their killer?" she pushed. "How can you not want revenge?"

He pressed a fist beneath her chin and gently guided her face up. "You think I haven't tried to bury the prick six feet under? You think I haven't thought about that very thing every day?" His eyes narrowed, and he visibly swallowed. "I've lost people who were like family—and I want vengeance for them all. And I'll never give up until I get it. For Jason. For Brad. For . . ."

The ellipsis of his unspoken words popped into her mind like little dots on repeat.

She sucked in a breath and closed her eyes. She couldn't put a lid on her emotions and contain them any longer. She'd been doing it for so long, but it was suddenly as if she'd forgotten how.

Her walls were even weaker than straw today, and she was pretty sure he was the reason.

Tears touched her cheeks as she struggled not to ugly cry.

"Shhh," he murmured, but he cupped the back of her head and pulled her against his chest.

And then, damn it, she did it. She broke down and cried. Not a hard sob, but any tears for her were like Everest for anyone else.

He stroked his fingers through her hair with one hand, while keeping her head close to the heavy beats of his heart with the other.

"You don't have to be nice to me," she cried.

"Yeah, well, I can be mad at you tomorrow."

* * *

"THE HOTEL WAS BOOKED, SO I COULDN'T UPGRADE TO A two-room suite. Besides, I'd rather be able to keep a closer eye on you." He set her bag on the bed. "My people are in this hotel. You'll be safe here."

She wet her lips and took a few uneasy steps across the room before sitting on the mattress. "You mean, the people from Scott & Scott?"

He angled his head, eying her with that same suspicious stare from earlier. "I didn't mention my company name. How much do you know about me?"

"Not enough, I'm guessing."

"The friend who did an *illegal* background check on me—is he the same guy who has the original picture?"

"No, my friend Javier works at the FBI crime lab. He has it."

"Hm." He kept quiet for a moment, studying her as if trying to unravel some complex mystery that had far too many red herrings. "And you work for the Intelligence Committee, right? You said your dad was a senator, but I had no idea he was Chairman McCarthy."

She lifted a brow and ignored the smile that attempted to touch her lips. "So, you looked me up, too, huh?"

"I've always known. I was keeping tabs on you, even if not directly. But I didn't make the connection between your name and face until today. It's been a long time since we've seen each other. You were young and had long hair at the funeral."

"You barely even looked at me."

He shook his head. "It wasn't exactly an easy day." He let out a quick breath. "I can't believe I didn't figure it out in Mexico, though."

When they collided in the lobby at the hotel, she'd nearly had a panic attack the second she realized it'd been him. And when he didn't make the connection, the truth got stuck in her throat. "I got so nervous, and every time I planned on telling you, it just became more difficult." *Because after talking at the bar—I didn't want you to be Owen York. I didn't want you to be off-limits,* but she couldn't say that aloud. Of course, she hadn't gone to Mexico for hot vacation sex, anyway, and so . . .

His Adam's apple bobbed in his throat, then he turned and moved toward the windows, drawing the curtains closed.

"Can I ask why you switched from being a Naval pilot to a SEAL?" Not that it mattered, but Emily's brother had only given her a fairly succinct rundown on Owen before Sam had chased him to Mexico. The glimpse into Owen York's life had left her itching for more details.

"No, you can't."

"Sorry," she said when the air became ice between them, and she could nearly see her breath puff out before her.

"Why didn't you go to the police about the picture? Was your first instinct really to come to me because Jason's in the photo?" He folded his arms, staring her down, and part of her wanted the ground to swallow her.

"My father would never let me look into this. The image would have been turned over to the Feds, and I'd have been left in the dark." She shook her head. "I couldn't risk that happening."

"So, you hunted me down in Mexico to pull me into all of this, huh?"

"You wish I hadn't?"

"I didn't say that."

"Then what are you saying?" She strode closer to him, trying to face the man who'd haunted her dreams last night.

"If we had fuc—" He let the curse hang in the air and

cleared his throat. "If we'd had *sex*, I would never have forgiven myself."

Me, either.

"Brad was like a brother to Jason. It'd be like sleeping with my brother's fiancée, and I just—"

"I know. I made a mistake." She eyed the floor instead of him. "I didn't mean for that to happen." She shifted her weight to one foot as she tried to claim some sense of mental clarity. "Can we start over? Work together to find out what really happened?"

"You won't get justice."

"What do you mean? What is it you aren't telling me?" She touched his bicep, but he staggered back a step.

"Nothing."

She considered his words, his mood.

"Just do me a favor, Samantha, don't tell anyone else about the picture right now."

Samantha? Was he worried he'd lose a shot at looking into the image, too? Was he as determined to find the truth as her?

His eyes veered to the lone bed in the room. "I need to look into a few things. Can you trust me on this?"

"I guess I owe you that much."

He looked back at her. "Get some sleep. I'll stay on the couch."

"I don't want to take your bed."

"I can't sleep next to you, even on top of the covers. It wouldn't be right."

She felt the burn of his words.

He couldn't stand her.

And maybe he'd never forgive her.

CHAPTER SEVEN

"WHO ARE YOU?" SAM CLUTCHED THE SHEET TO HER CHEST.

"I work with Owen." The woman rose from the couch and took a few steps closer to the edge of the bed. "I'm Jessica. He asked me to stay with you until he got back."

"You're capable of protecting me?"

"The pistol strapped to my leg should hold back any intruders."

Sam had no idea if the woman was kidding or not. "Did he tell you why I'm here with him?"

"I got the CliffNotes version." The light crease in her forehead deepened as her brows drew together.

"Where's Owen?"

"He needed to hit something." She angled her head, a pinch of irritation snapping across her face. "He's at a boxing gym with a friend."

"Oh." Guilt came down on her like a sledgehammer, yet again.

"Listen." Jessica held a palm in the air. "I'm sorry about Brad and everything you've been through, but I can't have anyone screwing with Owen's head. Not now. Not ever.

Don't lie to him again." She tipped her head. "Understood?"

Before Sam could muster an appropriate response, the door clicked open, and Owen came into the room, his gray V-neck drenched in sweat. He didn't make eye contact with Sam, and she had to wonder if his anger had gone back to nuclear now that the sun had risen.

"Thanks for keeping an eye on her," he said to Jessica. "Any news?"

"No word, but I've started looking into things on my end." Jessica glanced Sam's way. "You want me to stay, or—"

"No, you should work. Besides, I'm not ready to face Luke." He messed up his hair, swiping a hand over the shorter locks as if he'd forgotten his longer hair was gone.

Jessica sidestepped him. "I'll catch up with you soon." And she left without another word.

Sam dropped her legs to the side of the bed and stood as steadily as possible once Jessica was gone. "You told her, huh?"

He nodded and leaned against the TV stand. He finally found her eyes as she moved around the bed, only a foot away. "You sleep well?"

"Probably better than you on that couch." She took a second to observe the tee clinging to his muscled chest, and when she found his eyes, he arched a questioning brow as if she'd been caught cheating on a test.

"I've slept on much worse." He cleared his throat and pushed away from the TV stand. "I'm going to clean up, and then we'll go get the original photo back. We can't have this picture floating around out there."

"It's Sunday. I'll have to see if Javier has it at his home or not."

"Find out where it is. I don't want to wait." He brushed against her, and her skin tingled at the sensation of the slight touch, and it was as if he felt something too, because he paused mid-step for the span of a heartbeat before going into the en-suite, closing the door behind him.

She remained still for a moment, listening to the sounds of the water running, and she hated herself for even flashing back to Owen standing in a towel in the hotel room the other day.

Her fingers massaged her forehead as she tried to get a grip. A few seconds later, she forced away her guilty thoughts and grabbed her phone to text Javier.

Midway through typing it, her phone buzzed with an incoming call.

Blocked.

She slowly raised it to her ear. "Hello?"

"We need to talk." A deep tone touched her ears, as if altered by voice-changing software.

Shivers rushed over her skin, and she turned to check the bathroom door was still shut. "Who is this?"

"That doesn't matter right now. Check your phone—you just got a text."

She sank onto the chair by the window, her eyes widening as she scrolled through ten images. "Where'd you get these?" Her hand trembled as she brought the phone back to her ear.

The photos had been stored in only one place—her laptop at home.

Her stomach roiled, and she pressed her hand to her abdomen.

"Kill your proposal." The command had dropped through the line in a rush. "If not, these photos being leaked to the press will only be the beginning of what is to come."

She blinked a few times. "Screw you."

"Thought you might say that."

"Did you send me the photo to my office?" She shook her head. "Was it you? Why?"

Silence met the other side of the line, and she realized he'd already hung up.

Her heart thundered, the beat pulsing up and into her ears.

It took her a minute to pull herself together, and when she did, she hurried to the bathroom. "Owen!"

"Yeah?" he hollered from the shower.

"We need to talk. It's important."

"One minute." The water turned off, and a few seconds later, he opened the door wearing only a towel wrapped around his hips. The water dripped from his face and down his chest.

She backed up farther into the hall until she hit the wall. *Breathe*, she reminded herself as his smell touched her nose, reminding her of their time on the boat together a few days ago.

She hated that she missed the lie between them—when she had just been Sam, and he had just been Owen, and they hadn't been two people with baggage that pretty much exceeded airline weight-limit standards.

He propped a hand on the interior of the doorframe and angled his head, his eyes thinning. "What's wrong?"

Eyes off the happy trail. Focus. "I got a call."

"And?"

"It was from the delivery guy. Well, I think it was him. He texted me some photos."

"Why didn't you get me?"

Her shoulders rolled back. "I was too stunned."

"What'd he want?" Lines appeared in his brow.

The water kept rolling down the hard planes of his chest

and to his abdomen, and there was no way she could talk to him nearly naked. "Could we talk when you're dressed?"

"Fine." He cocked his head to the side, his gaze falling upon her chest. "Maybe you could get clothes on, too?"

She looked at her long tee, realizing her nipples pressed hard against the nightshirt.

The coldness of his hard stare sent blustery chills down her back, and then he turned, closing the door behind him.

She fumbled with the hem of her T-shirt as she walked to her overnight bag.

After throwing on a pair of shorts and a V-neck pink tee, she sat in the chair near the window and tapped her phone against her thigh as she waited for him to return.

Owen came into the room shortly after and dropped onto the bed. "You ready to talk?"

"Yeah." She handed him her phone to show the photos she'd been texted. "He's threatening to leak these to the press if I don't withdraw my proposal."

Owen stood and swiped through the images. "Where'd he get these pictures of you?" His eyes stayed on the screen instead of looking at her.

"They're *my* photos. The saved files from my computer at home."

"Well, they're mostly of you at clubs and stuff. A few guys in pics, but I don't see anything incriminating."

"Not with the event scheduled next week—a couple party pictures might seem like nothing, but it'd taint my reputation, and the work I'm trying to get done." *And my father would lose his mind.* "But I can't give in to him. If I abandon the proposal, I'd have to cancel the event in Russia on Wednesday." Of course, her dad still needed to land Senator Abrams's vote for the event to be considered a true success, so there was a chance everything could end up in flames next week anyway.

"What'd you say to him?" He clutched the phone tight in his hand.

She stood. "I told him to go screw himself."

"Did he mention the other photo he sent to your office?"

"He hung up just as I was asking about it." The hairs on her arms stood and chills passed over her skin. "It can't be a coincidence, though, right? But does that mean the picture is fake . . . or does it mean it's real?"

CHAPTER EIGHT

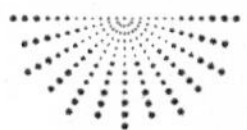

"I DIDN'T FIND ANYTHING. SORRY." JESS REMOVED HER glasses and pushed away from the desk. "Probably a burner phone, and he's since tossed it in the Potomac for all we know."

"You think that picture is somehow connected to the op from ten years ago?" Owen pointed to the photo the deliveryman had given Sam, which he'd turned over to Jess last night after he'd escorted Sam to his hotel room.

"Considering Canton is in the image with your brother and Brad, it sure as hell looks that way, but the location doesn't jive with the story we were given about how your brother died."

Yeah, that part was a bit of a mind fuck. "Whoever's threatening her must have our people, right?"

"We'll do our best to find out."

Owen checked the time. "When are we going to call in a manhunt for Handlin? It's not like him not to answer your calls, right?"

"He'll get back to me. He always does."

"Did it ever take him this long?" They needed to confirm

the photo was connected to the missing SEALs and the CIA officer. The wait was making his skin itch.

"No, but I'll try and get ahold of POTUS again if I don't hear from him by the afternoon. They must be held up in meetings about this."

He hoped that was all.

"Not sure how someone got that photo, but I'm having a hard time believing it was doctored. Well, unless they altered the background location."

"And that's fairly easy, right?"

"It'd take me all of two seconds." She was a cyber genius, though. "But the quality is damn good if it's a fake." She stood and turned on the single-server brewer. "One thing is for certain: Samantha is connected to this now. I'm not sure how we'll explain this to her."

"She knows what we do."

Jess glared at him. "What?"

He almost smiled. "Sorry, I mean she knows about our alias and wants our help."

"Well, whatever the hell went down on that op ten years ago, it must be pretty bad if POTUS can't share the operational details with anyone."

That was his line of thought, too, which made him wonder if the image of his brother in Kiev was real; damned if it didn't make sense.

Jess added a packet of sugar to her black coffee and turned to face him.

"How are you holding up?" he asked.

She waved a dismissive hand. Typical Jess. "Don't worry about me. I'm fine."

"Canton was your mentor at the Farm, and he's missing." He sent an exaggerated gaze drifting to the left and then slowly drifted his eyes to the right. "It's just me in here. You don't have to wear your brave-girl panties, you know."

She rolled her eyes. "My panties are perfectly fine. Let's just focus on your girl."

"She's not my anything." And she never could be, even if his body didn't seem to get the message. Even if his body was betraying him every time she was within arm's reach. And hell, how could he even have a reaction to her, or to any woman, at a time like this?

"I'm sorry she lied to you, but maybe she was just scared or intimidated." Her focus switched back to her screen, and she sat at her desk.

His gaze followed the swirl of steam rising from the coffee. "Anyway."

At the sound of the door opening, he straightened and almost sighed with relief at the reprieve. Then he stiffened at the sight of Luke entering with Liam and Knox.

"Anything from Handlin?" Jess asked once the door was closed.

"No. You?" Luke sat on the edge of the bed, and a band of tension filled the room.

Owen hadn't talked one-on-one to Luke since the meeting with Handlin yesterday. He didn't want to be pissed at his best friend, but the fact remained that Luke had known all along that Jason had been DEVGRU, and he'd never said a word. It'd take Owen a little time to shrug off the burn of that truth.

"Any hits on the image of Samantha's deliveryman?" Luke asked Jessica.

"I'm good, but I'm not a magician. The partial picture of that guy pulled up about five thousand hits at a twenty-five percent match each." She turned in her chair and looked to Liam and Knox, who now occupied the couch by the window.

"Tell me you guys got something helpful from the cameras at her office this morning."

Liam shook his head. "He couldn't just waltz into a federal building without ID. He had to have already devised a plan to infiltrate the building and bypass security."

"That's not something you come up with overnight," Jess noted.

"The blackmail photos and threat Samantha got this morning make sense, though," Knox said. "Hell, even the photo delivered to her office." His gaze shifted to Owen. "This shit happens all the time. Behind-the-scenes ways to make political change in D.C. But kidnapping two Navy SEALs and a CIA officer to force that change . . . not so much."

"You ever cross paths with the McCarthys?" Owen couldn't help but ask, especially since Knox had grown up in the same political spotlight as Sam.

Knox stood, the sudden political talk seeming to make him uneasy; he tucked his hands in his cargo pants pockets. "Nah. I've always done my best to avoid D.C. insiders—well, unless they're the ones writing us the checks."

Jess was on her feet again. "Even if whoever's threatening Samantha does have our guys, one question remains: how the hell did they know about Shaw, Robins, and Canton?"

"And what do they want with them? Torture for intel?" Liam's lips flattened as he laid out his question, allowing the others to gather ideas.

"If Jason and Brad really died in Ukraine instead of Iraq, that means the government lied about everything," Luke said. "And that'd be one colossal cover-up."

"It was a Russian nuclear scientist whom Jason and Brad were trying to save in Ramadi," Jess said.

Owen had memorized every detail about his brother's op. Well, the details which hadn't been redacted. Had everything been a lie?

"The scientist died in the explosion, right?" Liam asked.

Owen nodded.

"I'm thinking whatever happened was big enough to push Shaw into retirement, too. According to my research, he filed the paperwork within a few days of the end of that op ten years ago," Jess said.

"SEALs don't up and quit at that age unless severely injured," Knox added.

"Are we all thinking the same thing?" Jess folded her arms.

"Someone other than al-Qaeda killed that scientist, and the U.S. decided to cover it up." Owen hung his head. "That has to be the connection, right?" He thought about what Sam had told him. "She's trying to help broker a deal to end border conflict between Ukraine and Russia."

"What if whoever killed the scientist was from Ukraine?" Knox proposed.

"It'd blow whatever chances Ukraine has at entering NATO." Owen's mind raced as he considered what might have gone down ten years ago.

"Christ." Luke retrieved his phone from his pocket. "We've got to get ahold of Handlin and the president."

"We'll split up. This guy," Jess pointed to the partial image of the deliveryman on her screen, "is our best lead right now."

Owen's chest tightened. "I'll go get the original image from Sam's FBI pal. It looks like this situation needs containment more than we realized."

"Take Asher with you," Luke ordered. "Knox and I will

hunt down Handlin, and in the meantime, Liam and Jess can head to Samantha's and sweep her place for bugs."

"We should have you and Sam take a look at the security CCTV footage around her home and office, too. Maybe we can get a better shot of this deliveryman on camera," Jess suggested to Owen.

"Should we have eyes on her father?" Knox asked. "I mean, my pops never travels without a shit-ton of security, but what about her old man?"

"He's in Russia right now, and Sam said her dad is already heavily guarded," Owen answered.

"Good, because I don't want to raise any red flags about this, especially without knowing for sure everything is connected." Luke eyed Owen. "We're going to keep Samantha safe, though. I promise."

Owen gave him a quick nod. "Call me as soon as you hear from Handlin."

He left the room to grab Sam and Asher so they could head to Javier's place. He froze outside Asher's door when he heard Sam laugh, and the sound cut under his skin and created a warmth in his chest that didn't belong there. At least, not because of her.

Get your shit together. He blinked a couple of times and then knocked.

Asher opened the door with a shit-eating grin on his face.

Great. "Nothing from Handlin yet," he said in a low voice before entering the room and striding past Asher's large frame.

He tried to fight the jolt of his pulse at the mere sight of Sam sitting by the window. She caught her thumbnail between her teeth as her eyes found his.

How could he have slept in a bed with her? Kissed her?

She'd been Brad's fiancée. Brad had been Jason's best friend.

And now, Owen was the guy who'd seen her naked and shoved his tongue into her mouth on multiple occasions within the span of twenty-four hours.

He knew every little detail of her body; it'd been burned and stored in his memory bank. He wasn't sure how the hell he'd delete the damn thoughts.

And yet, why the hell was he even thinking about any of that now with everything he'd learned in the last day?

He was in the middle of an op. Well, not technically yet, since POTUS hadn't cleared them, but still, he shouldn't have been thinking about Sam. Period.

"Hey." Sam rose to her feet in her Chucks, which he found irritatingly hot paired with her khaki shorts.

She crossed the room to stand before him. She had on her jasmine perfume today, the one she'd worn on the boat when she couldn't blame alcohol for letting him kiss her.

He wanted to suck in a deep breath and pretend for a moment that all the bad shit of the world could get sucked into a black hole of oblivion.

She tucked her short hair behind her ears. "Javier texted me; he's at home." She grabbed her purse off the dresser and slung the strap over her shoulder, then maneuvered between Owen and Asher toward the door as if anxious to leave.

"Good. Let's do this." Owen turned toward the door and waited for both Asher and Sam to be out of sight before he could get his feet to move.

He needed answers. He needed the truth. And he needed to forget about Mexico.

* * *

"YOU HAVE ENOUGH HARDWARE HERE TO SPY ON THE ENTIRE Eastern seaboard," Asher mused while eying all of the turned-off screens and tech inside Javier's apartment.

"I work for the FBI. Of course, I have a lot of equipment." Javier swerved his attention back to Sam as he handed her the envelope.

"Since when do Feds let you bring your work home with you?" Asher pointed a finger at him. "You're a video-game addict, aren't you?"

Owen eyed Asher and lightly shook his head, warning him to leave the guy alone. Asher wasn't the biggest fan of the government with the exception of the military. He'd never liked the alphabet soup of agencies, and Asher hadn't exactly been candid as to why. Owen wasn't itching to ask, either.

"I'm sorry I couldn't help you." Javier pointed to the envelope in her hand. "I've been at the office nonstop, working some big case these last few days."

"Oh?" Owen wondered if Javier had been commissioned to help track down their missing people. Handlin had mentioned the FBI was working the case.

"Who'd you say you are again?" Javier asked, a threat of distrust in his tone.

"We didn't say." Owen's mouth tightened. He didn't like the guy for some reason, and when Javier turned to press his hand to Sam's shoulder and lean in toward her, he knew why.

The guy had a thing for her, didn't he?

"If you need anything, I'm here for you," Javier said.

"Thanks." She smiled, and even though he didn't know her well, it looked forced. "Please don't tell anyone about this picture. Okay?"

"Of course not."

"That's not a request, just so we're clear." Asher's voice had become low and gravelly.

"I don't take orders from you." Javier turned Asher's direction. "But I'll keep this thing under wraps for Sam."

Owen wanted to give him a few more reasons to shut his mouth about the image, but what could he say? He couldn't expose the truth of who he was; he'd leave that up to Handlin to deal with later.

Javier refocused on Sam. "Maybe, when my caseload is a little lighter, we can get a drink?"

"Sure," she quickly said. "But we should really get going. Thanks again."

He stole one last look at Javier, then he tipped his head goodbye and followed both Asher and Sam out the door.

"Well, that was awkward," Asher said once he was behind the wheel of the SUV.

"Why was it awkward?" she asked, and Owen resisted the impulse to look back at her; he kept his eyes pinned to the envelope in hand.

"Well, your boy Javier looks like he still has it bad for you. You two used to hook up, huh?"

This elicited a cough from Sam, and it had Owen glaring at him. "What the hell, man?"

Asher gave an innocent shrug. "Calling it like I see it."

"And my sex life is none of your business," she snapped.

Owen sure as hell didn't want to talk about it, either. The way her FBI pal had been looking at her, it was obvious Javier had a thing for her.

"I'm surprised Javier works for the government. I expected someone a little stiffer, without all the tatts," Asher said.

"And what do you do?" she asked. "Have you looked at yourself?"

Asher looked up, probably catching her eyes in the rearview mirror. "I'm sure as hell not government."

Well, technically speaking, they kind of were, but he wasn't about to call Asher on that with Sam in the car.

His racing thoughts came to a halt at the sound of his ringing phone. "It's Jess," he announced. "Maybe she has news."

"Did she go to my place already?" Sam asked.

"Maybe." He brought the phone to his ear. "Hey, Jess."

"I'm still at Sam's," Jess said straight away. "And you're not going to like what you hear."

The damn woman always built up the suspense, and it drove him nuts. "And?"

"We found a small dime-sized bug in her living room smoke detector."

"Shit." He dropped his gaze to the envelope and then hurried to open it. "If someone was listening, then it's possible—" His heart slowed at the sight of the correct photo.

"If this guy was listening to your conversation last night, he'd also know Sam made copies, so it wouldn't matter if you retrieved the original one he sent her or not."

Owen nodded in agreement, his heartbeat slowing back to its normal pace. "Well, did you learn anything based on the bug that was used?"

"It's an American-made device and not one you can exactly buy on eBay," she answered.

"Which tells us what?" Owen asked.

"What's going on?" Sam asked from behind.

He pivoted to face her briefly and mouthed, "One sec."

She nodded and sat back into her seat.

"There's not a serial ID on the bug, but there's a batch number. I might be able to pinpoint where this particular batch was sold. These bugs are normally sold in bulk. I should know since we've made similar purchases for Scott & Scott."

"Surprised it's American. Figured it'd be Russian."

"Yeah, it does throw us a bit of a curveball based on the phone call she got." The line became quiet for a moment. "But there's more I need to tell you."

His stomach tensed. "What?"

The line was silent for a moment, and he knew the blow would be heavy and hard. "Someone was watching her over a secure camera feed. The camera was positioned in the ceiling vent in her bedroom."

He hung his head, not wanting to tell Sam the news. He couldn't imagine how she'd feel to know someone had been watching her, in her bedroom, no less.

He pivoted to face her, trying to steady the angry pound of his heart before he spoke. "When was the last time the government did a sweep of your home and office?" Given her line of work, he assumed there'd be standard-issue checks to prevent intel leaks.

"They checked my apartment and office two weeks ago."

"We're looking at a two-week window then," he told Jess.

"Camera may not have popped up on their radar, though." She hissed through the line. "I'll do my best to track the feed, but for now, why don't you head back to the hotel and wait for news from Handlin. I'm also bringing her laptop with me."

"Right. Okay."

"Can you get her password?"

"Jess wants to check out your computer. What's your code?" He met Sam's eyes, and her browns softened.

"Rose 2008."

He thought about the tattoo on the inside of her arm. 2008, the year Brad and Jason had died. Now he knew her ink had to do with the loss of her fiancé, which wasn't terribly surprising, but back in Mexico, he'd just assumed she liked the flower.

He faced forward with a tightness in his chest and repeated the password.

"Luke checked out Handlin's home, and no one was there," Jess announced.

Owen clamped down on his back teeth then a thought came to mind. "Check the hospitals."

"What?"

"All that coughing yesterday. Smelled like he'd been in a hospital recently."

"Right," Jess said, her tone softening as if she was angry she hadn't thought of the idea herself. "Okay. I'll be in touch." She ended the call.

"What's going on?" Sam asked after he'd lowered the phone from his ear. She wrapped a hand over the top of his seat, her fingers skirting his shoulder.

How could he tell her what he'd learned without making her skin crawl? "They found a bug in your smoke detector."

Her eyes widened in surprise.

"But they also discovered a camera in your bedroom."

She scooted back onto her seat and cupped her mouth, her long lashes dropping down.

"I'm sorry." He wasn't sure what else to say on that matter, so he hoped to redirect her focus. "We should have enough to go on to try and figure out who the hell has been keeping tabs on you."

"Oh, God."

He patted the envelope against his thigh. "We're going to figure this out. I promise."

"What about my parents? Shouldn't I tell them now?"

Asher looked to Owen, his gaze hardening, and neither of them knew what the hell to say.

CHAPTER NINE

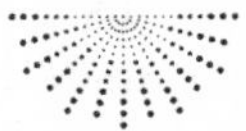

"YOU WERE JEALOUS IN THE CAR." ASHER LEANED HIS shoulder against the wall in the hall outside the hotel door.

Owen balked. "What?"

"I was testing you back there. You should've seen your face at the idea of Sam and that Javier dude hooking up."

Owen lowered his eyes to the floor, unable to meet his friend's stare.

"I get it. You guys hooked up in Cabo, and no one wants to think about a woman with another guy, but—"

"First of all, we didn't have sex, and second of all . . ." He'd already lost his train of thought, too pissed Asher had pulled him aside before going into the hotel room to have this heart-to-heart. What was with all his friends jonesing for these kinds of conversations lately?

"You stayed overnight in her room. Are you trying to tell me you didn't screw?" A dark brow arched in question.

Owen shook his head. "No, we didn't."

Asher's mouth tightened and curved down slightly in surprise. "Well, good. But you need to stop looking at her the way Luke looks at Eva."

"I don't look at her in any way."

Asher faked a laugh. "Don't lie to me, man. I know you."

"Maybe you don't." He turned, about to swipe his card to get into the room when Asher's paw of a hand wrapped over his shoulder.

"You can't go down this road with her. This whole situation is complicated enough without adding to the mix she was Brad's woman."

Owen slowly turned and expelled a deep breath. "I know that. Trust me."

Asher lifted his shoulders. "This could end badly, and I'm just looking out for you."

"Well, I'm good. And why the hell are we having this conversation, anyway? There's much more important shit to talk about than my love life."

Asher lifted his palms in surrender. "Love life?"

"Just get ahold of Luke—find out if Handlin's okay." He handed Asher the envelope with the original image inside. "I can't keep holding Sam back from telling her parents what's going on."

"Yeah, yeah, okay." He nodded then walked away.

Once inside the hotel room, he saw Sam pouring a mini blue bottle into a Styrofoam coffee cup. "You raided the mini bar?"

She looked up from the cup. "I'll pay you back. Promise."

He smiled. "You sure you want to drink at"—he checked his watch—"two in the afternoon?"

"Mm-hm." She settled onto the chair by the window. "My dad just messaged me. He got Senator Abrams on board. We got the last signature." She faked a laugh. "Everything is in place, but now . . . it may not matter."

"Don't think like that, Sam." He closed the distance

between them and rubbed at the tension at the base of his skull.

She rolled her lips inward, wetting them. "You called me Sam."

"Yeah?"

"You called me Samantha last night, and I was pretty sure you'd never want to . . ." She let her words die, and maybe that was for the better.

After a few blinks, she raised the cup back into the air.

"This is a celebratory drink, then." She hiccupped. "Cheers to my dad for getting Abrams on board." She took another sip. Actually, it was more like a heavy gulp.

He cocked his head, studying her. She was a beautiful and strong woman who was willing to go to bat with Russia—but right now, she looked fragile and a little broken.

"I also think I deserve a drink since I found out someone has seen me naked and been watching me for maybe two weeks." She stared down at the carpet in a daze, the realization possibly slamming into her at the moment, and then she tipped back the rest of her cup.

Yeah, he couldn't blame her on that. The idea had him wanting to fix himself a stiff drink, too. "Well, can I at least order room service, so you don't get shit-faced on an empty stomach? My hangover cure might not work tomorrow, otherwise." He lifted the phone. "What can I get you to eat?"

"Something greasy and unhealthy." She stood and retrieved another small bottle from the minibar. "And maybe some juice to mix with this."

"Sure." He forced a smile, even if it didn't feel right to wear at a time like this.

After ordering the food, he went to the bathroom, hoping to pull himself together.

He was hanging by a thread, and damn, he wasn't used to that.

The past twenty-four hours had been a bit much, even for someone like him.

He braced the bathroom counter, and memories from his past shot through his mind, which had him drawing his eyes closed.

Brad and I are going to head to Sin City for my birthday next week while on leave. Do you think you can make it? Brad's bringing his new girlfriend, so I need my wingman. Besides, you can tell the ladies you're a pilot. I can't exactly say what I do, Jason had said over Skype.

I won't be able to get off base. Sorry, man. I promise I'll make it up to you next year.

There hadn't been a next year, though.

His hand turned to a fist atop the counter as he peeled his eyes open.

He stared at his reflection for a minute, guilt twisting in his gut that he'd lived to see another day while so many hadn't.

Brad's new girlfriend: Sam. And now, here he was, in a hotel room with her.

When he found the energy, he left the bathroom, and the band of tension in his chest lightened a fraction at the song now playing from the music station on TV.

"Tiesto." He sat on the edge of the bed.

She looked up from her cup and smiled. "I almost forgot we have the same taste in music."

"You ever see him perform?"

"Yeah, once. You?"

"Nah, never had a chance. I'm sure it was an incredible experience."

She took another sip, this time, without wincing. "I saw

him perform when I went backpacking across Europe for three months." Her lids became heavy, but she kept her eyes open. "I was planning on blowing off law school after Brad died." Her chest rose and fell with slow breaths. "But I made a deal with my folks that, if they let me go to Europe, I'd stick with the plan to go to law school after."

It'd been a rough few months after Jason had died for him and his family, too. But he'd been in the service, and as much as he maybe wanted to, he couldn't take off and make the world go away.

"You ever hit up Ibiza?" he asked, needing to think of anything other than losing his brother at that moment.

"Of course."

"I assume your dad wasn't a fan of you going to places like that."

"He'd have a heart attack if he ever knew I went to raves."

"Sounds like your dad stresses about a lot of things," he noted.

"It's the life." She tensed then released a nervous light laugh before a somberness took hold of her face. "But, back then, the music sort of made me feel alive again. I'd felt so dead on the inside; it was like pressing one of those defibrillator things to my chest when being surrounded by free-spirited people and an electric bass."

I know the feeling. But he couldn't bring himself to say the words.

"It was hard coming back home after feeling so free." She wet her lips and pulled her bottom one between her teeth as she stared down at the floor.

He tried not to drop his gaze to her long, tan legs—but he couldn't help himself. He remembered how those legs had felt wrapped around his hips as he'd held her pinned to the wall in the hotel room a few days ago.

"Owen?" There was a velvety rasp to her tone when she said his name.

"Yeah?"

The knock at her door must've silenced whatever she'd wanted to say. He grabbed the room service and handed her the burger and fries before proceeding to make her a cocktail.

"You own the tavern now," she said softly. "You must know a thing or two about making drinks."

"Yeah, well, I don't work there much these days." He stirred the fruity concoction he'd made.

"That's where Brad and I met." She paused. "Where he proposed."

The hairs on the back of his neck stood, and her words had his hand stilling midair, the liquid dropping off the plastic spoon, splattering onto the desk.

"Crazy, right?" she whispered, her words light as air but heavy as fucking bricks in his mind. "My best friend and I went to Charleston for a weekend, and we were bar hopping. I met Brad there. He introduced me to Jason."

He slowly turned with the drink, and their eyes connected as he handed it to her, their fingers brushing during the exchange.

"I haven't been back there since . . ." She allowed her words to trail off, and they both remained quiet for a few minutes.

What was there to say, after all?

She'd met Brad in the bar he owned, a place he escaped to when he needed to pretend it was okay just to kick back and have a drink and chill—hoping the world wouldn't fall apart while he took a second to relax.

And now, that bar was a place of pain for her.

He tensed at the thought, then coughed into his fist, needing to change the subject. "So, uh, what's the deal with that Javier guy?" He wasn't sure how *that* question had managed to roll off his tongue.

She smiled, though. And hell, for a second, her smile managed to melt away the awkwardness, like she had a blowtorch in hand.

She shrugged. "We met at a political fundraiser two years ago, and he's been asking me out for months."

"Based on the way he was looking at you, I'm gonna have to say you've been turning him down?" He stole a fry from her plate since he hadn't ordered himself any food. His appetite had been less than stellar, and eating was the last thing on his mind.

"He's a good friend."

"You said back in Mexico you're not looking for a relationship. Some guys have trouble understanding a woman focused on her job, I'm betting."

"So many guys in D.C.," she said after finishing a bite of food, "are assholes, to put it mildly."

"Gotta be a few good men out there though, right?" He leaned back in his seat and studied the woman before him.

A woman who could probably bring D.C. to its knees.

Hell, she'd nearly had him tripping all over himself back in Mexico. On the plane home, he'd considered chucking his rules about dating out the window.

Within an hour of knowing her, he could tell she was a woman you didn't let go of. A once-in-a-lifetime kind of woman.

She was Brad's once-in-a-lifetime though, he had to remind himself. Surely she'd find someone else in the future, but he was crazy to think that someone could ever be him.

But it threw him off that even being within arm's reach of

her, somehow managed to dissolve some of the darkness that had consumed him for years. The darkness of what he learned yesterday, on the ten-year anniversary no less, should've swallowed him whole . . . and he wondered if she was the reason why he hadn't totally lost his shit and gone to the range to tear up a target, or maybe a hundred.

Of course, Sam had been the reason why he'd unleashed more intensity than normal in the boxing ring with Asher that morning. He'd been so damn pissed to discover she not only lied, but she was off-limits, that Asher about hung up his gloves, which wasn't like him, mid-fight.

"You're amazing, you know." Her whispered words had him peering at her.

The slow drum beat of his heart scaled up with each passing second of silence.

She sipped her drink. "I just don't know how you do so much. To go into the Naval Academy, which is like really hard to get into, then to switch from—"

"Your FBI pal told you all of this about me?"

"Um." She set her drink back down onto the makeshift dinner table. "Jason used to brag about you whenever the three of us hung out."

His stomach squeezed at her words, and the tight pressure in his chest nearly eclipsed every feeling inside of him, and he fought to catch his breath.

"Owen, are you okay?"

"I can't do this." He stood and dragged a palm down his jaw, blinking a few times.

"Do what?"

He shook his head. "I can't talk about the past."

She nodded a few times. "Okay." She rose and came to stand before him and gently touched his forearm.

He lifted his eyes to find hers, and it had emotion choking in his throat again, which further irritated him.

"We don't have to talk about the past, then." Her lower lip quivered ever so slightly, and he found himself wishing he could kiss the tremble away and make everything right. "I'm sorry."

She'd been apologizing nonstop since he'd learned the truth, but it still didn't make things right; it still didn't change the fact that now he felt something for her, and it was her damn fault.

"I didn't mean to upset you again. I'm—"

"Then you never should have lied to me back in Mexico." And the words scraped against his tongue as he said them, knowing he was so damn screwed.

CHAPTER TEN

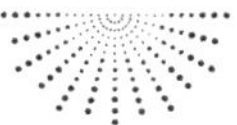

Owen glanced at Asher riding shotgun in the other SUV behind the Escalade, both of which had been sent by POTUS. He tipped his head in greeting, but when he redirected his focus to Sam, she remained a statue before the door with Luke standing impatiently waiting for her to get inside.

Luke had pounded on their door not even three minutes ago, alerting him to their sudden trip to meet with the president. Jess hadn't gotten ahold of Secretary Handlin, and Owen couldn't help but assume the worst now.

She peeked at Owen from over her shoulder. "I still don't get why we're going to the White House."

"Classified." Luke's jaw tightened, an obvious pinch of irritation. They were clearly in a hurry, and they needed to get their asses on the road, especially if they were being summoned by POTUS.

"This is Luke, by the way. Jessica's brother." Owen motioned to the door, hoping she'd finally slip inside the vehicle. "He's not normally so curt, but—"

"We're running late," Luke said brusquely and left their sides to hop into the front passenger seat.

Once Sam finally slipped inside, Owen got in next to her and glanced at the Secret Service agent behind the wheel.

Her fingertips rubbed up and down her goose-bump-covered thighs. "Don't you guys work in the private sector, though? I guess I'm trying to wrap my head around all of this."

Luke twisted around to view both of them as the SUV rolled out of the parking garage. "Yeah, we do." But the way he said it would've set off alarm bells for even the most naïve of people, and Sam surely wasn't one. "Secret Service will keep an eye on you while we're with the president."

Luke's words had Sam looking out the tinted windows, and she kept her gaze locked there as the city of D.C. scrolled by all the way until they'd circled around to a private entrance.

And within ten minutes, Sam had been whisked away by agents, and he'd been ushered in a hurry to the Oval.

His gaze skated the room, taking in the rest of his team, who stood firm before the desk in a line as if waiting for a commander to yell *at ease*. Being inside the Oval, he felt like he was on the set of the show, *West Wing*. It was surreal, to say the least.

"Thank you for coming on such short notice." President Rydell scratched at his chin and leaned forward, resting his elbows on his desk. "Unfortunately, Secretary Handlin is in the hospital, but he's not using his real name to protect his privacy." He allowed the information to settle in the room, for the team to absorb the news. "We're not optimistic he'll be back any time soon. We were speaking in my office last night when he collapsed. We'd been discussing bringing you onto the case." His eyes met Owen's, and the same look of concern in his eyes had been in Handlin's yesterday.

The president was worried about bringing Owen on the op, wasn't he?

Owen's mouth went dry as he eyed him, his stomach twisting into a sailor's knot.

"Will Secretary Handlin be okay?" Jess asked, speaking for the team.

"We'll have to wait and see. And I'm sorry it took me so long to meet with you, but I've been held up in briefings with the Joint Chiefs since last night to strategize how to best navigate the situation at hand." He paused for a beat and closed his eyes. "I've obviously decided to greenlight you for this op." When he opened his eyes, he looked straight at Owen. "*All* of you."

Relief settled hard in his stomach, and he took a breath.

The president's mouth tightened as he loosened his tie. "Yesterday, I commissioned all of our major agencies to double-check their servers to make sure they were secure—to make sure there wasn't a breach we were unaware of."

"We have the best cyber defense in the world," Jess interrupted, and Owen swiveled his gaze to her, and she rushed out, "Sir," at the last second.

"We do. But, in light of our current situation, Secretary Handlin and I had concerns someone may have hacked our systems and obtained the records of our missing men. We thought it was impossible, but we wanted to be sure."

Oh, God. Was the photo Sam received from the government? Was it possible? Had someone hacked their servers and was now using their own intel against them as blackmail?

"My hunch is that JSOC was hit, but we can't share the

details of the operation that are of concern with federal agents, which I believe Handlin already mentioned to you."

JSOC, the Joint Special Operations Command, was responsible for some of the most classified SEAL operations. But Owen had been under the assumption the government didn't even maintain records of certain missions to avoid such a breach of intel.

"I thought we didn't house entire operational JSOC missions within one server to safeguard the mission and the operatives?" Jess asked, her thoughts in line with Owen's.

"Right. Highly classified operations are broken into multiple documents and scattered over various servers, as you said, and they're heavily encrypted."

"If it was a hacker, there's only one guy in the world I know capable of pulling something like this off," Jess, their cyber expert, blurted.

"Lin Yan Cheng," Luke finished for her, then looked over his shoulder at Owen on his left, and he could tell Luke was thinking the same thing as him.

The picture of his brother from Ukraine . . . it was legit. It had to be.

Owen would follow Luke's lead, though, on the news—and wait for him to share what they'd learned since Sam came into his life like a bulldozer.

The president rose, and his palms flattened onto his desk. "I've been in talks with the Chinese all day. But, without evidence to prove he's our guy, especially since I can't even verify a breach, we're not making much progress with them. And I can't exactly send a team into Beijing to try and question him, either."

"Wasn't it Cheng who hacked Russia two months ago?" Well, Owen's source in Moscow told him, at least. Of course, the Russians denied the breach.

"And Israeli Intelligence, back in May?" Liam asked.

"Which is why we're thinking there's a connection to him and our missing men," the president answered. "But we doubt he's responsible for taking them."

Jess broke their line of formation and edged to the center of the group, turning to the side to both face the team, while also maintaining a visual on the president. "He's notorious for getting onto government servers, downloading whatever intel he can get, and all within the span of thirty seconds. He gets in and out quickly to avoid setting off alarms."

"So he doesn't go in with a specific objective?" Knox asked, and Jess glanced his way.

Her fingers slipped to her chest, and she rubbed the silver metal chain between her fingers as if channeling her thoughts. "No, it would take too long for him to search out specific intel."

"His MO seems to be grab and go, and then parcel off whatever he finds to the highest bidder later," Luke explained.

"This is just one avenue we've been pursuing," the president said. "We have to explore every possibility to determine who may have our people, and why they have them."

"Pick any terrorist. Who wouldn't want two SEAL operatives and a CIA officer?" Asher grumbled, his voice a half a dozen octaves lower than normal.

"Well, we might have the evidence you need to prove JSOC was hacked." Jess went over to where she'd set her computer bag by the couch at the center of the room.

"What are you talking about?" The president circled his desk to stand closer to the guys.

When Jess returned, she handed him the photo from the deliveryman. "A lot has happened since we met with Handlin yesterday, which is why we were trying to get ahold of him so desperately last night and today."

The president remained quiet, but Owen could hear the *fucks* going on in the president's head, flapping around, even if he didn't say them.

"Is this image from JSOC, Mr. President?" she asked.

"Where'd you get this?" The muscles in his jaw clenched tight, and he lifted his eyes to look at Jess.

Jess peered over her shoulder at Owen, giving him the go-ahead to tell POTUS what he knew.

"Sir, if I may?" Owen stepped forward to confront the commander in chief.

The president's eyes narrowed Owen's way, and he tipped his head granting permission.

"Someone dropped this picture off at Samantha McCarthy's office last Wednesday. She's Brad Thompson's fiancée, and her father—"

"I'm well aware of who she is," he said, his voice borderline raspy. "Go on."

Owen cleared his throat. "Someone's trying to blackmail Samantha to get her off a proposal she's working on."

"Ukrainian-Russian relations." The president's forehead creased, irritation slipping to the surface beneath his normally composed mask.

"We believe whoever sent that image is the same person who phoned her this morning demanding she drop her proposal," Owen explained. "Based on that photo, is it safe to assume everything is connected to our missing guys, and that JSOC was hacked?"

"This image isn't from our files," the president said, drawing collective breaths of surprise from the team.

Owen's brows slanted inward. "So, the photo's not real, sir?"

"Oh, I'm afraid it is, but it's not ours." He turned and set the image on the desk before re-facing the team and locked his arms tight across his chest. "I guess this would be a good time to tell you what the hell is going on." He surveyed the team, then his focus stopped and remained on Owen. "Every time a new president takes over, we're briefed on critical and highly classified operations that have previously taken place. Particularly, ops that could impact future relations with other nations. And, unfortunately, based on this photo"—he took a moment to swallow, as if the news was too unsettling to share—"I believe we have confirmation the mission relating to your brother's death is, in fact, connected to our missing guys."

The truth. Was he going to hear the truth about what happened to his brother from the commander in chief himself?

The thumping of his heart slowed, and everything damn near went calm inside of him so he could focus on what the president was about to say.

The president's face hardened. "Ten years ago, the CIA intercepted intel suggesting a Ukrainian militia group, led by Pavlo Teteruk, was planning some sort of attack against Russia. We couldn't risk tensions heightening, nor could we mobilize troops. It could risk tipping off the Russians." He shook his head. "So, four Tier One operatives, who were fluent in Ukrainian, were chosen to escort Canton into Kiev. The goal was to confirm the intel to decide on the best course of action."

Owen staggered back a step, his mind now reeling.

"While in Kiev," the president continued, "our people discovered Pavlo Teteruk was also responsible for the kidnapping of a Russian nuclear scientist who'd recently gone missing. Our former president relied heavily on the advice of his Chairman of the Joint Chiefs, General Mike Douglas, and the general proposed the recon mission turn into a rescue op."

"What happened?" Owen's body grew even tenser at the news.

He pinched the bridge of his nose as if gathering his thoughts. "The team entered Pavlo Teteruk's compound, and our men nearly got away with the scientist. But, outside the gates, a sniper spotted them and opened fired. Shaw, Robins, and Canton surrendered, and President Jones had to negotiate a deal to get them out alive and to keep everything under wraps."

The blood rushed to Owen's face. His brother should never have been there that day. It'd been a bad fucking call. "What kind of deal?" Owen couldn't stop the question from rolling off his tongue.

"Arms, funding, a show of support for continued independence from Russia," the president answered in a low voice.

"And they accepted?" Owen couldn't square up everything in his mind.

The president nodded. "The president had General Douglas's attorney coordinate the deal and ensure the money funneled to Teteruk was kept off the books."

"How could we make a goddamn deal with the man who killed Brad and Jason?" He needed to stand down. This was the president, and it hadn't been his call ten years ago, but how the hell had that happened?

"We don't negotiate, not normally," the president answered. "But, if we didn't, they'd have killed three more of our men, not to mention the blowback from Russia when they learned what happened over there. The Russians would've used this event to try and justify an invasion. President Jones weighed the risks, and chose to make a deal with Teteruk instead."

Owen turned his back, worried he'd lose his temper and break something in the Oval.

Black dots appeared before his eyes as rage filled him.

"What about the scientist?" Jess asked. "Even if our people survived, what would the U.S. have done with the Russian? They wouldn't be able to let her go home, right?"

The president simply shook his head, as if pained by it all, even though it hadn't been his call back then.

Owen took a labored breath. "And how exactly did we cover all of this up?" He faced the room again. Who the hell transported his brother's and Brad's bodies to Iraq . . . to have them blown the fuck up?

"Shaw, Robins, and Canton relocated York, Thompson, and the scientist to an old al-Qaeda stronghold. According to President Jones's records, Shaw and Robins faked an explosion in Ramadi and blamed al-Qaeda. The Russian authorities were then alerted our men died trying to rescue her when they'd discovered she was being held captive."

Lies. So many damn lies.

No one wanted war with Russia, not even another Cold War, but still . . .

"That's why Shaw retired, isn't it?" Owen came to the realization. "He couldn't handle what went down." Robins had come to the funeral, but Shaw—he couldn't look Owen in the eyes knowing what happened to Jason.

The president didn't respond, but he didn't have to. Owen knew the truth. The hard fucking truth.

"This will be a shit storm if Russia finds out." Asher's deep voice throttled the sudden silence in the room.

"What made our government think Pavlo Teteruk

wouldn't tell the Russians what had happened that day, anyway?" Luke asked.

The president dropped his focus to the rug beneath his polished shoes. "I'm pretty sure Teteruk didn't want Russia to launch a full-scale attack. And, the way I see it, I think he had all of this planned from the get-go. He knew the U.S. would come." He retrieved the photo from his desk and pointed at it. "He knew NATO would reject the Ukrainian bid for entry in 2008, and so he wanted to ensure the U.S. backed the country one way or another. He had people watching our men the second their boots touched the ground. I think he let them into the compound, just to take half of them out on their way out."

"That photo is Teteruk's?" Knox asked.

"One of many, I'm afraid." The president arched his shoulders back and cocked his head, the vein throbbing at the base of his neck.

"We're not still supporting this son of—" Owen cut himself off, nearly forgetting who he was talking to.

"He left Ukraine last year. We think he had a falling out with his group. We ended the funding to the party with his departure."

"You said *party*." Owen's eyes locked onto the president, his pulse spiking despite efforts to keep his nostrils from flaring. "Does that mean we're still paying off this cocksucker?"

"Owen," Luke warned.

The president held up his hand to Luke. "It's fine." He looked back at Owen. "We've been regularly monitoring his activity by way of drones since he left Ukraine, and he's kept to his compound in Georgia."

President Rydell had dodged Owen's question, but before he could bring it up again, Liam said with a hint of his normal casual posture, "I'm assuming we're talking about the country and not the state?"

Owen sure as hell wished the asshole was nearby so he could get to him quicker. Although, a little distance wouldn't stop Owen when the time came.

Owen tipped his head toward the photo in the president's hand. "That's why we didn't kill the prick? He has goddamn images stashed somewhere, and if anything ever happens to him, he'll let Russia know what the U.S. did? We're still channeling funds—just to him, instead of his party, right?"

Sometimes, the truth was ugly. And sometimes, the truth was so ugly it couldn't ever be exposed.

"Photos can be doctored," Jess began, "but the U.S. couldn't give Russia any reason to doubt the story about Iraq, right?"

The president's eyes journeyed over to her, and he gave a hard nod.

"Does that mean he's behind all of this? No hacking?" Luke asked.

"But why now?" Jess rubbed her temples before narrowing her eyes on Owen. "Why come after our men? He wouldn't need to pump them for intel; he knows what happened."

"And I don't think he'd want the truth out, anyway. He wouldn't want anything happening to his country, especially at the hands of Russia," the president noted.

"But clearly someone got their hands on his blackmail photos." Asher looked over at Owen and dragged his palms down his face.

"Before you got here today, I commissioned a SEAL Team to infiltrate Teteruk's place in Georgia. They'll be dropping in by helo at zero seven hundred tomorrow. We couldn't take the risk that someone would get to him if JSOC was hacked."

"Were we planning to protect this guy, or use him as bait?" Owen raised his brows, his pulse still spiking.

"Looks like we won't be doing either." Luke's words drew the attention of everyone in the room. "Clearly, he's already been taken or killed." He pointed to the photo in the president's hand. "How else would someone get ahold of that image?"

"Our guys will still go to Georgia as planned," the president announced. "We have to be certain."

Owen gripped the nape of his neck as he considered the possibility someone else beat him to the punch of killing the murdering SOB.

"Let's assume Cheng hacked JSOC, what kind of intel could he have downloaded and sold?" Luke asked. "And who would know the value of that specific intel?"

The president circled his desk, set the photo down and grabbed a USB off the top of a stack of files. "Teteruk's name wasn't in any files, but the longitude and latitude coordinates of his military compound our men infiltrated in Ukraine were listed."

"If that's the file Cheng got ahold of, what else could Cheng have learned from it?" Jess asked, as if trying to put the pieces together.

"The names of our fallen guys were in there."

"Cheng could do a quick search and discover Jason and Brad died in Iraq, and so, why the hell would their names be connected to a location in Ukraine." Luke eyed Owen, his lids becoming heavier.

"Cheng realized he was sitting on a gold mine that could fuck the U.S.," Knox said with a shake of the head.

"And if I were Cheng, I'd assume the Russians would be

the most interested in buying that kind of intel," Liam added. "And given the threat Samantha got this morning . . ."

"We need to find out who the hell has our men, and what they plan on doing with the intel. We have to contain the situation before it gets leaked any further." The president clutched the USB tight in his hand.

"We're assuming the Russian government didn't already buy the files from Cheng?" Asher asked.

"No, they can't be the buyer." The president shook his head. "Believe me, if they knew the truth, I would've heard about it already, and there's been zero chatter about this."

"Besides," Jess began, "with Cheng hacking the Russian servers before, I doubt he'd be speed-dialing Putin for a deal."

"Whoever bought the intel from Cheng, they're using it to try and thwart the McCarthys' plans," Owen said as Luke accepted the USB from the president and nodded.

"I have every bit of confidence in your team that you'll figure this out. The event the McCarthys are co-hosting with the Sven Group in Russia is Wednesday, right?" The president went back around behind his desk.

"Yes, sir," Owen answered. "But we're not still considering moving forward with it, are we?"

He sat in his seat and leaned back in his chair, eying Owen as he strode closer to his desk. "I'll need to think about it and assess the risks. I'm not a fan of being bullied into making political decisions or being blackmailed." His jaw strained with tension. "I don't want to give these people exactly what they want, do you?"

"I also don't want Samantha or her father in danger." No damn way could he let Samantha get on a plane for Russia. "Something could happen to her over there."

The president looked at his watch. "Then you're running out of time."

Owen fought the curse that tried to slip from his lips.

"We set up a secure location, which has all of the equipment you may need to get the job done." The president pointed to the USB in Luke's hand. "All the operational details from ten years ago are on that USB. The files are clean. Nothing redacted. Destroy it once you've looked at it. Understand?"

"Yes, Mr. President," Luke replied.

"I'll have some papers drawn up for Samantha McCarthy to sign. We can't let this information spread further. Please tell me she didn't share the photo with anyone other than your team." He scratched at his chin, dark stubble beneath his fingertips. "We're lucky she came to you guys with this instead of the Feds."

"Yes, but she did consult an FBI agent about the photo before coming to us," Jess spoke up.

"I'll need to have him brought here immediately. Too many people already know about this. The situation needs to be contained."

Contained? Like his brother's death was contained ten years ago? His hands instinctively tightened at his sides.

"We pulled an image off the security cameras at Samantha's office, but it was a shit angle. We're going to go through the footage tonight from both her apartment and office to see if we can get a better hit. The guy who gave her the photo is our best lead right now." Jess handed the president a new image after she'd retrieved it from her bag. "You recognize him?"

"Afraid not."

"What about Samantha's father?" Owen asked a moment later. "We don't believe he knows anything, but—"

"Everyone involved in the op ten years ago was already notified and given extra security, but before this meeting, we hadn't confirmed the extent of the threat." His nostrils flared a little, and he gave Jess back the security photo. "I'll make sure they're on board with what I need from them this afternoon."

"And what do you need from them?" Luke asked, but they all already knew the answer: *bait.*

"The former president, General Douglas . . ." Jess bowed her head. "How can we use them as bait?"

But before the president could answer, Owen asked, "How'd you know to alert Samantha's father already?"

The president's mouth tightened as he angled his head and looked straight into Owen's eyes. "Because he was General Douglas's attorney at the time. Samantha's father orchestrated the Teteruk deal."

CHAPTER ELEVEN

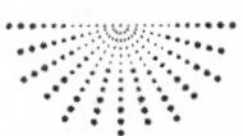

SAM EYED THE LAST DOCUMENT SHE'D SIGNED. "ALL DONE, Mr. President." Standing in shorts and Chucks felt a bit inappropriate in the Oval Office, but she hadn't been given a chance to change.

He slid the papers inside a folder, and she pressed her sweaty palms to her abdomen and swept her gaze around the room. She'd been in here before, but never with the president. Never *alone* with the commander in chief. They'd been in meetings together in the past, though, and most of the time, they'd never seen eye to eye, especially in regards to Ukraine and Russia.

"You understand the consequences if you ever tell anyone about the photo or the phone call from them this morning, correct?"

"Treason." She took a breath. "So, jail or death." She tried to spit out the words as casually as possible.

He rounded his desk to grab his blazer draped over a chair, and she swallowed her nerves at the proximity to the president. "Who else did you talk to about this photo?"

She inwardly groaned; she hated dragging them into the mess. "Um, Emily Summers and former FBI Special Agent Jake Summers."

"I know Summers. He's a good man." He gave a quick nod. "I'll have to bring them in."

"Understood."

"And please don't mention any of this to your father, especially over an unsecure line. I'll talk to him."

At least she knew her dad would be safe then. One less thing to worry about.

The president moved in front of her now and wrapped a hand over her shoulder. "There's something else I need to discuss before I go meet with the Joint Chiefs."

"Yes, Mr. President?"

"I need you to announce you're *not* going to back off your proposal. I want you in Russia as planned on Wednesday."

"What?" Her eyes widened, unable to hide the shock in her voice. "I don't understand, Mr. President. You didn't support the proposal before this happened, so why now?"

She thought back to the meeting she'd had with him in August. Because he hadn't backed her proposal, it had made getting support from Congress that much more difficult.

"Why don't you sit down?" He pointed to one of the couches at the center of the room.

"I'm fine," she said, and her words had him retracting his hand. "Mr. President," she rushed out at the last second.

He gave a curt nod and rocked back on his heels. "I don't bow to threats. I'm not like our last president."

She wasn't sure what that meant, so she kept her lips tight.

"I may not agree with your methods, but I do support the cause, and I'll sure as hell support you before I'll let some asshole try and manipulate the United States." He motioned for the door.

"There are a lot of important people who will be attending the event on Wednesday. Former President Jones,"—*since you wouldn't come*—"my dad . . ."

"We won't do anything to jeopardize their lives," he cut her off. "I promise."

It was one thing for her to be willing to put herself on the front line, but she couldn't risk others, could she?

"We'll be sure to increase security there, as well as inform our people of the situation. Don't worry."

How could she not worry? The event was her idea, and didn't that make her responsible for all of the people who'd be going? "And what is the situation? Don't I deserve to know what's actually going on?"

He released a ragged breath. "I can't go into detail with you on that, I'm sorry. But let's hope everything is resolved before your plane even leaves Dulles."

That doesn't give us much time, but she kept the thought to herself.

"The team outside this room will keep you safe. You can trust them." He opened the door, not giving her a chance to say more.

Owen stood waiting alongside the tight-lipped Secret Service agent who'd stayed with her while Owen and his team had been with the president.

"A word before you leave." The president motioned for Owen to follow him back into the Oval.

His eyes were dark and intense as he brushed past her.

And when he came out a minute later, he looked even worse.

What had happened in there? And what in the hell was really going on?

* * *

"ARE YOU SURE YOU'RE OKAY?" SAM STOOD BEFORE OWEN in the hotel suite as he sucked down a mini bottle of vodka. He was acting like she had earlier.

"What's the saying? 'Right as rain'?" He cursed under his breath. "What is right about rain, anyway?" He blinked and guzzled another bottle, his eyes narrowing as if fighting a wince.

When he started for the fridge for another, she grabbed his arm, but the way he peered at her from over his shoulder with a hard look to his eyes, had her retracting her hand.

"Can you tell me something? Anything? The president had me sign papers that could sentence me to death or life in prison if I talked about all of this."

He guzzled another mini bottle and then mumbled, "It's classified."

"Obviously, hence the treason insanity . . . but I need to know more. I deserve it. I work for the government. I'm not a—"

"Civilian?" He tipped up his chin. "Well, you are." His arm lazily fell to his side, clutching the now empty vodka bottle.

"And what are you?" she challenged, then closed her eyes as a hard knot fisted in her stomach, pumping hard and painfully steady. "I'm sorry I dragged you into this."

"You didn't drag me into anything."

She opened her eyes, finding his gaze on her mouth. "I've had a really shitty week," she said, her voice starting to break. "The picture. The threat. Then to learn some psychopath was watching me naked in my room and listening to my every word." She sucked in a sharp breath, her arms beginning to tremble. "Now, I'm pretty sure the president is stubbornly pushing my proposal because he doesn't want to look like a coward."

"I'm not letting you get on a plane to Russia. Just an FYI." His forearms went tense at his sides, the veins bulging.

"But the president—"

"Screw the president." He turned his back and pressed a palm to the wall. "Fuck all of them. They sit behind their desks in their suits putting lives on the line and . . ."

She touched his back, and the muscles tensed beneath her hand as he bowed his head.

He was in pain—she could feel it, practically absorb it through her fingertips.

"Look at me," she whispered.

He released the bottle at his side, allowing it to fall to the floor. "No."

"Owen, tell me what happened in the Oval."

His back lifted and fell with a heavy breath. "I can't."

"Turn around and look at me." Her voice nearly rattled, exposing her nerves at her question.

"I can't. I'm too angry. And right now, I just want to . . ." But then he did it, he slowly faced her, his hazel eyes darkening. "I want to—"

"Do it." Her words had her nipples pebbling, desire taking over her like a blazing fire, consuming every rational part of her. She needed something to take away the throb of indecision and the burn of anger—she needed him to do it, to take off the edge. "Kiss me," and the request sounded more like a broken cry.

When he didn't say anything, she started to turn, but then he captured her wrist, bringing her back before him.

"I think I hate you." His voice was low, and his eyes sharp on hers.

"I think I hate you, too," she lied.

And in one quick movement, he cupped the back of her head, pulling her tight against him, his mouth on hers.

His kiss had her backing up against the wall, and he boxed her in with his muscular frame, never losing hold of her mouth in the process.

She slipped her hands up his tee, running her fingers over the hard planes of his chest. She moaned as he deepened the kiss, his tongue sweeping into her mouth.

His palms pressed to her shoulders, and he edged back a moment later, which had her groin aching. The damn ache was going to kill her.

"I'm angry." He lowered his forehead to touch hers. "This would be an angry fuck," he rasped, his words like fire blowing heat over her already sizzling skin. "It'd be wrong." He didn't pull back to look at her, as if he couldn't handle the eye contact.

"I know," she whispered. "But . . . I'll lose my mind if you don't touch me again." She'd lose her mind if she were left alone to her thoughts, to muddle through the dark by herself.

He was like the light at the end of the tunnel, and she hadn't seen even a glimmer of light in so long—maybe it was a mirage. But what if it wasn't?

Nothing that had happened in the last week made sense, especially how she felt for this man, but she couldn't get herself to back down. Not now, at least.

His forehead gently tapped hers, as if he were trying to convince himself of what to do.

She slipped her hands down to his jeans and popped the button.

His hand bolted down to seize hold of her wrist, and he held her for a moment before stepping back to find her eyes.

"I really am angry right now. I meant what I said. I don't want to hurt you."

It was a warning, as well as his way of seeking permission from her. "I need this. I need one minute to just forget."

Her words did something to him—only for a moment, but it caused his lips to curve slightly at the edges. "It'd be a hell of a lot longer than a minute." The rough but almost velvety texture of his tone had her clenching her thighs tight.

The pad of his thumb brushed across her lips, and then he pulled her back in his arms, his mouth capturing her lower lip, tugging it between his teeth.

When he kissed her again, she was pretty sure her lids squeezed so tight she saw stars.

He peeled off his shirt before her back hit the wall again. He sucked at her neck, and she bit into his hard shoulder, unable to stop herself from rubbing up against him.

"Owen," she cried as he dragged his lips down the side of her neck, pushing her short hair away in the process, then gathered both her wrists in one hand and held them above her head.

Goose bumps scattered her flesh as he worked at her shorts with his free hand.

The man had skills. He'd managed to get his hand . . .

Oh, God. The moment his finger swept beneath her panties and touched her—she nearly buckled.

And when he looked deep into her now open eyes, a moment of indecision flared there, but only for a moment.

He released his hold of her wrists and dropped to his knees, yanking her shorts and panties down in the process.

She found his shoulders, her head tipping skyward, as his tongue licked and baited her into sweet ecstasy.

He grabbed hold of her ass cheeks, pulling her closer to

his face, and she bucked against him, so close to release—but then he stopped.

"Not yet," he said while standing, killing her with his words.

She kicked off her shoes and stepped out of her shorts, then tore off her tee and bra. When he lowered his jeans, she quirked a brow. "Boxers, huh?" An unexpected smile found her lips, a smile not supposed to be present during angry sex.

And when he freed himself of his boxers and grabbed hold of his shaft, which was roped in thick veins, she couldn't help but reach between her legs.

He heaved out a deep breath and groaned before grabbing hold of her.

He lifted her like she was a feather and then turned and tossed her on the bed. His hands balled into fists at his sides as she propped her head up with her elbow and stared at him.

Naked on Owen York's bed.

How was this happening? How was she *letting* this happen?

But she couldn't stop herself, either.

Her body had taken control, and her fingertips trailed a circle around her belly button before wandering to her smooth center, and Owen's impressive length seemed to grow even more as his gaze tracked her every movement.

He joined her on the bed with a condom he'd grabbed from his wallet. He braced himself above her, teasing her with the circular movements of his hips, his cock brushing against her.

She arched up off the bed, dying to have him inside of her—to have him do whatever the hell he pleased.

Somehow, their angry sex didn't feel so angry, though.

The way he looked at her—the way she looked at him. It felt anything but.

She felt as if she were a marionette and someone was pulling the strings of her heart, making it dance, making everything inside of her move and come to life. Owen was somehow capable of this, and she couldn't think about the how or the why; she only wanted to think about how damn good he felt.

His nose touched her chest. "You smell so good." And then his mouth came down over her breast, and he flicked his tongue at her nipple as his other hand caressed her inner thighs, torturing her with the promise of what was to come.

And when his fingers slipped inside of her, it was as if he were readying her for him—warming her up to the moment he filled her.

He continued to toy with her breast, eliciting moans from her as her body kept lifting off the bed, desperate for more.

A few minutes later, he moved to his knees and sheathed himself. Gone was any look of indecision in his eyes.

Lust. A hell of a lot of lust, mirroring how she felt.

And then in one swift move, he plunged inside of her, and her head fell back as she cried out a hard gasp.

He slammed into her again. Hard.

Then harder.

A minute? He managed to keep pounding into her for . . . well, she lost count of the many minutes as she became hot and sweaty.

His stamina was out of this world.

She was growing dizzy with the need to come while trying to hold back. Then, he flipped her to her knees and held onto her hips—delivering what he'd promised: angry and hard sex.

Her hands fisted the comforter as she moved with him, fighting to hang on without coming so soon.

She grunted like an animal in the wild.

Her body tightened, and his fingertips bit even harder into the flesh at her sides.

Then he leaned in closer and brought one of his hands around and to her nipple, pinching and twisting.

She couldn't last any longer.

She came, her voice deepening into what sounded like a lioness roar as everything from her core to her toes tightened and pulsed.

And then she could feel his release. Despite the condom, the heat of his orgasm warmed her, and she collapsed onto her stomach.

He grabbed hold of the flesh of her ass, squeezing it beneath his palms as he slowly slid out of her wet center.

She twisted her neck to the side to catch him walking toward the bathroom.

At the sound of a flush, she rolled to her back.

He came into the room, his cock still hard between his thighs as he moved toward the bed. He stood at the edge and dragged both hands through his hair and gripped at the ends as he eyed her.

She didn't know what to do or say.

She'd never had sex like that, and for that long. She'd never wanted it to stop, though.

Her palms landed at her sides as she forced herself upright. Sweat dotted her chest and spine, and she could really use some water.

He turned and grabbed two bottles from the fridge. *A mind reader?*

He tossed one her way, and she caught it and nodded her thanks. His eyes were on her chest, and she followed his gaze to find her nipples hardening beneath his stare.

He sucked down the entire bottle before lowering it from his mouth. Watching a naked and very jacked former SEAL drink water had been one of the hottest things she'd ever witnessed.

"I only had the one condom." He tossed the bottle in the recycling bin—because, of course, Owen York would be perfect and care about the environment. Another strike against him. A *strike* because she didn't want to want him.

"Just the one, huh?" She arched a brow and fought the smile at her lips. She was supposed to be angry, right? She couldn't allow any other emotion to reach inside and get to her. Not right now, at least.

"I don't want to be done with you yet."

I never want you to be done. She hated the thought that popped into her head, knowing being with Owen was impossible, but . . .

His hands went to prayer pose in front of his lips, and she tried to force her eyes to his and not on his incredibly distracting body.

"Don't be done, then." She hadn't meant to say it, but she had been unable to stop herself from voicing her thoughts.

She forced her legs to fall to the side of the bed and rose, even though she felt wobbly and her thighs already ached. She was pretty sure Owen beat every other guy's record in bed.

Every guy.

Brad.

She hung her head, and pain ripped through her hard and fast, but she didn't want to give in to it.

No. She needed more time to breathe.

"What are you saying?" He cocked a brow when his hands fell heavy at his sides.

She forced the guilt from her mind the best she could and swallowed the gap between them. "Angry shower sex?"

His hand found her hip, his fingertips biting into her, and

she liked it—his touch made her feel alive; it made her feel everything. "No protection, remember?"

She pressed up on her toes, trying to get closer to him. "Well, there are things we could do that would still feel good." Her mind raced with thoughts of having this man beneath the water with her—to have his hands back on her body.

His hand slipped from her hip to the curve of her ass, which had her feet going flat to the floor. His fingertips followed the slope of her cheeks, and she gasped when he found her center, holding her tight against him. "You're still soaked," he said into her ear, his breath sparking a new wave of desire within her.

"Think of all the things you could do to me."

He let go of her and stepped back, tipping her chin up with a closed fist, and she could smell herself on him. "You are wild, aren't you?" He glanced away and toward the alarm clock by the bed. "One more hour," he said in a deep voice as if trying to convince himself he could have one more hour with her—and then they'd have to face reality.

They needed to look at the security footage.

She should've been focused on the threatening phone call and the meeting with the president.

But instead, all she could focus on was Owen and the different ways he could make her come, make her live in the moment.

"Okay," she whispered, and then he took her hand and guided her to the bathroom as if she'd get lost on the way.

Once the dual showerheads were on and the room gathered with steam, she pointed to the tiled seat within the shower and motioned for him to sit.

Water dripping down her body, she lowered herself before him, dying to take his shaft into her mouth and taste him.

Once seated, he found her eyes, his eyelashes wet, and he rolled his tongue over his lips to catch the water there. “I really do hate you.”

“I hate you, too,” she said then took all of him into her mouth.

CHAPTER TWELVE

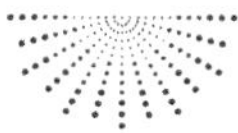

"WHY THE ROSE?" OWEN PULLED HIS TEE OVER HIS HEAD.

She zipped up her shorts and pressed a hand to her messy locks. "It's my middle name."

"There's more to it than that, right?" His hazel eyes narrowed.

She didn't want to talk about Brad right now. They both knew what happened any time they discussed their past. The mother of all Iron Curtains fell between them. But she didn't want to lie, either. She'd already made the mistake of lying before.

"Sam?" He stepped closer and started to reach for her arm, but then he pulled his hand back as if he'd made a mistake.

Their hour ended. Actually, it'd ended thirty minutes ago, but they'd extended it. They couldn't keep extending their hour, though. Reality had caught up with them when his coworker Jessica had called, requesting they join Asher in another suite where the security footage had been set up.

"Brad liked to call me his rose." There. She'd said it.

"And the rosary beads on your back?"

"I wasn't exactly a choir girl growing up, no matter how much my parents wanted me to be. But Brad, well, he was a devout Catholic."

"His grandmother raised him, right?"

"Yeah." She grabbed her strapless bra and hooked it on. "When she passed away, he decided to carry her rosary beads with him when deployed. Kind of his way of having her watch over him."

He surprised her by brushing his fingers over the tattoo.

"They weren't recovered on his body or at the base."

"Kind of your way of having him always watch your back, huh?"

He was perceptive, she'd give him that. But how long until he turned cold?

"When he died, I broke down. I barely survived it. It was my best friend, Emily's, idea to get the ink. The tattoo could be a reminder of the strength Brad had, and I guess I'd hoped I could absorb some of his faith, too." Emotion tightened in her throat, and tears threatened. She pressed a hand to her mouth to hold them back as her lids dropped closed.

"None of us can be saints, but we can do our best to be good people." He paused for a brief moment. "I only met Brad a few times, but he was definitely one of the good guys."

Her shoulders shuddered at the loss of his proximity. He must have stepped back—far enough back to reestablish boundaries or build a new wall between them.

Guilt at what they had done cut through her, and she assumed it was slicing through him just the same.

"I know what happened to them on their op."

She tensed at his words, unable to move or think.

"But I'm not allowed to tell you."

Her stomach fell, and she spun to face him. "What?"

He cupped his mouth and looked down at the floor. "I'm going to tell you, though."

She staggered back until she found the bed and sat, her legs unable to hold her.

His hand converted to a fist, and he tapped it at his lips a few times. "I'm going to break every rule in the damn book and tell you because Brad would want you to know the truth, and because I'm so goddamn pissed at the truth, that I don't care what's right or wrong anymore." He visibly tensed and blew out a sharp breath. "He and Jason died in Kiev trying to prevent a war with Russia."

"So, it's true? The picture?"

He nodded. "The U.S. placed their bodies in Iraq so the Russians wouldn't find out the truth."

"And what's the truth?"

"The scientist was kidnapped by a Ukrainian militia group. She was probably used to bait the U.S. there, though—to force our hands to supply them with weapons and cash, knowing we'd try and cover it up to stop Russian retaliation for the kidnapping—as well as keep the other three men from the op alive."

"Oh, God." She finally stood and wrapped her arms around him, burying her face in his chest.

"Brad, Jason, and even that woman got caught in the crossfires of it all, and now whoever is threatening you is trying to use that mission against us." He grabbed hold of her arms, pulled them down, and looked into her eyes. "But the motherfucker who orchestrated the entire thing may still be alive, and I'll be damned if I'm going to let him stay that way."

"Owen." She knew what he was trying to say, what he was suggesting—and as much as she wanted him to get justice for Brad and Jason, she couldn't let him commit murder. She couldn't let him get locked away for the rest of his life.

Before she could find the right words, a hard knock at the door had her hands landing on her hips, her head bowing.

"Yo, you guys okay?"

She recognized the voice: Asher.

"We need to talk about this," she whispered.

"No. I told you because I need you to know that I'll keep the promise I made ten years ago."

The promise?

Owen's words from the funeral blasted to the forefront of her mind like a BB from a slingshot.

I'll never stop until I find the SOB who did this to them. I won't rest until their killer is dead, Owen had said, his voice grave, his eyes bloodshot.

She scrambled to grab her shirt off the floor as he walked to the door to let Asher in. "Wait. Please, we need to finish this conversation."

He peered at her from over his shoulder. "There's nothing left to say."

"You told me this so I'd stop you." She pulled her shirt on as she approached him. "You can't do this. You don't owe anyone anything. Jason wouldn't want you in jail because of him," she whispered so Asher wouldn't hear her through the door.

He looked away from her and opened the door, effectively ending the conversation.

For now, at least . . .

CHAPTER THIRTEEN

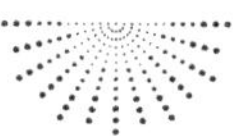

"YOU GOOD?" ASHER ASKED OUT IN THE HALL.

Owen wasn't in the mood for another hall chat. "How can I be good?" He cocked his head and glared at him.

"I know what you're thinking because I'd be thinking the same damn thing." Asher wrapped a hand over his shoulder. "But we have to handle this situation first. We need to get our people back alive before anyone else gets hurt."

"I know." He flexed his forearms at his sides, trying to control the burst of anger popping through him. Teteruk could already be dead if he'd been captured, and for some reason, the idea was maddening. Owen wanted to take vengeance into his own damn hands. But . . . "I can't put Sam in danger." He shook his head.

"Then let's end this before she goes to Russia." Asher pointed to the door. "Jess and Luke are handling the operational files and coming up with a list of potential assholes who might have our men. In the meantime—"

"Look at the footage," Owen finished. "The blackmailer is our only lead right now." He turned and reached for the door handle.

"Just a sec."

He dropped his hand and slowly eased back around.

"You didn't tell her anything, did you?" He looked Owen square in the eyes.

"No. That's Luke's way, remember? I don't divulge classified details like he did with Eva." The lie slipped a little too easily from his lips.

He hadn't told Sam everything, though, especially not about her father.

He wasn't sure how the hell to bring up the fact her dad had not only sat on the truth about Brad's death for ten years, but had helped orchestrate a deal to provide money and weapons to the man who'd killed her fiancé.

Asher took a step back and looked at him with new eyes. "You up and did it, didn't you?"

He couldn't face Asher and lie again. His gaze cut to the floor.

"You pulled a Luke, and you fell for someone off-limits."

The words had him slowly dragging his eyes to his friend's face—although the friendship was suddenly a little touch and go.

"Maybe you haven't fallen yet, but damned if I think you jumped from a plane without a chute." He shook his head. "You're going to hit the ground and hard."

"We don't have time for this," Owen snapped because he honestly had no clue how to respond without the lies getting stuck in his throat this time.

He stormed into the hotel room to find Sam already seated at the desk, positioned behind one of the two laptops Jess had supplied Asher.

"You think you can recognize the guy, too?" Asher's eyes narrowed on Owen a beat later, and a dark brow rose.

"I'll do my best." Owen tried to draw up an image of the

guy from the street in his head, but all he remembered were sideburns and dark hair.

"Are you staying here?" Sam asked Asher, peering at him over her shoulder.

"Nah, I have shit to do."

"And by 'shit,' you mean covert stuff for the president?"

He stroked his beard and looked at Owen, a warning in his eyes: *don't tell her anything else.*

The lines were becoming murky, and today, he was beginning to wonder which side they were even on. How could he be working for a country that allowed traitorous murderers to live?

Owen eyed the chair alongside Sam and hesitantly dropped down next to her. He hated the first thing he noticed was her smell. No perfume—just the orange-scented soap they'd scrubbed on each other not even an hour earlier.

He glared at the second laptop's blank screen. What in the hell had he been thinking? How could he have had sex with her, especially after what he'd learned in the Oval?

"Let's find this guy." Owen pressed play on the screen.

"I need to go meet up with the others," Asher said. "Sorry we can't bring you with us, Sam, but there will be classified intel there."

"I'll be in touch if we get a hit," Owen said.

Asher dug in his pocket and then tossed a cell phone his way. "In case the SOB calls, Luke thought you should hang on to her phone."

He gave a quick nod and then focused on the computer screen.

"Well, should we divide and conquer?" she softly asked once they were alone. Her words were whisper-light, as if she were suddenly holding back tears.

He leaned back and rubbed his tired eyes. "Sure, but

we're going to need coffee." He spied the single-server brewer and rose to turn it on.

"Owen," she said as the black liquid began to pour a minute later.

From that one word, he knew a lecture was about to follow. "Not now." He pinched the bridge of his nose and took a breath. "Let's focus on the cameras."

"But we should talk about what happened."

He folded his arms. "The sex, you mean? The mistake we made earlier?" If only he were Catholic, like Brad, so he could go to mass and have someone absolve him of his sins. How would he ever shake away the guilt of what he'd done?

Sam's lips parted before snapping shut.

Yeah, that's what he thought. She wouldn't want to talk about their total screw-up, either, and he didn't want to engage in any conversation that involved her trying to convince him to back off from taking down Jason and Brad's killer—if the guy was still alive.

Of course, first, he had to get his people back while keeping Sam safe. But after that? It was game on.

"Let's just not talk at all, then," she said, her voice surprisingly deep.

Armed with two coffees, he strode toward her and handed her one. "I wouldn't go that far." He lifted one shoulder and brought the drink to his lips.

Her long lashes fluttered for a brief moment. An attempt at self-control, maybe? He could well imagine the hot and heavy words she longed to hurl his way. "You're frustrating." She focused her gaze back on the screen and set the coffee alongside the keyboard.

"It's not the first time I've heard that."

He returned to his seat next to her and checked his desire to inhale that damn orange scent, hating the reminder of soap lathered all over her body. She was squeaky fucking clean now, and all he wanted to do was get her dirty again.

"I can't work next to you." He sprang from his seat, snatched the laptop, and brought it to the bed.

"What? Do I smell?" She glanced at him as he returned for his coffee.

"Yeah. That's the problem." *You always smell so damn good.* A moment later, he had his back to the headboard with his legs stretched out. With the computer on his lap, he began scrolling through footage, doing his best not to steal glimpses of *Brad's fiancée.*

Jason and Brad—they were the reason he was currently in that hotel room with Sam. If she hadn't gotten the photo—if she hadn't been working for the Intelligence Committee—they may have never run into each other again.

"You know, your mother sends me an invitation to the gathering for Jason every year."

Her words were like whiplash to the spine. "What?" He sat up straight and glowered at the back of her head.

She didn't turn to face him. "I've never RSVP'd. I never even returned a *no, but thanks* note. I'm a coward, I guess. She offered to have the celebration-of-life party be for Brad, too."

Shit. His mom had never told him that.

"I assume you go?"

He shook his head, then realized she still wasn't facing him. "Not in a few years."

Finally, she turned in her chair and gazed at him. "Why not?"

He faked a laugh. "A couple of years back, I tossed a guy in the cake." This elicited a smile. He held up a palm to stall her question. "I had a good reason."

She lifted a disbelieving brow.

"The SOB mocked the SEALs."

"What could he have said that would be bad enough to get tossed into a cake?"

"*SEALs get hard-ons when they're killing.*"

Her mouth rounded in surprise. "Oh. Yeah, I'd probably knee him in the groin for that since I wouldn't be able to throw him."

"I don't know. You look pretty tough to me." The quick curve of his lips caught him off guard.

"Well, next time you talk to your mom, could you send her my apology?" With a plea in her eyes, she swallowed and swiveled to face her computer again.

"You could call her, you know. I'm sure she'd love to hear from you."

"Do you guys talk often?"

"Not as much as she'd like. I'm fairly busy."

"Looks like it."

He could hear the soft sigh even with her back turned.

Regroup. Focus.

He looked back at the screen. *Focus.*

After twenty minutes of speeding through footage, he paused the video. "You went into your apartment building with a guy and a woman, but then twenty minutes later, you left alone. Do they live in the building, or did they come with you?" He carried the laptop over to her.

"That's my best friend, Emily, and her boyfriend, Blane. I had them over for dinner, but then I got a call from Senator Drake to have a drink to discuss my proposal. So I had to leave them." A light blush crawled up her cheeks. "Horrible hostess, I know. But Drake was one of the few people I had hoped to get on board." She brought her lip between her teeth for a brief moment. "Of course, he shot me down, anyway."

"So, your friends were alone in your apartment? For how long?"

She tilted her head. "I don't like where you're going with this. Emily is my best friend. Hell, she's being summoned to the White House as we speak." She pointed to her cell. "She texted me ten minutes ago, and I didn't want to bother you—but she's pretty confused, and I feel like an asshole. Her brother is on a flight back from London because of me."

"That doesn't change the fact that she was alone with her boyfriend in your apartment. There were no signs of forced entry into your place, or you would've noticed. Someone got in using a key." He cursed under his breath. "I don't know why we didn't ask you this before. Shit." His entire team had been so stunned with the recent turn of events, none of them had thought to ask.

"What?" She stood and rubbed her forearms.

"Who has access to your apartment? Who has a key? Who has been alone with your purse and keys? They could have made a copy."

"You'd need a key fob to get into the building unless someone buzzed you in."

"Those can be easily replicated. Or, hell, anyone could wait near the entrance and slip in behind a person going in."

"Okay, point taken. My parents have a key. Emily, and one of my interns because he drops off my dry cleaning." She held up a palm. "I know, I know. I shouldn't let my intern do grunt work, but—"

He shook his head. "That's a lot of territory to cover. I need a list of everyone who comes into regular contact with your mom and father, as well as you." He grabbed a notepad off her desk. "We need to check to see if any of those people ever entered your apartment without you. It'll be someone who knows your schedule, too."

Five minutes later, she handed him a list of names; he snapped a picture of it and texted Jess the photo. "We should focus on Emily and your intern and see when they've been in and out of your building while we wait for Jess to look over the list."

He eyed his watch. A SEAL Team would be hitting Teteruk's compound at 7 a.m.—not even eight hours from now. He'd give his left nut to be there. Surely Teteruk was already gone, but still.

"Tell me about Emily's boyfriend. How long have they been dating?" He set his laptop back on the desk, and they began looking over footage together.

"Hm. Maybe four weeks. His name's Blane Davis. I already did a background check on him, though."

He peered at her out of the corner of his eye. "Come again?"

"Emily doesn't make the best decisions when it comes to guys. So I had my friend Javier look into him." She innocently lifted her shoulders. "He came up clean, minus a few parking tickets."

Shit. That made him like her that much more.

Maybe she misunderstood his expression because she replied, "What? Wouldn't you do the same for a friend?"

"None of my friends date. Well, not until recently." Not until Luke up and fell in love, on an operation no less.

"No? Too busy? Too dangerous, given the covert work you do for the president?"

"I—" Swallowing the retort, he hung his head, and a smile found his lips. "Funny."

"Can't blame a girl for trying." She blinked her long lashes a few times.

"Bat those eyes all you want. I'm not falling for it."

She offered a nonchalant shrug. "I guess that's a dose of truth you can't deliver, huh?"

He grumbled and pointed back to the computer, hoping to quiet the sudden onslaught of thoughts that battered his mind —thoughts of his team, of the people he'd lost . . . of what he was giving up for his country. A real home—a woman to love . . . But if Luke could do it, maybe it was possible to find a balance? "Let's focus," he said, more so as a command to himself.

"Are you thinking this deliveryman had someone else plant the bug and camera?"

"I'm not sure, but we'll figure it out, and hopefully, soon." He paused the screen a moment later. "Who's that?"

She leaned closer to the computer. "My intern, Phillip. He's the one who delivers my dry cleaning every Monday morning."

He sped up the tape. "Why would it take seven and a half minutes to drop off your clothes?"

"I, uh . . . don't know."

"Will he be delivering your dry cleaning tomorrow?"

"Yeah, but there's no way someone got to him. He was vetted by the FBI to gain clearance to work with my team."

"Everyone has a weakness. This game is all about finding and exploiting it."

She was quiet for a moment, staring at him. "And what's your weakness?" Her voice had dipped lower at the question.

His palms landed on the desk as he gathered his thoughts and tried to slow his pulse, which began to peak. "I think it's fairly obvious." He stood and strode to the window, then peeled back the floor-length drapes to view the city he'd spent every waking breath to protect.

"Your brother?"

He caught her gaze in the window's reflection and fought the urge to bow his head and hide his eyes like a coward. "Him." He paused. "You."

Her long fingers drifted to the nape of her neck.

"Ever since you bumped into me in Mexico, my mind has been all kinds of messed up," he admitted.

"I'm guessing learning the truth about Jason didn't exactly do wonders for you, either."

He faced her and crossed his arms, leaning against the window.

Words were unnecessary.

He watched as she bunched her hands at her sides and lifted her gaze toward the ceiling. "I was doing fine until that picture showed up." She faked a laugh. "I mean, I was getting pretty good at appearing to be fine, I should say. I was a hot mess at first after Brad died—with the partying and drinking—but then I redirected my focus on revenge." Her eyes briefly fell closed. "On justice."

When she opened her eyes, he could almost see right through her, to the very core of her being.

"When my dad became the chairman of the Intelligence Committee, I thought maybe that was my chance. I could use his clout to access classified intel—to find out if there was any news or hope that the terrorist who'd killed Brad and Jason would be taken out." She gave a half-hearted shrug. "So, I pulled myself together and worked my ass off to land a position with him."

And your dad knew the truth, all that time. "That's why you ditched being a lawyer, huh?"

"Yeah, at first." A long sigh left her lips. "But every time I tried to look into the operation, my dad shut me down. So, I started to redirect my attention. I guess it was unhealthy to have such an obsession over revenge, anyway."

The truth about her father was on the edge of his tongue, but Sam had already been through the wringer. Could he really deliver the blow right now? Maybe he was beginning to understand why she'd kept her identity hidden from him for so long.

"Anyway," she said, tipping up one shoulder, "I started traveling and visiting areas hard-hit by war, and it made me realize I had to move on. Other people needed me."

He knew how that felt, but doing it was easier said than done. "And then you got the picture."

She gave a slight nod. "And it blew my glass world to pieces," she said, her voice a mere whisper of sound.

He wasn't going to tell her about her dad right now. Instead, he took a breath—and a chance. "I was always the adventurous one. My brother was the book-smart kid who stayed out of trouble. And when he told me he was going to try and make it into the SEALs, I honestly didn't believe him. I thought he was trying to prove something to me. He was the older one, so he was 'supposed' to be the tough guy. Maybe he thought he had to look out for me." He shook his head. "But he needed someone to look out for him, too."

"You couldn't have saved him."

His gaze pierced right through her. He was actually talking about his brother. He never did this. Not with the shrinks. Not with his friends. Not with anyone. And yet . . .

"I thought if I joined the Teams, I'd be able to get justice for him. Sort of like you, I guess."

Maybe they had more in common than they'd realized—way more than what they'd discovered during their flirty rapid-fire questions down in Mexico, which felt like ages ago.

"Some similarities," she admitted. "Only you went into combat zones to fight, and I went to war-torn countries once the dust had settled."

He offered her a fleeting grin. "Not so much at first. Flying hawks and jets wasn't enough. I needed to be on the ground in case the green light ever came to catch Jason and Brad's killer. I needed to be one of the guys called in to take down the terrorist."

The quiver in her bottom lip gave him pause. His eyes remained focused on her mouth for a long moment.

"I gave Jason a hard time when he was in BUD/S, but in truth, I was worried about him. Worried about him going to war. And damn, when I joined I almost missed the cut-off age —I was the one who barely made it."

"I have a hard time believing that."

"I'm just lucky." He shrugged. "I've always been the lucky one. But I wish I could've given all of my luck to him." An unfamiliar lump of emotion gathered in his throat. "I'd trade my life for his in a heartbeat."

"Of course you would." She took a hesitant step his way. "That's the kind of man you are." Her palm rested over his heart, which began to pound harder. "The kind of man I'd expect you to be."

He tried to shake off her words, but she lightly tapped at his chest. "Jason would be proud of the man you are." Her voice shook, and then he realized something inside of him was shaking, too.

"I was flying when he died. I was in the air, and I know it sounds strange—but damn, it was like I could feel him pass through me—going up." He wasn't sure if he believed in the afterlife, but he also hated the idea of there just being nothing, which would mean his brother was truly gone. "When I landed, I was told he'd died."

"I'm so sorry," she whispered.

A hardness in his chest had him gasping for breath, and

then she did something . . . something that had him locking his biceps tight at his sides.

She wrapped her arms around him and pulled him into a hug.

He wouldn't cry.

He was a thirty-seven-year-old man.

He was a SEAL.

But fuck if his chest didn't hurt.

He scooped his hands free of his pockets and pulled her even tighter against him.

"You're supposed to hate me," she said through a broken laugh a few minutes later when she pulled back and swiped at her cheeks.

"Yeah." He nodded and found her eyes, his palm cupping her face. "But you're making it really hard."

* * *

"They tossed the place, but someone had already got to him." Jess's words took Owen's breath away.

"Any blood? Sign of a struggle?" He rose from his seat and cupped his mouth, as the possibilities raced through his mind.

He wanted Teteruk to live.

He needed him to still be alive.

Then, he could kill the bastard himself.

"Yeah. Hard to tell when his compound was hit, but the SEAL Team guesses he's been gone at least a week. Four guys, eight days ago, bought one-way tickets from Russia to Georgia and then rented a car. The ID used to rent it was bogus, and the plane tickets must've been under aliases. We think they took Teteruk and then drove him over the border and into Russia."

"No faces? Nothing to nail these bastards down?" he asked in a quiet voice since Sam was in the en-suite.

"The security cameras at the airport aren't stellar. Pretty pixelated, and these guys did a good job hiding from them. I'm doing what I can, but I'm not optimistic." Jess tightened her blonde ponytail before folding her arms.

"Teteruk's photos probably ID'd our men."

Jess cleared her throat when Sam exited the hotel bathroom.

He looked over to see that she was dressed for work in a red skirt, white silk blouse, and nude heels. She smoothed her hands down the sides of her skirt, and he tried to forget the soft, sweet flesh beneath the stiff fabric.

It hadn't taken him long to discover this woman was just like him. Hard on the outside, but packing a lot more on the inside.

He could see through her walls, maybe because they were so similar.

"We should've been checking who had access to you and your father's keys sooner." Jess flicked her index finger at the notepad of names on the desk, drawing Owen's attention back to the mission. "With everything else going on, we overlooked the obvious."

Her father. He wondered how Senator McCarthy's talk had gone with POTUS yesterday. Wouldn't he be worried about continuing the event, with his daughter's life on the line? Maybe he'd convince the president to, at the very least, postpone Wednesday's benefit.

"We've all been a bit out of it," Owen professed a moment later.

Last night, for instance, had taken an unexpected turn. One minute he had been observing security footage, and the next, he'd been confessing his feelings like a guest on some talk show.

After their heart-to-heart, he had jerked himself back to business, forcing his gaze onto the camera footage until he'd felt his eyes practically bleeding. But despite his efforts, his mind had remained stuck on Sam.

He gave an internal shrug as he thought about it. Maybe his response was some sort of self-defense mechanism. Nature's way of preventing him from losing his mind with everything going on.

"Did you have a productive night?" Sam asked, directing her question to Jess.

Owen knew she wouldn't answer with anything other than a generic statement.

"I made some progress on tracking the bug in the smoke detector, actually."

And Brad and Jason's murderer is gone. He couldn't tell Sam about that, though—not in front of Jess. "What'd you discover?"

"Five vendors received bugs with that batch number. The thing is, those vendors feed into about one hundred other companies. I'll work on narrowing down the list this morning."

"Good." Owen strode to the desk and pressed play on the footage he'd saved last night. "See this guy?" he said to Jess. "He's in a hoodie, and he's keeping his head down and away from the camera. He's not quite as tall as the deliveryman, but he's hanging back near the door, waiting to get in."

He fast-forwarded a couple of minutes later to show one of Sam's neighbors entering the building; the guy in the hoodie followed her in. "My money is on either her intern or this guy."

"I'd prefer the intern since Hoodie Guy has no face." She

checked her watch. "Liam and Asher are downstairs waiting for you guys." Jess turned to Sam. "Your intern should be arriving at your apartment by eight, right?"

"Yeah. He usually makes it to the office by eight thirty."

Jess nodded. "Well, you guys will be inside waiting for him."

Owen rose and stood alongside her. "I don't think we'll need four of us to face a twenty-three-year-old intern."

"No, but it sure as hell will scare him." Sam smiled. "The guy's even intimidated by me."

Owen cocked his head to the side. "Can you blame him?"

"If he knows something," Jess began while jerking her thumb in Owen's direction, "these guys will get him to talk."

"If he's innocent, which I think he is, what's to stop him from telling the police about this chat?" Sam asked as she crossed to the bed to grab her phone.

When she passed by, he could smell her perfume. It was sharper and more distinct. Heavier. It must be the take-no-prisoners scent she wore to work.

He still hated the idea of sending Sam to her office later. It was too exposed. Even though he'd be watching, he knew the odds. What if someone got to her first?

All this risk because the president wanted her to publicly announce that her proposal now had *his* support.

"We'll make sure Phillip doesn't tell anyone about us." Jess gave her a reassuring smile, smoothly covering for Owen's silence. "Our people started cross-checking the other lists of names you sent me last night. Nothing yet, but we'll keep at it."

"Okay." Owen turned to Sam. "Ready?"

Sam nodded, but hesitation flitted over her features. She was a civilian, he had to remind himself. She was a woman not used to being caught in the crossfires of a mission, even if she had originally joined her father's team to get retribution for Brad—a gutsy move that most people wouldn't have taken.

Owen forced his booted feet to the door. He needed to get out of that small room and breathe in some fresh air. If he could just clear his head . . . then, somehow, he could reset his focus.

CHAPTER FOURTEEN

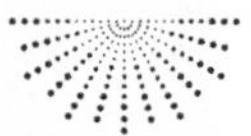

ASHER AND THE AUSSIE LIAM WERE SITTING ON HER COUCH, and she couldn't help but smile at the two Navy SEALs occupying nearly every square inch of the piece of furniture. Muscles upon muscles. Tattoos. If they didn't fit the stereotype of a Teamguy with their swagger and looks, she didn't know who would.

Why am I thinking about this? Then again, it was better than facing the reality, that her intern could've invaded her privacy and watched her naked. *Ugh.*

"Your place is pretty eclectic." Liam eyed the pouf in front of her leather chair near the couch. "That Moroccan?"

"How'd you know?"

"Been to Marrakesh a few times."

"Of course you have." She thought back to her trip to Morocco and the vendor who'd insisted she buy the pillow-like seating slash table. She had a habit of bringing items back home from all around the world, and now her apartment was filling up—she'd need a bigger place soon. "Got it in Casablanca."

"Ah, a romantic city," Liam said as if remembering something, a grin teasing his lips.

Asher rolled his eyes. "Ladies-Man-Liam, what can I say?"

"What?" She smiled, but then her skin popped with goose bumps, and her whole system seemed to suddenly slow down at the sight of Owen exiting her bedroom.

He had a funny way of calming her when she needed it—but he also had the ability to excite her body to epic proportions at insane times.

She must be on an episode of some dramatic TV show. This couldn't really be her life.

In real life, would two people have sex in the middle of everything going on? Maybe she and Owen were both equal parts screwed up, so much so they couldn't even respect their own limits. Would they be able to reset the boundaries?

It'd been easy to avoid messy and complicated relationships over the years since she hadn't wanted a new relationship. But, in a few days, this man had blown through every one of her barriers and had left her only wanting more of him.

"No new bugs, right?" she asked when Owen stood before her with the same device that federal agents used to sweep her home and office during their random checks.

"We're good."

Her cell began buzzing, and it had everyone whirling toward it as if the device were an explosive. She grabbed it off the bar counter and grimaced.

"Who is it?" Owen came up behind her.

"Javier. He just sent me a text. He says I owe him drinks because he got dragged to the Oval Office last night." She set the phone back down. "This whole thing is getting out of hand." She'd never thought a photo would have tangled her up in a spider web of such proportions. “It’s ten past eight. He should be here soon.” She turned to face the room, noticing Asher’s booted foot propped on her two-thousand-dollar coffee table. She wasn’t pretentious, but she could imagine her mother’s jaw hitting the floor.

Liam flipped through a copy of a women’s magazine that had been on the end table. He spun it lengthwise and angled his head. “Sixty-nine ways to spice up your bedroom.” He flicked an index finger at it. “It’s got graphics.”

“Is that porn?” Asher snatched the magazine.

Liam’s eyes nearly twinkled before he winked at her. His second wink of the morning. She was beginning to wonder how many women he’d wooed with that wink. “Damn, I thought men were bad.”

She rolled her eyes, but then sucked in a breath when Owen’s hand wrapped over her wrist and pulled her closer.

“You have a hell of a lot of red lingerie in your dresser,” he whispered into her ear.

Liam’s gaze swerved away from her; he cleared his throat and looked out the window. Asher kept his eyes on the magazine, his brows drawn together, scrutinizing it as if it were a book written in ancient Chinese.

“You noticed that while checking for bugs, huh?” She knew what else he’d probably found: her vibrator.

“Makes it hard to do my job with that kind of distraction.” His voice, low and rough, scraped over her skin.

“I’ll be sure to”—she took a breath, forgetting where they were and *why* they were there—“remove such distractions if you ever need to check again.”

He parted his lips to speak, but no sound came out. The apology shone in his eyes, though. It was as if he had just done a quick reality check, heard his own words, and realized they had no business exchanging sexual banter at a time like this.

At the sound of a lock turning in the front door, her heart climbed into her throat.

"It's time," Owen quietly announced to his buddies.

The men were on their feet, more intimidating than ever with their black military boots paired with jeans, and tees that showed off biceps roped in veins.

Owen pointed to the hall, motioning for her to get out of sight.

Surely Phillip wasn't dangerous, but she'd follow his orders.

The door creaked open before she heard Phillip shriek, "What the hell!"

"We need to talk," Owen growled, and from her vantage point, she saw Asher and Liam lunge toward the kitchen in two quick strides.

"Don't make this hard," Asher yelled, and she could hear urgent gasps for breath.

She peeked around the corner and found Phillip pinned to the floor.

"Why the hell did you run?" Owen's knee pressed down into the center of Phillip's back.

"Phillip?" She rounded the hallway for a better view.

Phillip pivoted his head to the side and looked up to find her. Her dry cleaning lay crumpled inside the plastic on the floor.

Asher kicked the door shut and blocked the exit, while Liam helped Owen lift Phillip to his feet.

"What's going on, Miss McCarthy?" he asked, his eyes narrowing.

"Why'd you run?" Owen asked again.

Sam held up her palm. "You guys did scare the shit out of him. He probably thought you were going to attack."

Phillip nodded his head. "Yes."

"I think you can let him go," she said softly and folded her arms.

Owen and Liam released their hold and then took a step back as Phillip smoothed his hands down his dress shirt.

Owen nodded his head her way, which she interpreted as an offer to take point. "Phillip, do you remember that deliveryman from my office last week? The one you chased down?"

He squeezed his eyes closed, and sweat dotted his hairline and the sides of his face. "Yes, ma'am."

"Did you ever see him before that day? Did he ever ask you to do anything for him?"

"I-I think I need to sit." He slowly walked toward her living room and dropped down on her couch, covering his face with his palms.

"You can talk to me. Please, this is a matter of life and death." She hadn't expected to get anything out of him, but now, looking at him, she knew she'd been wrong.

His black shoe tapped against the rug beneath the coffee table, and his leg trembled.

"Why were you in Samantha's apartment for so long last Monday?" Owen came up alongside the couch. When Phillip remained silent, he added, "Someone bugged this apartment."

His eyes darted to Owen's face. "What? No! It wasn't me."

"Then why are you so nervous? What were you doing up here for so long?" Owen folded his arms, his biceps popping. Cue the extra intimidation factor.

He swiped the sweat from his face and looked up at Sam. "I was looking around. Being nosy. I'm so sorry."

"You were looking through my things?" Like she needed another creep invading her privacy. "What the hell, Phillip?"

"You're this strong, powerful woman, and I can't help but . . . but be attracted to you." A mortified flush raced up his neck and over his cheeks. He shrugged. "Being in your home is the closest I'll ever get to being with you."

She pressed a hand to her mouth and turned away, not sure what to think or feel.

"You didn't answer the question about the deliveryman." Owen's voice was rough and intense; it even had the hairs on her arms standing up. "Answer me. If you lie to me, I'll find out."

"No, it wasn't him." Phillip's voice was little more than a squeak.

"But *someone*?" Owen raised a brow.

Phillip finally nodded. "I'm sorry. I wanted to tell you, but he threatened me."

"Who? What'd he say?" she rushed out, her spine bowing at the news.

"Four weeks ago, some guy showed up at my apartment with a mask. You know, the scary kind? With only the eyes cut out?" He cringed. "He offered me a lot of money to make a copy of your key."

"Oh my God. How could you?" Betrayal cut through her tone. All this time, she'd thought he was just a nervous guy, but one of the good ones.

"I didn't! I refused." He shook his head, his brows pinching together. "I was worried he'd kill me if I didn't cooperate, but, uh, surprisingly, he only said he'd kill me if I ever told anyone about the offer."

"I'm not sure I believe you." Owen motioned for Phillip to stand, and he obeyed. "Did anyone else ever approach you? Make threats?"

"No. I swear." His gaze darted back and forth between Sam and Owen.

"Do you believe him?" Owen glanced back at Sam.

"I honestly don't know," she murmured.

Owen scrubbed a hand over his jaw and stepped back from Phillip. "I want you to go to work and pretend like this morning never happened." He cocked his head to the side, staring into Phillip's eyes. "That man who showed up at your house, he's nowhere near as scary as I am. You got it?" His voice could pave a road, it was so hard and heavy.

Sam stepped forward. "What? We're letting him go?"

"Fire him after we catch the bastard. If this guy is keeping tabs on you, he'll suspect something if Phillip doesn't show up to work," Owen explained. He turned back toward the intern. "And if you're lying to me—"

Phillip's palms went into the air. "I'm not," he half-cried.

She glared at Phillip. "You should've told me. I could have protected you."

"When we started, you warned me that we could get threats," Phillip said. "But I was too scared to report it. I'm sorry."

She didn't know what to say, so she left the living room and went to her bedroom, closing the door behind her, in desperate need of space.

Her hands landed on the door, and she tapped her forehead against it a couple of times, trying to regroup. Out of the corner of her eye, she spotted her dresser and saw that the top drawer was ajar.

A hard sigh fell from her lips as she went over to it. Hesitation passed over her; instead of closing it, she pulled it open. Owen's hands had been in that drawer not too long ago, and she could still smell his cologne in her room. She was becoming as heightened to smell as he was. Somehow, that thought lightened her mood.

Her fingertips skimmed the lace inside, and she shifted the garments back to reveal the silver and pink object her friend had gotten her for a gag gift on her last birthday.

Two sharp raps at the door had her shoulders flinching. "It's me."

"Come in." She could get used to hearing Owen say *it's me*, like he was hers and she was his—like it was natural for him to be there, to be part of her life.

"You, uh, need to pack a few more things before we get out of here?" His eyes fell upon the dresser before journeying back to her face. "Although, I don't think I could handle watching you pack that piece of hardware you've got in there. The idea of you in bed doing that, with me sleeping on the couch . . ."

"Funny." The word teased over her tongue and between her teeth as she closed the drawer and faced him.

He leaned into the frame of the doorway. "But in all seriousness, if you need to let loose again, I wouldn't blame you. I could take a shower or something while you're, eh-hem, taking the edge off." He lifted a brow. "It'd be a very cold shower, but I'd do that for you."

Desire surged hot and hard in her chest and spread through her limbs, a sharp contrast to her feelings just minutes ago, when her intern had been pinned to the floor. "Oh you would, would you?"

"A sacrifice I'd be willing to make. I couldn't stand between a woman and her needs."

She stopped just shy of him and folded her arms. His gaze dropped to her cleavage. "And what about your needs?"

He slowly dragged his focus back to her eyes. "My needs don't matter right now. All that matters is keeping you safe."

Her lips twisted at the edges as she tried to conceal the threat of a smile. "Well, sex should be the last thing on my mind right now, don't you think? Given what's going on."

He shifted his stance and pulled the door closed, which had her hands bunching into fists at her sides. The brooding swirl of lust in his eyes pierced right through her, and she backed up against her tall dresser, a dresser that had been her great-grandmother's—passed down over the years. Generations of lace . . .

He pressed both palms to the mahogany, and she merely gaped at the biceps in her line of sight. "Owen, what are you doing?"

"We shouldn't be thinking about sex; you're right. With what's going on, it should be the last thing on our minds." He found her eyes. "I shouldn't be thinking about bunching up that tight red skirt you're wearing and feeling just how wet you are . . . because you are, aren't you?"

A twitch between her thighs had her closing her eyes and taking a breath. "Since my intern is out there, along with your two SEAL buddies, I definitely shouldn't be thinking about how it'd feel to have your tongue inside my mouth, then."

His hand dropped to her hip, and he pulled her against him. She could feel his hard length pressing into her. "I shouldn't still want to bury myself inside of you, even if everyone outside of this room were to disappear."

"But you do," she whispered and opened her eyes.

His jaw clenched as he studied her. "But I do."

"Am I a bad person to want to have sex with you? Even if sex is the best possible way to take my mind off the sick shit in this world—it's not natural to want you like I do, right?"

His lips rolled inward, and his brows pulled together. "I—"

"You two ready to rock and roll? Phillip's gone."

She blinked at the sound of Asher's voice on the other side of the door.

Owen quickly released his hold and staggered back. "Be right out."

"Hurry up," Asher responded. Sam could hear the heavy footsteps of his boots as he left.

Owen adjusted his jeans, and she bit her lip as she watched him try to hide his desire. "I might need a second." He turned away.

She stepped behind him and trailed her hand up his hard back, her fingers slipping over his now closely cropped hair.

"You think touching me will get me to calm my dick down?"

"It must be the adrenaline of everything going on that's making me lose my mind," she said apologetically.

He faced her, his jeans still tented from his massive erection. "Adrenaline can definitely increase your sexual appetite." He eyed her while taking a hard swallow.

"It happens to you a lot?" She didn't want to think about him with other women. She didn't have time to decipher the brief flicker of jealousy that had crossed through her, either.

"Sex on an op?" He shook his head. "You'd be a first." His eyes thinned when he stepped closer to her. He caressed her cheek, and she turned into his palm, relishing in the way his touch made her feel.

Adrenaline, sure. "We should go . . ."

"They can wait." His thumb ran over her lips, and her tongue peeked out of her mouth to catch his skin. His nostrils flared slightly. "I just need one more second alone with you, one more second to ignore the 'sick shit of the world.'"

When his fingers found her short locks, he gave a slight tug on her hair, tipping her chin up. His other hand skated down her throat before dropping underneath her blouse and grazing her nipple.

"Owen," she whispered, arching her pelvis with the need to feel him. "I don't think this will be an arousal killer, either. Just an FYI."

He lifted his mouth to her ear, and his breath there had her breasts puckering even more.

"You can't fight nature," he said before claiming her mouth as if her very breath belonged to him.

His tongue touched her lips like a command, seeking entrance, and she gave it to him.

Seconds? A minute, maybe? At some point, he staggered back and dragged both palms down his face.

Her trembling fingers fixed her blouse and bra strap, so she wouldn't expose a nipple to Liam or Asher.

He lightly scowled. "I shouldn't want to fuck you six ways from Sunday right now."

"Only six?"

Her words had him catching her eyes. "I can't get enough of you, even though I don't *want* to want you."

"We have a million different reasons to stay away from each other."

His brows pinched tight. "And yet, why aren't we?"

"I guess we don't have time to figure that out right now."

"In my line of work, there's never a right time." And with that, he started for the door.

To hell with his erection, apparently.

He held the door open and waited for her to walk out. She forced the heavy breath to remain in her lungs as she moved past him.

She caught sight of Liam and Asher down the hall. They both abruptly whirled away from her, as if they'd caught Sam and Owen doing naked limbo.

"Let's go," Owen said as they caught up to the men.

She tried to ignore the bulge still present beneath his jeans.

"Let's take the stairs," Asher said outside her apartment door.

Liam unlocked the Suburban once they were in the parking garage, and she scooted onto the back seat.

Sam strapped on her belt, and her gaze skated to Owen now next to her. His hard-on was almost gone, but his hand rested atop his jeans, concealing whatever was left of it.

If Owen was a distraction for her, did that mean she was throwing him off-balance, too? Was she impacting his focus? Was she dangerous to him?

She'd lost Brad. She couldn't lose him, too.

She inwardly sighed. She didn't have Owen in the first place, though. *I can't have him.*

"This is a normal day for you guys, isn't it?" she asked.

Liam pulled out of the parking garage. "We're usually a lot more fun."

"I get the distinct feeling your version of fun might vary slightly from mine." She wondered if they were "more fun" on the ops that weren't so personal.

"With what we do, if we don't lighten the mood every once in a while, shit could get ugly pretty fast." Asher's admission had her looking at him in surprise.

Owen looked out his side window, and it was as if any humor or buzz of desire she'd felt went right out the glass with his gaze.

All that was on her mind now was Owen and his thirst for vengeance.

He wouldn't really kill a man in cold blood, though, would he?

She'd wanted justice for years, but she never thought

she'd have the chance to do it herself. No, she'd sat safely in the comfort of her home while men had suited up in combat gear to handle the evil of the world. Men like the three guys in the car with her.

If it was okay to take out a terrorist with a drone in the blink of an eye, would it be okay to take out Teteruk, the man who'd murdered two Navy SEALs and a scientist?

How did anyone really know which lines were okay to cross?

"It'd be a lot easier if we could all meet up at TOC," Asher said as they pulled out onto the road, scattering her thoughts.

"TOC?" She arched a brow.

"Old habit." Asher waved a dismissive hand.

"No exceptions for me, though, huh?"

"Sorry, darlin', but no," Liam answered.

"Are we thinking it was the deliveryman who threatened Phillip?" Asher pivoted to face the back again.

"Maybe." Owen's face was drawn tight when he looked Asher's way. "But we still need to find whoever the hell hired him."

"I'm thinking the friend, Emily—"

"No way," Sam cut Asher off.

"I didn't mean her, exactly, but I'm betting someone close to her copied your key."

"The boyfriend would be too easy," Liam said from behind the wheel as if disappointed by the idea. "But my money is on him."

"I doubt Blane could pull all of this off," she said.

"He's probably the small fish, sweetheart," Asher said before facing forward. "But we need him to catch the whale."

"Not a shark?" Liam glanced at Asher.

"We're the sharks, bro," he said with a laugh.

"Nah, we're the SEALs," Liam replied, and their banter had her smiling.

Smiling. I'm smiling right now. She touched her cheeks, shocked by the warmth there. "And you're *still* SEALs, aren't you?"

Liam glanced back at her. "Of course." He smiled. "You don't ever stop being a SEAL."

That wasn't what she'd meant, and he knew it, but she wouldn't push. One thing was for damn sure: the rumors floating around the upper echelon of Washington were true: there really was a top-secret black ops group working for the president. And these guys sure as hell were it.

* * *

SHE SWALLOWED THE LUMP THE SIZE OF A BOULDER. "IT'S really Blane?"

She could practically hear Jessica's nod over the speakerphone. "I'm doubting it's a massive coincidence that his company received a shipment of the same batch of bugs."

Sam shifted her gaze to Liam as he pulled the SUV to the side of the road and began inputting a new address into his phone's GPS. "That's Emily's place." She pressed a hand against the back of Asher's seat. "Blane's at her place right now?" She thought about the text she'd gotten from Emily that morning. Emily's brother had been picked up by Secret Service and taken to the president an hour ago. Emily must have skipped work since Jake had flown in from London. "What if he hurts her?"

"Based on our intel, this guy just influences policy decisions in D.C.; he's never actually hurt anyone. Plus, he has no way of knowing we're on to him," Jessica explained.

She tried to let Jessica's words reassure her, but still,

Emily was alone with the guy responsible for having bugged her apartment. And, oh God, he'd spied on her in her bedroom. Her stomach wrenched at the reminder.

"We need to find out who the hell hired this guy," Owen said, and his voice sounded almost hoarse, as if a brush of anger had painted strokes inside his throat, clenching his words.

"And we're sure he's at Emily's apartment?" Sam asked again.

"Traffic cams picked up his plate. He's still parked outside her building," Jessica answered. "Be safe. Call me when you have news."

"Always, Peaches," Asher said. Then the call ended, and an eerie silence claimed the vehicle.

"Are you guys carrying?" Sam asked as they neared Emily's townhouse.

Owen looked over at her and gave a curt nod. "We're strapped. Don't worry."

She hadn't remembered seeing him hide a weapon beneath his clothes that morning, but he was a covert operative, so of course, she wouldn't have noticed.

These guys were probably trained to blend in, but hell, there was nothing ordinary about the muscled men in the car with her, especially Owen. Since meeting him last week, he'd somehow managed to remind her that life could be so much more, more than she'd ever thought it could be.

I want you to have everything in life. I want you to be so happy your cheeks hurt from smiling. Her mind kept replaying those words, spoken during a Skype call from Brad when he had been deployed. The message now had her tensing from head to toe.

Owen's knuckles tapped at the side of her thigh a second later. "You good?"

Her thoughts rattled around in her head for a moment, before she could finally look at him. “Nervous,” she said softly. “I don’t want anything happening to Emily.” *Or you.*

“What’s the plan?” Asher asked once they’d parallel parked in front of Emily’s townhouse.

A memory popped to mind. “Emily has a gun. It’s in her bedroom safe.” She unbuckled and looked expectantly at Owen.

“Good to know. Do you think she gave Blane the code?”

“I . . . I don’t know.” She pursed her lips in thought. “I still can’t believe this is happening.”

“I need you to try and hold it together, okay?” He pointed to her purse, sitting on the floor by her heels. “Call Emily. Tell her you’re outside, and you need to come in to talk to her.”

She nodded and retrieved her cell.

“Try to determine if Blane can overhear your conversation, and if not, tell her we’re all coming in,” Owen told her.

She squeezed her emotions down her throat, and when the line connected, her eyes fell closed. “Hey,” she said as casually as possible when Emily picked up. Emily was okay. *Thank God.* “Is Blane around?”

“In the shower. Why?” Emily was quiet for a moment, and Sam mouthed *shower* to Owen.

The four of them stepped out of the SUV, and Owen motioned for her to stay sandwiched between him and Asher. Liam trailed behind them to the door.

“Can you let me in?” she asked Emily, the phone trembling in her hand. Somehow, she felt like she was betraying her friend. “I’m outside. It’s important.”

“Um. Yeah.” Through the phone, she could hear the

sound of the chain being slid from its lock a few seconds later.

"I have Owen with me, and his friends," she sputtered, right before the door opened.

Emily's eyes widened in surprise, and she nearly dropped the phone.

Sam sidestepped Owen, needing to get to her best friend. "Is Blane still in the shower?"

"Uh." Emily blinked. "Maybe." Her focus drifted back to Owen and the other two guys. "What's going on?"

"Blane sent the photo. He's been spying on me." Sam swallowed. "They need to talk to him."

Emily's face blanched, and Sam could tell she was on the brink of denying the possibility, but when her eyes swept to Sam's face, she took a breath and stepped out of the way.

It was the kind of trust only a best friend could give, and Sam was grateful. "I'm sorry," Sam mouthed as the three men moved past them and entered the foyer of her townhouse.

Emily slowly shut the door and tucked her phone into the pocket of her long pink silk robe. "He's in the shower upstairs."

"In your bedroom?" Liam asked, and she nodded.

Owen looked at the stairs before glancing at Emily. "Does he carry a gun? Or know the code to your safe?"

"No." She cupped her mouth and leaned against the interior wall as her eyes lifted to the flight of stairs off to her right.

"Stay here," Asher said. "We'll be down with him in a minute." Liam and Asher moved so quietly up the stairs, she could barely hear them creaking in the twentieth-century historical townhouse.

Owen pointed to the hall, which led to the living room and kitchen area. "Come on."

Sam reached for Emily's elbow and guided her, knowing her best friend was shocked at the moment.

"I don't understand." Emily hunkered down on one of the couches and pulled a pillow to her lap.

Sam sat next to her and gently squeezed her forearm. "This whole thing is such a mess. I'm so sorry you got dragged into it."

"Get your fucking hands off me!" a man shouted a moment later.

Sam jumped in alarm at the thuds pounding above her.

"They're fine. Don't worry." Owen gave a reassuring nod, and a moment later, Asher and Liam came into the room. Between them stumbled Blane, dressed only in boxers. Blood trickled from his lower lip.

Emily gasped and clutched the pillow tighter.

"What's going on?" The man's gray eyes darted around the room. He looked even more frazzled than Phillip had earlier.

"Sit." Owen issued the command and pointed to the lone leather chair opposite the couch. "If you move, they'll shoot you in the kneecap."

It was the first time Sam had noticed a drawn weapon.

Asher held a silver and black gun. She wasn't sure what kind it was, but God . . . everything just suddenly felt a hell of a lot more real.

Blane lifted his hands as he walked to the chair and sat.

Mr. Drago. Maybe Blane wasn't Russian, but now her nickname for the guy was fitting, particularly if he was taking money from someone to try and block her efforts to effect peace between Ukraine and Russia.

Blane gripped the arms of the chair. His calf muscles tightened as his toes dug into the carpet beneath his feet. "Emily?" He took a ragged breath.

"Don't act like you don't know why we're here." Owen glanced at Sam before moving past her to confront Blane. "You started dating Emily to get close to Samantha. You used her. You tried to buy off Sam's intern, Phillip, and when you couldn't, you had to take care of the job yourself." He paused. "How am I doing so far?"

Emily scooted closer to Sam. This must have been unbearable for her. She'd been sleeping with the asshole.

Sam couldn't take her eyes off the bastard, though. She wanted to slug him across the jaw herself.

"I don't know what you're talking about." Blane lifted his palms, but Owen rushed toward him, yanked him by the arm, and pulled him to his feet.

Owen's back and neck tensed as he gripped Blane's jaw, squeezing. "Don't lie to me. We know it was you, but we want to know why, and we want to know who hired you."

When Blane didn't respond, he let go of him and shoved him back into the chair.

"I promise. I have no idea what you're talking about," Blane rushed out.

Owen peered over his shoulder. "Liam, could you take Sam and Emily out of the room, please? Upstairs?"

She didn't want to go.

She wanted to see the truth spill from his lips.

But Emily—she'd leave for Emily.

"What the hell is going on?" Emily covered her face once they were in her bedroom. Liam stayed in the open doorway on guard, probably half-listening to whatever was happening downstairs.

The sudden crash from below had her cringing, but he didn't move a muscle.

Sam moved toward the bed and then noticed the rumpled comforter that lay along the edge.

Awkward.

Emily and Blane had probably just recently had sex. *Why'd this have to happen?*

She couldn't tell her friend too much, especially with Liam in earshot. "You were right about the picture and my proposal. I think someone hired Blane to force my hand. He pursued you to get to me, and then he copied your key to my place." She squeezed her eyes closed, hating this moment. "He put a camera in my bedroom and a bug in my smoke detector, too."

"Oh, God." Emily wrapped her arms around Sam. "I'm so sorry."

"No, this is my fault. I brought you into all of this." She gulped. "And now you and your brother—"

"I'm going to kill him," Emily growled and pulled away.

Liam held up a hand and shook his head at her fierce approach. Shoulders slumped, she faced Sam again. "Are you okay?"

"Don't worry about me." Sam stepped over Blane's strewn clothes, her stomach roiling at the sight, and reached for her friend's arm. "We'll make him pay for this."

Emily softly nodded, still in a daze.

They sat back on the bed and remained there in silence, because, honestly, what was there to say at a moment like this?

"Liam! I need your help!" Asher's voice rang through the stairwell, and everything inside of her went numb.

CHAPTER FIFTEEN

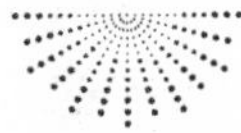

Owen kept his hands wrapped tight around Blane's throat. The slow tinge of red crept up the man's face; he could feel the blood in his own body heating.

"You're going to kill him!" Asher roped his hands around Owen's arm and yanked on it, but Owen didn't want to let go.

He lost sight of the man as his own eyes clenched shut, feeling like he was traveling at a high speed and low altitude, and he'd have a G-induced loss of consciousness soon.

He wanted to kill him. He wanted to stamp out the life in him, to make him pay. He should pay for everyone who'd ever died. For Jason. For Brad. Hell, even for his buddy Marcus, whose death had nothing to do with the case.

Scum like Blane didn't deserve to breathe when good men had been taken from the world.

"Owen, you have to stop," Asher yelled.

He heard Liam's voice in the distance, too, but he couldn't make out his words.

Anger boiled deep inside, and blood rushed to his ears.

But at the sound of Sam's voice, his hold loosened. He

finally shot his hands into the air in surrender and stumbled back.

Asher sidestepped him to check Blane's pulse.

"Owen." A hand wrapped over his shoulder.

He flinched and slowly pivoted to face Sam. Her eyes were wide, and she was probably scared shitless, even if she didn't show it.

He wiped a hand over his mouth before locking his hands into fists at his sides. Maybe she should be scared. Maybe she should fear him.

He'd almost deep-sixed him, hadn't he?

Sam pressed both hands to his cheeks, guiding his eyes to hers, and something changed inside of him. A damn switch flipped, and when their eyes met, the burn inside of him, the desire to kill, was extinguished. The red mist was gone, and all he could see was her.

"What happened?" she asked softly, her lower lip trembling, her eyes now welling.

"I, um—" He reached for her wrists and lowered her hands from his face as he tried to find the words.

"This asshole," Asher explained, "wasn't paid to plant the camera in your bedroom. He did that for himself, in case you slept with someone important in D.C. or did something he could blackmail you with later."

His words had Owen's skin burning again.

"You son of a bitch." Emily suddenly appeared and blew past them, lunging for Blane, but Liam grabbed hold of her waist and spun her around. "Easy, darlin'." She squirmed in his arms for a moment before finally giving up the struggle.

"That's why you almost killed him?" Sam asked him, disbelief echoing in her tone.

Owen guided his focus back to Sam but found himself unable to speak.

"He wouldn't have gone through with it," Asher assured her, giving Owen a slap on the back.

Owen wasn't so sure, though. The second Blane had begun sputtering about watching Sam get herself off this past Saturday—only an hour before Owen had shown up on her doorstep—he'd snapped.

"But someone did hire him to blackmail me?" Sam rubbed her arms.

He turned away, unable to face her. But the second his eyes fell upon Blane, sitting on the floor, gasping for breath, some of the anger began to resurface.

"He wouldn't give us the name of the person who'd hired him; he says he didn't know it," Asher said when Owen remained quiet. "He did admit to downloading the pictures from your computer, though, and making the blackmail call yesterday."

"And the delivery guy? He worked for Blane? Where'd he get the photo of Brad and Jason?" Sam faced Asher, since he was the only one giving her answers.

Owen grabbed his phone. He had to call Jess. He'd let Asher explain everything to Sam; he didn't have the stomach to tell her.

Jess answered straight away. "You've got something for me?"

"Blane claims he doesn't know who hired him, and when I showed him the security image of the deliveryman, there was zero recognition in his eyes." He let out a breath. "He says he takes jobs like these all the time to prevent certain bills from getting passed in D.C., and he never knows who writes the checks."

"What kind of money trail are we talking about?" she asked.

"Cayman accounts."

"That's doable," she responded. "I've got Knox working on accessing all of the security cameras in and around Blane's office. If the deliveryman did show up at Blane's, we'll get eyes on him."

His stomach squeezed as his mind circled back to Teteruk. He walked into the hall and away from Blane as Liam zip-tied his hands behind his back. "Do we have a rough idea of when JSOC was hacked by Cheng yet?" he asked in a low voice. He turned and faced the room, observing Sam now talking to Emily, probably trying to calm her down. "Blane was hired four weeks ago, so NSA needs to widen their search time. Someone may have been sitting on this intel for a while."

"And plotting."

"We'll bring Blane your way and resort to some more colorful ways of getting him to talk." Not waterboarding, but Owen wouldn't mind—

A red laser beam . . .

"Get down!" he yelled. Dropping the phone, he raced to Sam and Emily as a bullet shattered the window—pegging Blane in the head.

Emily screamed as Blane crumpled to the floor, and Liam barreled toward her, blocking her with his body.

Owen tackled Sam, trying not to crush her while keeping her safe. "Find the shooter," he shouted to Asher while reaching for the firearm strapped to his ankle.

Asher army-crawled out of the room and to the hall before disappearing from sight.

"Let's get them to the hall," Owen said to Liam. "Stay low," he whispered to Sam, even though the gunfire had ceased. "You hear me? I'm right behind you."

* * *

Owen eyed Luke as he placed his hand over a palm scanner near the door, then lowered his face for a retinal scan.

"Jess will get you set up with access to the place in a bit," Luke told Owen, and he nodded.

The bark of the gunshot was still in Owen's ears every time he'd looked at Sam in the last hour—she'd been far too close to getting hurt, or worse.

"You're certain the shooter didn't follow us here?" Sam asked.

"Even if he did, he'll just assume we're meeting with the FBI since we're at their headquarters. Well, beneath it." Luke stepped back from the door once it slid open and allowed Owen and Sam to enter. "He won't know we're down here."

Luke locked up behind him and then pointed down a long, narrow, and dimly lit hall.

Owen hadn't had much of a choice in bringing Sam with them. The plan to have her show up to work had been blown to pieces the second someone had fired a rifle. No way in hell could she go to her office now.

Thankfully, Emily's former FBI brother had been on his way to the townhouse after his meeting with the president, and he had taken charge of Emily's safety.

"And what about the FBI? Do *they* know we're here?" She trailed behind Luke, keeping pace with Owen.

"No, they don't, and the president wants to keep it that way." Luke rounded a corner and opened the first door on the right. "There's a bed and shower in here."

Sam peered inside but didn't step into the room. Instead, she turned to face Luke and Owen. "How long will I need to stay here? Will I still be going to Russia tomorrow?"

"I'm not sure yet," Luke said. "I think the shooter has been following your every move. It's possible he even tracked you to Mexico. We'll check the passenger list for your flight, and we'll look at every security CCTV you ever walked by in the last few weeks to see if we can catch him."

Owen wanted to reach out and hold her hand, to do something to comfort her, but at the moment he didn't think she needed it—maybe she wouldn't even want it.

She'd remained surprisingly calm, given what had gone down. She'd been Emily's rock, and even though she had some intense endorphins pumping through her now, she was taking it like a champ, like a woman who'd served in a combat zone before.

He'd thought she would've been pissed at him for nearly killing a man in cold blood, but she'd yet to look at him differently. No judgment in her eyes.

Her fingers brushed down the column of her throat. "If he wanted me dead, why didn't he kill me before, when I was alone? He had plenty of opportunities."

Owen's hand swept to the wall at his side. "Because he wasn't trying to shoot you this morning."

"Blane, then?" she asked.

"Let us worry about that. We'll figure it all out," Luke said, a definitive grit to his voice. He hated being in the dark as much as Owen.

Sam looked at Luke with a cocked brow while pointing a finger at her chest. "How can I not worry about it?"

Luke cleared his throat and sent a pointed glance toward Owen. "I'll let you two talk. Meet you in a couple minutes? Third door down on the left." Luke's blues pivoted to Sam. "We have enough security and alarms for the SEALs all the way at Dam Neck to hear, so, there's no way anyone will get inside here. But please, don't leave the room."

Once Luke had disappeared to their temporary work site, Owen motioned for her to head into the room. He took a few measured breaths as she eyed the suitcase on the bed and sat next to it.

Now she looked nervous.

A whistling bullet by her head hadn't seemed to rock her so much as whatever was on her mind now.

"The team brought your stuff from the hotel." He leaned against the doorframe, trying to act casual, even though his heart was scaling higher and higher.

She kicked off her heels and rubbed her calf muscles.

His eyes lingered longer than necessary on her fingers as they smoothed over her tan legs.

"This is just too much," she said softly. "I'm in what feels like a bunker that could withstand a nuclear blast, and some guy blew a hole in my best friend's boyfriend's head." Her hands rested atop her thighs. "And then, there's Russia," she said, almost sarcastically. "We can't forget about that possible war if the Russians discover the truth about what happened."

"Sorry," he said, as if that could mean anything. "And I'm sorry you had to see someone die this morning, too."

She lifted her hand to the base of her throat. "You almost killed Blane before the shooter did."

He strode a few steps deeper into the room, which had a full-size bed against one wall and a small end table and lamp next to it. It felt sort of like a prison, although he doubted penitentiaries had bedside lamps. "Yeah, I guess I snapped." The admission felt good, surprisingly.

"You beat me to it. I would've throttled the guy myself for using Emily like that."

Her words had his gaze flying north to find her eyes.

"They had sex," she said, as if she'd taken a bite of something sour. "She was being used because of me."

His mind veered to the vibrator in her bedroom, and it had

his blood boiling again, thinking about Blane watching Sam use it.

"I think death is a bit of a harsh punishment, but right now, I can't feel bad for him." She shook her head, her eyes falling in a daze to the floor. "I watched him die, and I don't feel sorry for him. Does that make me a horrible person?"

He ate up the space between them in two quick steps. The old bed squeaked and sank a little as he lowered his weight onto it. "Of course not. What he did was inexcusable, and it's natural to be angry."

He had to do it now, he had to reach for her hand and comfort her. Now was when she needed it. It wasn't because she was scared for her life, but because some part of her felt the way he did on the inside right now—justice had been delivered for a wrongdoing.

"You stopped me from killing him, you know." He allowed his heart to slip back into its rightful place before speaking again. "I may have gone through with it. I was so furious. But at the sound of your voice . . . thank you." He squeezed her hand. "I don't want to be a killer, even if the guy is an asshole. It shouldn't have been up to me to decide his fate."

Hearing his lofty words, he tensed.

Teteruk was a different story. Teteruk was an enemy of the state. He had murdered Jason and Brad, and God knew how many other people. His fate had been decided the second he took the lives of two Navy SEALs ten years ago.

But was Sam's father any better for helping broker the deal that had allowed a killer to live?

That would be like blaming every defense attorney in D.C. for doing their jobs and representing criminals, but . . .

"Does that mean you've reconsidered going after Tet—"

"Let's focus on finding our people first." She could read his mind, apparently.

Her brow furrowed. "What people?"

He hung his head and released her hand. He was having trouble keeping track of the parts of the op she knew about and the parts she didn't.

He stood, gently closed the door, and leaned against it. With crossed arms, he studied the beautiful woman sitting before him. She didn't belong in a place like this, or in the mess of a situation they were all now in.

"Was someone taken? More than one someone?" she asked softly.

He didn't want to answer her, but hell, he was going to have to. In his mind, he'd be off the team soon, anyway.

The second he found and killed Teteruk, if the guy was alive, at least, Owen would be done.

He knew Sam would never betray his team, just like Luke had known the same about Eva. "Two Navy SEALs and one CIA officer were taken last week. And as of this morning, I learned Teteruk is missing as well."

"They were involved in the op from Ukraine, too?" She pressed her elbows to her knees and leaned forward. "When we were on the boat . . . that's when you got the call, right? That's why you came to Washington?"

He nodded. "And then you wound up being placed at the center of it all." He lightly shook his head, still in disbelief at how everything had gone down. "We thought the image you got came from our government files."

"What do you mean?" She was on her feet now.

"The U.S. Joint Special Operations Command servers were most likely hacked, so we assumed the photo you got was from the mission files."

"But it wasn't?"

He looked skyward for a moment to corral his anger. "It was from one of the blackmail photos Pavlo Teteruk used to extort money from the U.S.—the reason he remained alive, even after what he did."

If there were ever a time to tell her about her father, it'd be now, but for some reason, he didn't think he could do it.

"Shit." Her hands went to her hips.

"It looks like Teteruk was taken before our men were, which means they used his photos to ID our guys."

"Was Teteruk's name in the JSOC files?"

"Close enough. The location to his compound was in the file. He's been living in Georgia, not far from the Russian border. He was taken from there eight or so days ago."

She scratched at the side of her long neck, as if in thought. Perhaps she was sweeping through the details in her head, trying to make sense of it all. "I, uh, shouldn't keep you, then. I should let you get to work. You need to find your people. You need to put an end to this."

"That's the plan." He closed the gap between them and wrapped a hand over her shoulder. "Will you be okay while I'm gone?"

Her lips rolled inward. "I'll be whatever I need to be."

"That's not what I want to hear." He smoothed the pad of his thumb over her cheek, holding her eyes. "Don't tell me what you think I need to hear. Tell me the truth."

"The truth," she whispered, nodding her head ever so lightly. "When I know the truth about how I feel, you'll be the first one I tell."

His chest grew heavy, as if his heart was growing in size and competing for space. "I'm here for you. I haven't been for the last ten years like I should have, but I'm here now." He stepped away from her and withdrew contact. "I promise."

"You don't owe me anything. You never did." She turned and reached for her suitcase.

She was using her actions as a buffer between them. He knew a thing or two about that, but for some reason, he didn't want her to do this with him; he didn't want her to feel like she had to wear a mask, which he was pretty sure her father had forced her to do for years.

His hand slipped to her hip and then skated around to her abdomen, pulling her back against him. He had her gently pinned to him, his way of letting her know how he felt. Even if he couldn't voice his feelings, he wanted her to know.

She leaned into his touch and tilted her head against the top of his shoulder. Her hand fell over his, and their fingers locked tight against her stomach.

Her powerhouse work perfume was subtle now, and beneath the flowery layers, the beautiful scent was simply her. He could breathe her in all day.

"We'll get through this. I promise," he whispered into her ear.

He released his hold of her and left the room without looking back. Because he couldn't look back.

He'd never be able to leave her side if he looked into her brown eyes even one more time.

Once the door was shut, he paused in the hall, pressed his fists to her door, and bowed his head, trying to gather his control before entering their makeshift TOC.

He wasn't used to dealing with so many emotions, and it was throwing him off. He needed to get his shit together, or he'd be of no use to his team.

An agonizing minute later, he entered the room where everyone was assembled.

Knox, Luke, and Jess were behind computers, and Liam

and Asher were standing in front of a whiteboard at the back of the room near a conference table.

"Did we ID where he got the shot off yet?" Owen closed the door behind him and approached Jess.

Asher touched a set of blueprints taped to the whiteboard. "Feds are crawling all over Emily's place now, but it looks like he was on the roof of the home behind hers."

"This whole situation is becoming harder to keep out of the public eye. The press is going to figure out something is up, and soon," Knox said.

"Well, the shooter took Blane out for a reason," Liam noted. "He wouldn't suddenly take the risk to possibly expose everything unless Blane knew something."

"The shooter was either planning on taking Blane out anyway, or he followed you to Emily's. We've been scouring every bit of security footage we could access to see if we could catch him tailing you," Knox said. "We think we got a hit outside our hotel late last night." He approached Owen and handed him a photo. "This him?"

Owen narrowed his eyes. "I think so." He turned to Jess. "Can we upload this image to your program?" His heart began to race, hopeful for a lead.

"Already done. If he's connected, we should know within an hour or so," she said before returning her focus to her screen.

"Thank God." Owen handed Knox the photo.

"How's Samantha holding up?" Asher faced him, squaring his stance and folding his arms.

"Crazy morning for her, but I think she's solid." Somehow, the woman was a damn rock. Of course, he had to remember she'd learned to be that way; and she didn't necessarily want to constantly be tough. When she'd cried against his chest Saturday night, he was pretty sure her slip of emotions had taken even her by surprise.

Owen's hands settled on his hips as a sudden idea breezed through his mind. "We need Sam's help. We need to bring her in."

"You do know the definition of *covert*, right?" Asher whirled his finger in the air, simulating helo blades. "The thing we're supposed to be?"

Jess looked over at them, then to Luke. "Owen might be right."

"She and her father are the masterminds behind the Ukrainian–Russian deal. They know the timeline, and now that we know her blackmail threat is related to the mission ten years ago, we might be able to put all the pieces together with her help."

"We'd be breaking protocol." Asher peered at Luke as if expecting him to reject the idea.

Luke stood from his desk, and the way he was looking at Owen told him one thing: Luke knew the truth. He knew Owen had already divulged classified intel to Sam because Luke himself had broken the rules not too long ago for Eva, the woman who now carried his child.

"Can we have a minute?" Luke pointed to the door.

Once they were in the hall, Owen waited for the door to close before making eye contact with his boss. Of course, Luke and Jess never made him feel like they were anything less than equals.

Luke wrapped a hand around the nape of his neck and eyed him. Words weren't needed; the grimace on his face revealed his discomfort.

Yeah, him, too.

Luke glanced down the hall in the direction of Sam's room. "Are you sure you want to stay on and work this op?"

Owen's eyes widened. "Where the hell is that coming from?"

"We haven't had two seconds to talk since all this shit has gone down, and I'm worried about you."

Owen's booted feet inched back a step. "I didn't see you backing down when Eva was in danger."

"That was different," he grumbled, "and I'm not asking you to back down. I'm thinking of having you stick by Sam's side while we take care of the situation."

He folded his arms. "Yeah? And if POTUS makes her go to Russia?"

"We won't be sending her overseas, not when someone got a shot off so close to her head this morning."

"Tell that to the president," Owen seethed, his anger toward authority projecting onto Luke right now. He released a pent-up breath, trying to calm down. "Listen, I know I haven't been at the top of my game, but I have to be part of this op."

Luke's Adam's apple moved in his throat. "I know I promised you if the time ever came to find who was responsible for Jason's death, I'd fight for you to be on the team, and I did." His hand patted his own chest. "But now, well, I'm just wondering if that's the best idea."

"Asher told you about Blane, didn't he?" Luke had to be concerned that Owen might snap again.

His brows furrowed. "What about Blane?"

So, Asher didn't talk. He owed him a case of beer when this was over. "I want to get our men back," he said instead.

"Are you sure that's all?" He shot him a pointed look. "Because I know if I were you, I'd be thinking about going after Teteruk. And I know this because I still think about what I'll do when I find the men who killed Marcus." A dark stain slowly rose up his neck and into his face. "I won't hesitate to take them out."

"What are you saying?" Owen's brows pinched tight.

"I'm saying if something were to happen to Teteruk during this op," he found his eyes, "Command won't know it was you."

His eyes narrowed. "I thought we don't murder people. I thought we were supposed to let the law decide justice."

"In this case, fuck the law." Luke clenched his jaw. "That asshole killed our men. Killed your brother." He released a heavy breath.

Owen nodded, not sure what else to say. He didn't want to verbally admit that he had every intention of committing murder.

"What I'm trying to say is that, whether you're on this op or not, I'll make sure you get justice. So, if you'd feel better hanging back with Sam when we're commissioned to go wherever the hell POTUS needs us, I'd understand." He shrugged. "If anyone could understand, it'd be me. You saw how crazy I got when Eva was in trouble."

"But you were also falling in love with her."

"What do you think is happening to you?"

He sounded like Asher now. What was with his team? "We just met, and she's Brad's . . ." He couldn't say it out loud. He didn't want to hear the truth right now. "The timing is shit, and she's off-limits, anyway."

Luke shook his head. "The timing is always shit, and no one is ever off-limits."

"Even your sister?" Somehow, a near-smile almost snuck up on him.

"Except her." Luke lifted his hands and wrapped one over Owen's shoulder. "Brad would want her to be happy. You know you'd feel the same if you were in his position." He patted his shoulder once.

He shook his head. "I'm in. I have to be."

He nodded. "Fine. Figured. Go get her, then. I'll deal with the consequences of that decision later."

Luke returned to the room without another word, and Owen dragged his palms down his face, thinking about Sam. From the dimple in her cheek when she smiled, to the sexy huskiness in her voice, to her gorgeous brown eyes that darkened whenever she gathered her lower lip between her teeth and stared at him . . . she was all he wanted to think about.

He didn't want to think about the three Americans possibly being tortured; he didn't want to think about war with fucking Russia.

Or even vengeance for Jason and Brad.

He shook his head.

No, all he wanted to do was think about her. Samantha Rose McCarthy.

And what the hell did that mean?

CHAPTER SIXTEEN

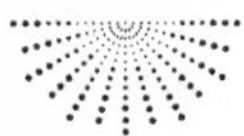

"You startled me." Sam clenched the towel tight in front of her chest as she eyed Owen standing before her in his black tee, jeans, and boots—with laces loose—looking every bit as intimidating as he probably should've been.

"Sorry. I knocked, but you didn't answer. I forgot there was a bathroom in here." He tilted his head, his eyes skating down her still wet body.

She hadn't even had time to dry off; she'd just stepped out of the shower and whipped the towel around her at the sound of his voice. "It's fine. Better you than someone else, I suppose." Her fingers darted through her wet locks, and she bit into her lip when his eyes connected with hers.

He visibly swallowed and lightly shook his head. "Yeah, I'd prefer the guys not see you like this."

"Um, so, how's everything going?" she softly asked a moment later. "You weren't gone long."

He scratched at his cheek. "We're sort of stuck."

His words pelted her skin and put her even further on edge. "Oh," she whispered. "Something I can do?"

"Actually, yes. We're thinking it's time we bring you in."

"You want my help?" She blinked, trying to corral her thoughts.

"We're short on time, and you might be able to better assist since you're—"

"At the center of it all?" Her gaze shifted to the towel. "I, uh, should get dressed, then."

"Need me to wait in the hall?"

She kept the towel around her as she went to the bed and grabbed some clean clothes. "No, I'll be out in a second."

Once inside the bathroom, her palms went to the counter, and the towel fell to her feet. She had to mentally prepare herself before going back into the room.

A man had died that morning. An asshole, at best, but still—he was dead because of her.

More people could die. Good people.

What if she couldn't do anything to save them?

A few deep breaths did nothing to calm her nerves, but she slipped on her skinny jeans and a white V-neck anyway before heading out to face Owen.

He was on the bed with his elbows resting on his thighs. When he spotted her, he shifted upright and pressed his palms to his legs.

Her eyes remained steadily on the veins of his forearms. Those same veins had been so pronounced that morning when his hands had been wrapped around Blane's throat.

She took a tentative step his way, her bare feet cold against the concrete floor.

"Can you sit?" He shifted her overnight bag to the floor and scooted over to give her room. And when she sat, he pivoted to face her and rested his hand atop her thigh.

Her breath hitched when he looked up to meet her eyes.

"There's something I have to tell you before we meet up with the team."

Yeah, that's never good to hear. Based on the grim look on his face, he was about to level her with something.

"Your dad knows about what's going on," he said quickly. "He knows because he helped form the deal between the U.S. and Teteruk ten years ago."

She couldn't possibly have heard him right. Then, the hard blow of a memory blanketed her mind.

Your dad said yes, Brad had told her. *I asked him for your hand, and he said* yes. *So, what do you think? You want to marry a Navy man?* That'd been Brad's proposal, and then, after he'd died, her father had seemed to distance himself from her. She often wondered if he somehow had felt guilty for giving his permission, only for Brad to die three weeks later. But now . . . could there have been another reason for his guilt?

"Sam?" Owen squeezed her hand, pulling her back to the present.

She blinked a few times, bringing him into focus. "You're telling me my dad knew the truth about the operation ten years ago? He knew how Brad died?"

Memories continued to whirl around her mind like a dust storm, making it hard to see.

Every time her father had warned her to stop looking into the mission, he'd already known the truth.

But no. It couldn't be possible. Could it?

She retracted her hand from his and slowly rose, needing space to think, to get her thoughts together.

"Aside from Brad, Jason, and the other three members of the team, no one outside of a select group of people knew about the deal presented to Teteruk." He grimaced. "Hell, even Brad and Jason's commanding officer wasn't made aware of the deal. Shaw, Robins, and the CIA officer, Canton, had to swear an oath that they'd never share the details of the op. And that paperwork they signed—your father typed it up."

Unwelcome tears welled in her eyes.

Betrayal sliced through her, and it hurt too damn much.

"How long have you known?" she asked with a broken voice. She cupped her mouth, trying to stop the quiver in her lip.

He stood, and a deep breath left his lungs. "The president told me yesterday. I wanted to tell you sooner, but I didn't know how to do it. It was part of why I was so angry yesterday."

Our angry sex. Her lids dropped closed. "You had sex with me knowing this?"

"I'm sorry."

She could hear the apology, even in his tone. But could she be mad at him after what she'd done in Mexico?

A tear managed to break through her defenses; she swiped it away. "Is that why they chose me to send the photo to? Not because Brad was my fiancé, but because of my father?"

"I think so."

A heaviness filled her chest like lead pouring inside of her, filling her lungs. The realization suddenly hit her. "This isn't just about my proposal, is it?"

SIX DESKS OCCUPIED THE ROOM, THREE FACING THREE WITH A walkway between them. A laptop inside a heavy-duty case was positioned on each desk among a bunch of other unfamiliar devices and cables. This was the closest she'd ever come to an operation, and it had a rush of unease settling in the pit of her stomach.

Everyone in the room had been busy working when

they'd entered as if they were preparing for war—and maybe they were. But once their gazes landed on Sam, fingers lifted from keyboards and bodies tensed.

She was an outsider, and they were a team of elite operatives used to working in secret, she reminded herself. She couldn't let the sudden scrutiny of their watchful eyes upset her.

Owen was bringing her in for a reason, and if she could help, she'd do her best.

"You guys can relax." Owen stepped forward, looking to the left side of the room before shifting his gaze to the right. "She doesn't bite."

His words almost induced a slight twitch of her lips. She came up alongside him and attempted to stand her ground—a formidable task with all eyes pinned on her.

"Does she know who we are?" Asher slowly rose and pressed his fists on the desk in front of him.

"Yes, but you have my word I won't tell anyone anything, not even my father." *Especially not him.*

Owen and his teammates were still SEALs, and they put their lives on the line, but, if something ever happened to them, no one would know what they'd done or what sacrifices they had made.

Sam continued to survey the room, hoping to find acceptance in their eyes. She hadn't realized her heart was racing until it stilled at Owen's touch. His fingers laced with hers. Hands united.

He was making a statement to his team.

She tried to ignore the tight band of pressure gathering in her chest at the pull of emotion from such a simple touch.

"Well, do you think you can help?" Knox leaned back in his swivel chair and pressed his clasped hands atop his chest.

"I'm going to try," she said as steadily as possible. "I get threats all of the time. And honestly, the texts to my phone—that kind of stuff isn't that abnormal for anyone in my position." She eyed Knox specifically, recognizing him as the son of a major political player. She assumed *Knox* was a nickname since she remembered him as Charlie. "You know what I'm talking about, right?"

He nodded. "What's the protocol for such threats?"

"Usually security handles it, or we pass information over to the Feds." The warmth of Owen's touch continued to ground her, enabling her to block out the betrayal from her father and to focus on the issue at hand.

"If I were going to blackmail you to get you off your proposal, I'd do something a hell of a lot more extreme," Asher remarked.

Liam nodded. "Hell, they could've sent Teteruk's images straight to POTUS to try and get the president to force Samantha off her proposal or cancel the event in Russia."

Knox wagged an index finger in the air, one eye narrowed. "Or tell Samantha's father he'd kill her if he didn't call the whole thing off. My dad has dealt with shit like that in the past."

Luke glanced at his sister next to him. "The threat, the texts, the bug in her apartment—hell, Blane . . . everything was purposefully planned."

Jessica removed her black-rimmed glasses, and her gaze cut straight to Sam. "It was a distraction."

"A distraction?" Sam echoed, her brows slanting inward as she processed the thought. "Distracting us from what?"

"What they're really after." Owen released his hold and pressed a hand against his forehead. "Justice." He nearly hissed the word. "You got the photo the same day our men were taken." He faced her. "Whoever took them wanted us looking one way instead of where it mattered."

"But how would they know I'd come to you?" A dull, achy throb had her rubbing her chest as Owen held her eyes.

"Someone knew about your past. They knew the picture you got would be personal, and you'd react differently this time than you had in the past to other threats," Owen explained. "They probably wanted you to go to the Feds, so they'd tie up their time looking into the photo and the blackmailer."

"Chasing false leads, like with Blane," Asher gritted out.

"If they didn't really want the event canceled, why take the risk and let Sam know anything?" Liam rolled back from his computer. "How'd they know POTUS wouldn't call everything off once he discovered the op had been compromised with Teteruk's images out there?"

Owen looked at Liam, off to his left. "As soon as our men were taken, all bets were on the table, anyway. By dragging Sam and her proposal into this, maybe they got exactly what they wanted."

"They practically guaranteed the event." Sam's fingertips brushed across her lips as everything began to come together. "President Rydell now supports my proposal when he didn't before."

"Everyone knows President Rydell's stubborn," Asher said. "If someone tells him not to do something, he usually does the opposite."

"POTUS also ordered more security for the event. A bunch of last-minute additions, and whoever planned this shit storm could now use that as a way to get his guys inside," Owen pointed out.

Jessica slipped her glasses back on and began typing. "I'll pull up a list of everyone recently added for security and see what I can find."

"Why use the event to get everyone together, though?"

Sam asked. "Why not just take everyone, like they did with your SEALs and the CIA officer?"

Owen wrapped a hand over her shoulder. "Because everyone else is heavily guarded all of the time. You can't just grab the former president."

"And I'm assuming Shaw, Robins, and Canton weren't on the guest list for the event on Wednesday, right?" Liam asked.

"Whose idea was it to host this event?" Jessica asked.

"Mine. At the NATO Summit in July, my father and I got to talking to the CEO at the Sven Group, Viktor Gromov, and we realized not *all* Russians are opposed to Ukraine being in NATO, and so, the idea to host bilateral talks about border peace came into being. It's been on the calendar for eight weeks now."

"The timing doesn't work, then." Jessica glanced Owen's way. "While you were gone, the NSA let us know they'd narrowed down the hack to a two-week window. Looks like JSOC was hit, but it was only five or six weeks ago."

"So, whoever has our guys didn't help orchestrate the event, but that doesn't mean they're not using it to get at our people," Owen said.

"The attendee list is online." Jessica whipped her long blonde braid to her back and shook her head. "And it looks like all the high-ups involved in the Teteruk op will be there."

"Then this has to be it. Someone wants justice for what happened." Knox pinched the skin on his throat.

"Samantha's dad worked for General Douglas, and he worked for President Jones. It wouldn't take a rocket scientist to pull together a list of who they deem guilty," Owen said.

"And they could easily Google the name of the CIA director at the time," Knox added.

Owen edged closer to his team, but Sam remained stuck in place, close to the door. She wouldn't bolt and run like a coward—but she wanted to wake up tomorrow and discover this was some wicked, alcohol-induced dream.

The entire room was in jeans and tees, but she could see *military* carved into every inch of them, from the way they moved, to how they processed information—anyone could observe the wheels of their minds working at hyperspeed. There was something about them that gave Sam a sense of safety, a sense of hope that somehow everything would be okay and her nightmare would end.

Brad had worn the same aura. He'd been a decade older than her, and she'd thought maybe the age difference had made her feel such a commanding presence from him, but now she knew it was something more, something that each person in this room had inside of them. Maybe she couldn't put a finger on what it was, but she sure as hell could feel it.

"Someone has been planning this for weeks. A month, maybe. Watching you and your father." Owen's words scattered her thoughts. "They waited to get Teteruk at the last minute."

"And lucked the fuck out that he had blackmail on the U.S.—pictures that could ID the other operatives." Asher sat back at his desk between Liam and Knox.

"But what are the chances that everyone involved in that op ten years ago would end up together in Russia?" Knox asked. "They couldn't have just gotten *that* goddamn lucky."

Owen turned to look at Sam, his face drawn tight. "How did you decide who to invite to the event?"

Sam inhaled sharply, trying to fight the sting of guilt. She inched closer to him and the group. "Viktor Gromov called me last month to discuss the honorary guest list. We were coordinating everything together." She thought back to the call. "He said many of his guests would drop out if we didn't have presidential support. He asked specifically for former President Jones."

"Did you ask why?" Owen's brows snapped together.

"I didn't have to." A slight tremble in her shoulders had her shaking her arms out at her sides. "He already knew President Rydell didn't support my efforts in the region, and so I assumed he just wanted the next best thing."

"Since we know you were working with Gromov before the hack, we have to assume someone was whispering in his ear about getting Jones there." Faint lines appeared in Jessica's forehead as she observed Sam. "Some important guest or a member of his own board, maybe."

"How'd you get Jones to agree to come?" Luke asked.

She thought back to the conversation a month ago and exhaled a sharp breath. "General Douglas is a family friend since my dad used to be his attorney." Her stomach knotted. "I called in a favor to see if he could convince President Jones to come."

"Fuck," Owen said under his breath.

"This is my fault." She pressed both hands to her abdomen to try and quell the nausea.

"No. We've just all been played," Owen said, a bitter bite to his tone. "We've been chess pieces on their damn board, and they're planning on calling checkmate soon."

"If this is about justice, someone wants everyone from the operation together, and in territory that's not as friendly to the U.S." Luke faced Owen.

"Someone wants to make a statement—to expose the truth about what happened ten years ago," Owen added.

"And I'm betting their vengeance will end in a massacre," Liam said and lifted his eyes skyward.

"This is exactly why Americans should start staying the fuck out of everyone else's business. We try to stop a war, and now we're going to look like the assholes." Asher's voice dragged her eyes to his.

"We'll discuss the consequences of U.S. politics later," Luke grumbled. "Let's focus on who the hell wants to have a public execution."

"When someone dies, who hurts the most?" Owen asked the room.

Sam's lids dropped closed at his words, at his implication. "Enough to plan all of this? To kill?"

"We all thinking the same thing?" Liam asked.

"The scientist. Her family should be at the top of the list," Asher replied.

"I looked at Tatyana Kozak's file this morning," Jessica said.

The tap, tap, tap of her fingers over the keys had Sam finally opening her eyes to face reality.

"Tatyana left a husband and son behind," Jessica announced. "Her husband, Laszlo Kozak, retired from a low-level government position after she passed away, and he became a law professor in Moscow."

"Last time I checked, teachers don't make enough dough to—"

"He has money," Jess cut off Knox. "He and his son inherited ten million dollars worth of Russian rubles when Tatyana died. She came from a wealthy family, but the Kozaks didn't live like typical rich people."

"What else do we know about the Kozaks?" Owen asked and then motioned for Sam to have a seat at the empty desk on the other side of Jessica.

She nodded and sat, staring in a daze at the screensaver, a little white cube bouncing around the screen like a ping-pong ball—basically, how her insides felt at the moment.

"Laszlo Kozak's a do-gooder," Jessica said. "He's on

multiple charity boards. He's donated a ton of money and time to the fight against the Taliban and al-Qaeda."

"Of course, he would," Owen said. "He thought his wife died at the hands of terrorists in Iraq."

"And their son was eighteen when his mom died. He joined the Russian Armed Forces right after that," Jessica added. "He fought in Syria just last year before he retired to work in the private sector."

"It has to be them, right?" Knox asked. "Cheng tells them the last ten years of their lives have been a lie, and Ukraine and America are to blame for Tatyana's death." He lifted his shoulders and held his palms in the air. "They want payback."

"Seems a bit extreme." Liam pinched the bridge of his nose. "But if I learned my mother's body was placed in another city and then purposefully blown up after . . ."

"We get the idea." Knox glanced at Liam with wide eyes, warning him to stand down.

Owen's stance became more rigid, and he looked to the ground.

Sam noticed Liam's grimace, as if he'd forgotten for a moment that the same explosion had involved Owen's brother.

"I'm sorry, man," Liam said, starting to stand, but Owen patted the air, motioning for him to sit back down.

"It's fine." Owen glanced at Sam as if checking to see if she was okay, and she gave a slight nod. He couldn't afford to be worrying about her at a time like this.

She did her best to stuff away her emotions—it was her specialty, after all—and refocused on the team.

"But what about the connection to the Sven Group?" Owen placed his hands back on his hips as if he didn't know what the hell to do with them.

"You said Laszlo Kozak sits on charity boards, right?" Sam asked.

Jessica turned in her chair to look at Sam. "You're thinking that's Laszlo's way into your event?"

"Maybe," she said, and a new thought blew through her mind. "The date was changed." Her hand rested on her stomach. "The event was going to be in October, but Gromov called and said we needed to move it up." Her body tensed. "He requested for it to be last Saturday."

"The anniversary." Owen's whispered words had the hairs on her arms standing.

"I couldn't handle the idea of the party being that night, so I lied and said President Jones was tied up that day. We settled on Wednesday."

"Motherfuckers," Asher hissed.

"I need to cross-check the guest list and see if we can get a hit. The Kozaks have to be in attendance," Jessica said.

Owen circled the desks to stand behind Jessica. His palm curved over the back of her chair as he observed her screen, but then his gaze swept to Sam, and the eye contact had her sucking in a breath.

The way he looked at her at that moment, it was as if the rest of the room fell away, and they were alone.

His eyes narrowed, and his lips parted a fraction as if words were dancing on the tip of his tongue, but he couldn't bring himself to say them.

Once his team stopped the world from burning, they would have to face their feelings for each other—and they wouldn't be able to blame anger or alcohol next time.

CHAPTER SEVENTEEN

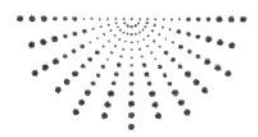

OWEN'S BODY REMAINED RIGID, LIKE A SOLDIER OUTSIDE Buckingham Palace. His gaze was as tight as his stance, and his eyes were glued to the rose on the inside of her wrist—a permanent reminder of the man she'd lost.

Sam had never revealed the truth about her tattoos before.

The day I'm ready to tell someone about Brad and the ink, that's when I'll know he's the one, Sam had told Emily. It felt like yesterday when she'd said those words, although it'd actually been years.

She had opened up to Owen, though. So, did that mean . . .

She couldn't let her mind wander in that direction, not when the world felt like it was crumbling. And besides, she barely knew Owen. They had a connection because of their loss, but that didn't make him "the one"—even if every fiber of her being was shouting to give him a chance.

"I'm not sure how much longer I can wait." Her hands were tucked beneath her thighs as she sat on the bed. "You don't need to stay in here with me, though."

Owen's brows stitched together as his eyes fastened on

hers. "I want to be in here." He relaxed his stance a little, his arms loosening at his sides. "With you."

"You just want to convince me not to go if POTUS decides he wants me in Russia." Her head angled to the side as she tried to get a read on him. "But you should know trying to convince me to stand down is the same as my asking you not to kill Teteruk if you have the chance on Wednesday."

He immediately dropped his eyes to the concrete floor. "You'd be at the center of it all, and something could go wrong." He edged closer without lifting his eyes, as if he couldn't stand to look at her. "I can't let you get hurt." He cradled his neck, his elbows meeting in front of him as he slowly dragged his gaze to her eyes.

She pulled her hands free and stood before him. Her fingers trailed up the back of his right arm, which had him lowering his hands to her hips.

"I've been lucky over the years, but my luck doesn't always extend to the people around me. I'd rather you stay here."

"If you're sent to Russia, you'll need me there, too, and you know it. How else will you all get into the event without raising red flags?" Her eyes squeezed closed, her chest tightening in terror at the idea she could be walking Owen and his team straight into some psycho's trap.

"We can find another way," he said with grit in his voice.

"No, you can't," she whispered. Peeling her eyes open, she found his hazel irises on her mouth.

His hand slipped up her side before greeting her chin. "I feel like . . . it took me ten years to find you; I can't lose you now."

She forced a smile, hoping to ease whatever burden of guilt he was feeling. "You didn't even know you were looking for me." Her shoulder lifted. "And I found you, by the way."

"Because I was an idiot to walk away from you at the funeral and never look back." He released his hold of her.

"I wouldn't have been ready for you back then; and you wouldn't have been, either," she softly admitted.

The muscle in his jaw squeezed. "I meant as friends."

Her stomach muscles banded tight at his words, at the suggestion. "Is that what you want now? I mean, after this is over, and we're *both* okay come Thursday, do you really think we can be friends?"

He rubbed a hand over his jaw, his eyes steady on hers as he nodded. "I won't be stupid this time. I promise."

Friends. Friends with Owen York, a man she probably shouldn't have slept with—but that didn't mean she didn't want to do it again.

"Sam?"

"Hm?" She dismissed her thoughts.

He brushed the pad of his thumb over her cheek. "I won't let anything happen to you in Russia." He gave a light nod, as if he needed to say it aloud to make it come true. "But if something goes sideways, and I don't make—"

She pressed her finger to his lips, silencing him. "Don't say that. I need a chance to get to know you when this is over."

"Really?" He bit into his lip, studying her.

She nodded. "Yeah," she whispered. "As friends."

"As friends," he echoed, and his face edged closer to hers. "Do friends kiss?" His brows rose, and the beautiful shade of his eyes captured her focus.

She smoothed a hand over his beard. "Not normally." Her throat tightened. "No."

"So," he bent his head and brought his lips a fraction from

hers, "if I kiss you right now, I'd be breaking all kinds of rules, right?"

There was so much more to his question, and they both knew it, but to hell with it. She met his lips, pressing her mouth to his as the blood rushed through her body.

He guided her legs up to wrap around his hips as his hands settled beneath her ass, holding her in place as his tongue dipped into her mouth.

He swallowed her moan with his lips and urged her body even closer to his, not that there was any space to fill as she rubbed up against him.

The heavy metal door screeched across the floor, and the sound had Owen lowering her to the ground, breaking contact.

She pressed a hand to her shirt, smoothing it back in place before looking over at Knox in the doorframe.

"Sorry." Knox scratched at the back of his neck and looked at Owen.

Owen expelled a deep breath and faced him. "What's up?"

"POTUS is about to stream live on a secure feed."

"Tell me you found something." Owen strode closer to his friend.

He glanced over Owen's shoulder to look at Sam. "We got the confirmation we needed to prove the scientist's family is behind everything." He tipped his head. "You guys need a minute?"

"No, we're good." Owen glanced back at Sam. "Let's do this."

They followed Knox down the hall a moment later, and the quiet walk gave her a chance to collect herself. She needed to shift gears before she faced Owen's team and, apparently, the president.

"We have a few minutes before we'll be live with POTUS." Knox opened the door and stepped out of the way to allow Sam to walk through.

"Thanks." She smiled at him and shifted her attention to the team assembled around the conference table.

"What do we have?" Owen pulled out a chair for Sam, then sat next to her.

Jessica was working on the laptop, maybe setting up the call with POTUS. "We got a hit on the deliveryman from that photo we pulled," she said. "Gregoff Voyesky. He served in the Russian Armed Forces with Alexander Kozak, Laszlo's son."

"They work together now doing mercenary shit under the guise of a PI firm," Liam said with a lopsided smile from across the table. "Ironic, right?"

"We also confirmed the transaction between Cheng and Laszlo Kozak," Jessica said without looking up.

"Any connection between the Kozaks and the Sven Group?" Owen asked.

"Laszlo's name isn't officially on the list," Jessica said, "but one of his charity houses is on the guest list, and they were a late addition. No names provided, just two guests attending to represent the charity."

"Probably the son and father." Luke eyed Sam; he was the only one standing, positioned behind Jessica.

"Would he have that much pull to manipulate decisions with Gromov?" Sam asked, hating how easily her strings had been pulled to manipulate this entire thing.

Jessica stood and positioned the laptop at the far side of the table. "Laszlo Kozak and Viktor Gromov grew up in the same town. Their sons went to private school together. They've known each other forever."

"So Gromov *is* in on this?" She found that hard to believe. He seemed like such a good man.

Jessica shook her head. "Gromov may not know anything, and Laszlo is just using his friendship to manipulate the event. Maybe he mentioned to Gromov that he should have presidential support at the event, so that the Sven Group looks impressive. Who knows? But this is the best lead we have."

Sam covered her face, hating that someone turned an event meant to encourage peace into a possible bloodbath for justice.

"We're still not sure how our guys were smuggled out of the U.S., but at this point, it doesn't matter because we know where they're being brought." Asher's hand curled into a fist, bearing down on the table.

"You think they're still alive?" Sam's hands fell to her lap.

"They want everyone at the event so they can tell the world about what happened ten years ago," Liam said, looking at her. "Maybe they'll kill everyone after—maybe not. Who knows to what extent these people are willing to go, but if they killed Blane just to deflect our attention . . . I'm guessing they're more than willing to kill others."

"The son is hardcore," Jessica said. "He was nicknamed the Grim Reaper—well, the Russian name for it—when in the military."

"Shit, and that was before he learned the truth about his mom." Knox braced his hands against the table and leaned back in his chair, connecting his eyes with Sam and shaking his head lightly.

"We're canceling the event, right?" Sam's stomach fluttered as all eyes turned to her.

"We have to rescue our men." Owen looked over at her, a

hard set to his jaw. “We can’t let more men die because of what happened ten years ago.”

“And if we cancel,” Luke began, “the Kozaks will probably go ahead and announce the truth about the op to the world, and then we’re fucked in more ways than one.”

“So tell the truth.” Sam stood, trying to maintain her confidence. “Maybe Ukraine will have to wait on NATO, but it’s the cover-up that got us all into this mess. Do we want to take the risk that we’ll always be living in fear of the truth getting exposed?” She tried to hide the tremble to her tone as she surveyed each person in the room before her gaze stopped on Owen at her side.

“She’s right,” he whispered and slowly rose. “But we do it on our terms.”

Luke’s hands went to his hips just as the line over the computer suddenly connected to showcase the president’s face.

“Mr. President,” Owen said, a gravelly depth to his voice, “could I start?”

“Are you going to explain why Samantha McCarthy is in the room?” the president asked, looking right at her, and her stomach squeezed.

“I promise I’ll get to that,” he responded, “but first, could I ask, have you had any luck with the Chinese about Cheng?”

The president leaned back in his chair in the Oval. “It’d involve a deal in tariffs I’m not exactly itching to make. What’s your point?”

Owen glanced across the table at Luke for a moment before casting his eyes back to the screen. “I think I have an idea.”

CHAPTER EIGHTEEN

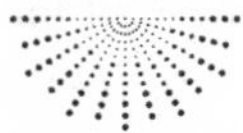

"This morning, Building B had a maintenance guy arrive to fix the central air-conditioning unit." Jessica rubbed the nape of her neck and looked at the team gathered in the hotel suite.

"That's where the event is being held. What the hell do they need air-conditioning for?" Asher looked up from the computer screen sitting atop his lap. "It's sixty degrees out, and tonight it'll be cooler."

"Exactly," Jessica said. "What if the Kozaks aren't planning on blowing the place up, but they're going to use the building's ventilation system to release some sort of toxin or gas?"

"And who knows what kind of bio-agents the Russians have on hand." Luke went around behind Jessica's desk to view the screen. "Can you hack the feeds to see if we can get a look at their maintenance guy?"

"Doing that now." Jessica's fingers deftly moved over the keyboard like some cyber-pro, and, apparently, she was.

Sam swiped a hand through her messy dark locks. She'd

been combing her fingers through her hair for hours—ever since the plane had landed in Russia that morning.

"It's our deliveryman. Gregoff Voyesky." Jessica turned her screen to show the team.

"Looks like he made it home," Knox grumbled.

"Still no luck identifying which guards the Kozaks paid off or planted at the event tonight?" Sam stood from the red-tufted, velvet chaise lounge positioned near the couch where Asher, Liam, and Knox were sitting.

Owen was by the window, eyes sweeping outside, as if on alert. He'd barely spoken since Jessica and Luke had assembled the team.

"I've made some progress," Knox announced. "I found one guy who wasn't a last-minute add, but he had a major transfer of funds into his account this morning, and it's not the kind of money a guard would make."

"Get me his name, and I'll have a word with him," Luke said to Knox. "I want eyes on a swivel tonight—assume everyone is an enemy until confirmed."

"What if you tip off the guard when you speak to him?" Sam asked.

Before Luke could answer, Asher said, "This isn't our first rodeo, honey." He rose from the couch and set his laptop on the nearby table.

"I do have a favor to ask, though." Luke faced her. "Do you think you could get us waitstaff uniforms? Jessica's working on creating IDs, but it'd be easier to move around the building if we look like we work there."

"Yeah, I think so. Are you planning on going in early?" She crossed her arms, her nerves catching in her throat.

"Asher's the only one of us who speaks Russian fluently and won't raise alarms, so he'll go in early and scope out the scene. He can try and get access to their ventilation system and see if it's been tampered with." Luke glanced around the room at his team. "But the rest of us will do a clothing swap once you get us through security."

"You know how to diffuse bombs?" Sam pivoted to face Asher now, her pulse climbing at the idea of a bomb detonating tonight. "Don't the SEALs have EOD guys with them for stuff like this?"

Asher eyed her, a smile in his eyes. "You know about explosive ordinance disposal?"

"I do work for the Intelligence Committee. I know a thing or two about what you do." *I've just never been this close to the action.*

Asher grinned. "Well, I'm not an EOD guy, but I know my way around weapons of all kinds." His gaze suddenly darted to Jessica. "I'm a bit of an expert at handling volatile"—he coughed into a fist, and Jessica's eyes met his—"situations."

Jessica rolled her eyes and returned her focus to the screen.

Sam had no idea what that was all about. "I'll make a call and see what I can do." She nodded. "But what if someone spots you guys in part of the building tonight where you shouldn't be, even in server uniforms?"

"We've got it covered," Jessica replied. "I'll loop the security feeds, so our guys won't be caught on tape, but first, I'll try and get eyes on the Kozaks and any other enemy combatants."

"I hate going in without ISR first." Knox's nostrils flared.

"We can't exactly send one of our drones over Russia," Owen said, speaking for the first time in a while. "What kind of weapons will Secret Service provide us once we're inside?"

Liam stood, taking point on the question. "They couldn't

get us rifles without raising alarms. We'll be working with pistols."

"Better than nothing," Knox grumbled.

"You really think your taken men will be in that building? Even Teteruk?" Sam asked. "I mean, how would they get them in there unnoticed, especially if Gromov isn't in on the Kozaks' plans?" Sam's fingers curved around the back of her neck.

"The building blueprints date way back to the old Soviet days when not everything was clearly defined, and purposefully so. I'm betting some tunnels connect to the nuclear bunkers," Jessica explained. "That will probably be their way in and out."

"And the Kozaks are really willing to give up everything for revenge?" she asked in disbelief.

"People have done shit like this for a lot less," Luke said with a touch of anger to his voice.

She was sure, as Asher had said, this wasn't their first time in this kind of situation. And so, she'd have to trust the team of experts to handle everything.

"You want to back out?" Asher cocked his head to the side and edged closer to her.

"No." She looked at Owen instead of Asher, though. "If you're in, I'm in."

* * *

LUKE CLOSED THE STIFF RED FLOOR-TO-CEILING DRAPES, blocking out the afternoon sun, and then switched on the floor lamp by the couch in the hotel suite. "When you see your father later, you can't mention the plan, okay?"

Her dad had been tied up with Russian dignitaries all day, and she hadn't yet seen him. She dreaded any conversation with him, especially now that she knew the truth.

Sam's eyes journeyed to the gold-framed image of the famous Russian poet Pushkin above the couch, a reminder of where she was—Rostov-on-Don.

The city was at a crossroads—stuck between old and new. That's how she felt. Wedged between the past and maybe a future she could see herself having.

"Should we let my dad know about what's going on tonight?" she asked. They were one hour away from leaving for the event—and *that's* what she should've been focusing on.

"We can't let anyone know the plan, not even your father's security detail." Owen strode closer to her, fingering the collar of his pressed black dress shirt as if it suffocated him, the black tie remaining untied and draped around his neck.

"We still haven't ID'd everyone whom the Kozaks have on the inside." Luke stood alongside Owen and tucked his hands into his black slacks pockets.

Both men standing before her looked just as dangerous in a suit as they probably did in combat gear, only right now, they had more of the James Bond look going for them—quietly deadly.

Her fingers fanned against her collarbone when Owen's stare fell to the deep V of her black velvet dress. It wouldn't have been her first choice to wear on a night like this, a night when she may need to run. Although her high heels allowed the fabric to drift off the floor, the material was tight and clung to her curves, limiting quick movements. Of course, when she purchased it three weeks ago, she hadn't been worried about a life-or-death scenario.

"I just don't want my father to be in danger." She

swallowed the hard knot in her throat and lowered her hand to her side.

"We'll keep him safe." Owen's hazel irises connected with her face briefly before he glimpsed Luke out of the corner of his eye. "The rest of the team is getting set up. Did you double-check to make sure the locker has everything we need in it?"

She nodded. "There are three server uniforms inside the staff room. Locker seventy. Combination: five, two, three, five."

"Thank you," Luke said. "Once you get us into the event, Knox, Liam, and I will head to the staff quarters and swap our clothes for the uniforms."

Sam looked at the clock. "Asher is about to head inside with the staff, right?" Her nerves were bunching in her stomach now, and so, she crossed her arms over her chest, not sure what to do with her hands.

"Yeah." Luke strode closer. "We've got this, okay?" He was trying to reassure her, but hell, she wasn't sure if that was possible right now.

If anyone dies tonight . . .

"I wish you had more backup." Her fingertips bit into her biceps as she continued to hold her arms locked across her chest, a chill fluttering down her spine.

Luke wrapped a hand over her shoulder. "Don't worry." He cocked his head, his eyes narrowing as if he could tell she was still nervous. "I have a baby due in November, and I have no intention of leaving him fatherless."

"A boy?" She exhaled when Luke's hand left her shoulder.

"He's hoping." Owen smiled, and Luke rolled his eyes.

"Well, thank you for doing this."

"Thank me when it's over." He winked and brushed past

her, heading for the door. "We'll all rendezvous in the lobby at nineteen hundred hours. Hopefully, I'll have good news from Asher by then."

"If the Kozaks weaponized the ventilation system, will Asher really be able to diffuse it?" she asked once Luke opened the door.

"Yeah, most likely, but we'll need to wait until the start of phase two," Luke answered. "We can't tip off the Kozaks. But we'll have time. The Kozaks want to make a show of tonight."

"We have to beat them to the punch," she said, nearly under her breath.

Luke smiled. "And we will."

She turned to face Owen once Luke was gone. "I trust you guys, I do, but this is all just pretty intense."

"You're handling it damn well, I'd say." He came up to her, and she mindlessly reached out and pulled at the ends of his tie.

"I wish you weren't here, though." He placed a palm on top of her hand holding his tie.

"You need me." Her teeth sank into her lip at the words because there were layers of meaning packed into them.

He quietly regarded her, his eyes thinning.

"You look handsome."

He smirked. "I can count on one hand how many times I've worn a suit."

"You should do it more often."

"Hard to fight bad guys in this get-up." His eyes crinkled at the edges with another hint of a smile.

"Yeah, I can't imagine trying to do anything in this dress." She released his tie and glanced down at her outfit.

"You look stunning, by the way." He brushed the pad of

his thumb over her bare shoulder and up the column of her throat. "More than words can describe, actually."

"Thank you." Her cheeks warmed, and she started to turn, not sure how she'd remain standing so close to him, but a hand on her arm stopped her. She twisted back to face him. "Are you sure you don't need to be with your team, planning?"

"I'm where I need to be." He angled his head slightly, and his gaze drifted down the length of her dress before slowly returning to her face.

"We have an hour to kill, and since we're both already dressed—any ideas what we should do? We can't go gallivanting around the hotel and getting into trouble, so . . ."

"No gallivanting?" He cracked a smile. "Damn it. You chucked my plans out the window."

She couldn't help but grin. "I have one idea." It was a crazy, stupid idea. *Probably. Maybe. Or maybe not?* "I think I got dressed too early." Her red lips rolled inward briefly as he held her eyes. "This thing isn't that comfortable." Her heart raced in her chest as she slowly turned, offering him her back. "Would you mind getting the zipper for me?"

What am I doing?

Her eyes shut when the dress parted and slid down her body. The thick material gathered around her ankles, her strappy heels now hidden.

His finger slid beneath the thin strap of her thong before cupping her ass, and a pulse of desire burned through her at his touch. "No bra?"

"The dress has a built-in bra. Don't worry, the world doesn't need to see my nipples poking through a gown."

"Mm. Good call."

She stepped out of her dress and faced him.

Owen rubbed at his cheek as he observed her, from her toes up to her eyes. "Do friends have sex, by any chance?"

Friends? The conversation on Monday in the basement of the FBI building seemed to have taken place a month ago. "I don't think they're supposed to." She pinched her brows together. "And we probably shouldn't, but I could die tonight, and so—"

"Don't say that." He maneuvered around the material on the floor and reached for her arm, gently guiding her closer to him. "I can't have sex with you because you're afraid you might die tonight." A gritty edge to his voice had her blinking a few times.

Her eyes cut to his as she decided to bare the truth. "And what if I told you that was just an excuse, so I didn't seem so crazy for wanting you at a time like this?"

The crease in his forehead disappeared, and his lips twitched at the edges. "I thought we already established at your apartment the other day we're both pretty damn nuts. So"—he reached between their bodies, his hand unexpectedly shifting the tiny strip of fabric out of the way—"if you want me because we're both a little crazy . . . I could work with that."

Her eyes rolled upward before closing as he caressed her sensitive flesh with his thumb, and she nearly stumbled into his body at his continued touch.

"I must seem like some sex-starved woman." She arched her hips, the desire for him to be inside of her dulling her thoughts.

"You say that like it's a bad thing," he said with a laugh. "A woman like you deserves to be pleasured all day long." His tone was deep and breathy as if he were hanging on the edge as much as she was.

"I don't know about that, but we have an hour." And

maybe she was afraid tonight would be her last time, but it wasn't because she truly thought she'd die—no, she trusted Owen would keep her safe . . . she was just nervous Owen would be gone from her life when this was over; she was afraid that this could be *their* last time together.

He retracted his hand and stepped back, absorbing the sight of her. "I'd give anything to have the entire night with you, but I can't be greedy, I suppose." He flung his tie to the floor and slowly began working at the buttons of his starched black shirt.

Her thumb went between her teeth as she hungrily eyed his flexing muscles as he removed the fabric. His abdominal muscles seemed to tighten as he unbuckled his black belt, and his heated stare had her lungs filling with air. She released her breath once he was fully naked.

He was hard as a rock as he stepped around his clothes and scooped her into his arms. He gave her a quick kiss on their way to the bedroom.

She kept her arms slung around his neck, feeling safe there, feeling like she belonged to him.

A pinch of sadness tried to brush inside of her, light strokes at first, before a harder knot curled tight in her stomach. Not from guilt this time—but from the sudden fear that she could lose him someday, even if they only remained friends. She could lose him the way she'd lost Brad.

When he set her on the bed, he sank to his knees before her, his fingers skating up the insides of her legs and to her panties. She braced herself against his shoulders as he removed the last bit of clothing she wore, tossing the thong—and with the panties went her thoughts.

She needed to survive tonight and make sure no one died on her watch, and so, she'd have to worry about her feelings tomorrow.

Right now, all she needed to worry about was how he made her feel in the moment—*complete.*

"Keep on the heels." He planted sucking kisses to the inside of her thighs before his mouth found her center, and it had her falling back onto the bed. He grabbed hold of her legs and pulled her closer to him.

"Owen," she whisper-cried his name as her back arched off the bed.

"Come for me," he demanded.

Her core clenched. "It's . . . too . . . soon." Her breathing became ragged as she fought the compulsion to give in to him.

"I'm going to get you off again. Don't worry." His words were like vibrations against her skin, and his facial hair teased her sensitive area. "Come for me, Sam."

Her body tensed, and she moaned and grunted as her fingertips clawed at the comforter.

Owen's lips lazily dragged north to her belly button.

She lifted onto her elbows, noticing a satisfied smile on his face once he was on the bed with her.

"Thirty seconds," she mumbled, dropping her head back onto the bed. "You got me off way too fast. Not fair."

He held his body above her. "And I also got you nice and wet for me, so it'll feel better for you while I'm inside of you for the next hour."

Her stomach banded tight at his words. "An hour?"

He winked and slowly lowered as if he were doing a push-up, his lips hovering above hers. "The last time was angry sex. This time, I want it to be . . ."

He let his words hang in the air for her to decipher.

"Do you still hate me?" She lifted her chest a little, so her nipples touched his muscled body.

His brow furrowed, an expression of intensity sweeping across his face. "I could never really hate you."

She brought her legs into the air, locking them around his hips, connecting her heels at the ankles to hold on tight. "Good, because I sure as hell don't hate you," she whispered, and he plunged deep inside of her, making her forget what was about to go down tonight.

CHAPTER NINETEEN

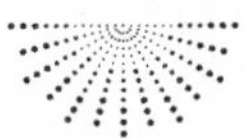

"LET ME HELP YOU. I WATCHED MY MOM DO THIS FOR MY DAD many times growing up." She smiled and knotted Owen's tie.

He captured her wrist before she finished and held her eyes. He couldn't help but catch the fact she was wearing her powerhouse work perfume, which was fitting, because he sure as hell hoped they'd kick ass tonight.

"I'm sorry about earlier," he found himself saying.

Her lips parted in surprise.

He released his hold of her slim wrist so she could finish with his tie. "The protection," he clarified. "I forgot to strap something on, and I never forget things like that."

"Always prepared," she said with a smile. "So am I, though. Birth control." She stepped back, eying his tie to assess her handiwork.

He released a hard breath. "Okay. Good." He wasn't ready to be a father. First, he needed to make sure she got through the night without so much as a scratch.

"We got caught up in the moment. It's okay." She smoothed her hands down the sides of the velvet dress. "Just so you know, I'm really not a sex addict." She swallowed, fighting her nerves. "Apparently, though, around you, I just can't get sex off my brain."

You sure that's all it is? He left the thought to himself, though, and edged closer, his brows pulling together. "Just with me, huh?"

"Must be your devilish good looks and insanely ripped body that have my hormones taking control of my brain."

He stroked his beard, but the air changed between them. Maybe it was because they both realized they were five minutes away from the start of the op. "You ready?"

"Hope so." She turned as if to hide her nerves, and it had him taking a hard breath, wishing they could return to their casual banter.

"You can back out. It's not too late."

"No way," she said quickly but bowed her head.

He spied the rosary beads tattooed at the base of her neck, and an idea brushed across his mind.

He strode past her to his black duffel bag and crouched to zip it open.

"Forget something?"

"Almost." He stood and faced her with a small box in hand. "Not a ring. Don't worry," he half-joked to ease some of the tension, then felt like kicking himself in the ass for the comment because Brad had died a few weeks after proposing to her.

The guilt that had beckoned him after they'd first had sex didn't creep up on him tonight, though. He wasn't sure why, or what that meant, but he'd take it because he couldn't afford to lose his focus on the mission, not with Sam's life on the line.

"What is it?" She bit her lip, curiosity in her eyes.

He crossed the room to meet her again and opened the jewelry box.

She reached inside and lifted it out. “A Celtic cross.” Her lips teased into a slight grin. “My grandfather was Irish.”

“With a name like McCarthy, I kind of figured.” His stomach tensed at the sight of the chain in her palm. “My dad moved from Dublin to the States when he was fifteen after his dad died. His mom had family in the U.S., and she came here.”

“I’m sorry,” she whispered and found his eyes. “Was this his?”

“Before he gave it to Jason, yeah.” The lump in his throat didn’t want to go down. “Jason was the oldest, and since he joined the military before me, he got it.” He turned and set the box on the TV stand and then tucked his hands in his pockets, trying to stand as casually as possible, given what he was about to tell her.

“And now you have it . . .” She cupped her mouth with her free hand, and he could already see the tears brimming in her eyes, which wasn’t what he wanted to happen.

“Yeah, but Jason gave it to me.” His words had her eyes darting to his, surprise there. He tried to smile, to shrug away the emotions before he bared his feelings to her.

But he couldn’t get his lips to curve.

“Jason had an idea,” he said while blinking back to the past, to his brother’s words spoken so long ago.

“What was it?” She closed her hand around the necklace, holding it tight as if to channel the strength to hear what he was about to say.

“After I got out of the Naval Academy, he grabbed my alumni ring and told me if I wanted it back, I’d have to get it from him myself when I finished my first deployment.” His stomach muscles tightened. “So, I made him give me something.”

“His necklace,” she whispered.

He nodded. "And then we decided we would hang onto the stuff until we were both retired. We had plans to run Dad's bar together when we hit our forties. I'd give him the necklace back then." He swiped a hand down his jaw.

"What happened to your ring?" She opened her palm, offering him the necklace, but he shook his head.

"I never got it back. I think Teteruk took it off him because I know Jason always carried it with him as a good luck charm."

She blew out a breath, a tear rolling down her cheek.

"I want you to wear that necklace tonight. It's kept me safe for a long time. I've never gone on an op without it."

"No," she rushed out. "You need it." Her hand trembled as she extended her arm to try and get him to take back the necklace.

"I need *you* safe, and I'll feel better knowing you're wearing it." He gave a stiff nod. "You can give it back to me when this is all over."

"Owen."

He held a hand between them. "Please, do this for me?"

She took a long breath, as if considering his words, and then she turned around. "Help me put it on?"

He ignored the slight shaking of his hand as he connected the clasp, noticing the spread of goose bumps over her skin.

When she faced him again, she took him by surprise by slinging her arms around his neck and hugging him. He held her cheek to his chest, his heartbeat probably loud in her ear. "Everything ends tonight," he said under his breath.

Teteruk wouldn't be leaving alive.

* * *

THE WAY SAM'S FATHER HAD LOOKED AT HER IN THE LIMO

tonight told Owen one thing: he knew Sam was aware of the truth about Brad, even if she hadn't said anything.

Senator McCarthy didn't offer up an excuse or an explanation, not with Owen, Luke, and the others inside the limo, but he could see the apology in his eyes. He knew what regret looked like.

Once inside the function hall, Owen's gaze darted to Sam's fingertips as they dug into the material of her dress at her sides. He'd give anything to reach down and hold her hand, to comfort her, but they were in a room of a hundred fifty people, and he had no idea how many were enemies of the United States. Plus, his cover was as her bodyguard, so they couldn't be seen hand-holding.

"You really pulled this off."

Sam sipped her champagne and glanced at Viktor Gromov, the CEO of the Sven Group, who'd stepped up next to her. Two sharp lines cut through his forehead, and he scratched at the side of his dark hair. "You had doubts?"

"No, of course not," he said, his voice blending with the Russian words drifting around them. "And who might your friend be?" The man's brows slanted as he extended his hand.

"Bodyguard." Owen shook his head, still not sure if the guy was in league with the Kozaks.

"You do not feel safe here?" Gromov directed his question to Sam and then snatched a flute of champagne off a tray as a waiter carried it by. "Kidding. I have ten men to protect me. We both know not everyone is a big fan of Russia and the U.S. throwing this—how do you say?—shin-dig together?"

Sam smiled, maintaining her cool like a damn champ, and Owen couldn't be prouder—even if everything in his chest hurt at the idea of her being here and in danger.

They'd been inside for just twenty minutes, and it felt like twenty minutes too long.

Owen surveyed the room. His heart took a quick climb into his throat at the sight of Laszlo near the stage at the front of the room. He did his best not to make eye contact, but it was hard not to stare at the man at the center of Sam's nightmare.

Owen wanted revenge, too, but Laszlo had taken things to another level. "Be right back," he said and moved out of earshot of Gromov. He cupped his jaw, so it didn't look like he was talking to himself. "Eyes on the king."

Jess's voice popped into his ear. "Still no signs of the prince?"

"Negative. You?" He peered around the room, searching for Alexander Kozak.

The security guard confirmed Alexander had entered the building ten minutes before Owen and Sam arrived, but it made him nervous as hell they didn't have eyes on him, especially since surveillance cameras had already been looped to hide the team's movement throughout the building.

"Third and second floors are secure. But they have to be here," Jess noted. "We have forty-three minutes before the weapon releases the gas into the air ducts. Bravo Three is in the wings, waiting for the go-ahead to dismantle. We'll give our guys twenty more minutes to find our people, but if not . . ." Jess let her words trail off because Owen knew what she was saying.

They'd have to start phase two of the op, regardless of whether they recovered their missing men.

"Copy that."

"I'm looking into a few things on my end while I'm out here, though. Something just feels off now that we're here."

"You care to explain?" Owen looked back at Sam, and her

eyes connected with his, her fingers smoothing through her hair as she faked a smile at something Gromov had said. He could already tell the difference between her real smile and the pretend one she used with the outside world, the one that hid her pain.

"Can't yet. I'll be in touch soon."

Owen returned to Sam's side but kept scanning the room, trying to locate Alexander Kozak.

"You're the real brains behind all of this, aren't you?" Gromov asked Sam. "Your dad is the face, and you're the smarts."

Owen glanced at Sam. A soft blush touched her cheeks as she finished her drink and set the glass on one of the nearby tabletops. "I'll never tell." She lifted her shoulders and winked at Gromov.

"Why Ukraine, though?" Gromov rubbed the whiskers of his beard, his eyes narrowing on her. "What makes you so interested in peace there?" He opened his palms. "You never did tell me."

She smiled. "You never asked."

"We have them." Jess's sudden words in his ear were like a shotgun to the chest—so damn powerful his heart nearly exploded.

He took in a sharp breath, and his eyes widened in Sam's direction.

Sam reached for Gromov's shoulder and pointed toward a group of Russian dignitaries not too far away. "Well . . ."

"What's going on?" Owen asked Jess once Sam redirected Gromov's focus away.

"They're okay. Alive," Jess said. "Can't say the same for the guys guarding them, though. Gregoff Voyesky is dead, too."

Relief slammed into him. "What about—"

"He wasn't with them, but we're switching to phase two now."

Teteruk. Where are you?

"Still no eyes on the prince."

"We'll find him. Going dark now," Jess announced.

"Copy that."

Jess would be jamming every frequency and killing all cell service within a twenty-mile radius in case the Kozaks had a remote detonator and decided to set off the weapon early while Asher was in the middle of disarming it.

Owen went over to Sam and leaned forward to whisper in her ear, ignoring Gromov's eyes in the process. "Phase two."

"I have good news," Sam said a beat later, as planned.

Gromov arched a brow. "And?"

"It's a surprise." She pointed to the screen slowly lowering from the ceiling where the stage was positioned at the opposite end of the large room. "President Rydell has decided to support our efforts, and he recorded a message he'd like to share tonight."

Owen stared at Gromov, trying to get a read on him. Was the guy in Laszlo's pocket or not? Then he noticed Laszlo out of the corner of his eye. He was talking to a tall blonde, and from the way he was smiling and touching her arm, he was flirting.

"Now this is something I look forward to hearing. I'll gather everyone's attention." Gromov gave a light nod to Sam, as if saying, *nice work.*

When he left their side, Sam quickly faced Owen. "Are they okay?"

"Our people are alive," he said.

She breathed a sigh of relief. "Thank God." She glanced to the stage, where President Rydell's frozen face now filled the screen. "It looks like Jessica managed to access their servers to upload the video."

"We'll be going radio silent the second the video begins." He wrapped a hand around her elbow at the sight of Gromov pulling Laszlo away from the blonde. "I think he just informed Laszlo of the president's message."

She followed his gaze. "Where's his son, though?"

He peered around the room again. "We didn't get eyes on him from the security feeds before we had to loop them." He gently squeezed her arm, his quiet way of telling her everything would be okay.

His people were safe.

Asher was disarming the weapon.

And now all they had to do was admit the truth to the world . . . and take out the Kozaks without any innocents getting hurt.

A few seconds later, Gromov made his way to the stage, and the room quieted down. "We are thrilled to have President Jones here with us tonight, but we were just informed that the current president of the United States would like to share some news with you all."

"Here goes," Sam said under her breath.

"Did you know about this?" It was Samantha's father in his stiff three-piece suit, his eyes sharp on his daughter.

"Um, yeah." She looked over at him and to the two guards flanking his sides.

Before Sam could say more, the video began.

The president made his introductions and discussed his support for better Ukrainian–Russian relations before his voice grew somber, and the prominent wrinkle in his brow creased even more.

"What I am about to tell you is not easy," the president began, clasping his hands on his desk in the Oval. They couldn't live-stream the video since Jess had to jam all incoming and outgoing signals, so POTUS had to record the tape ahead of time.

Owen kept his hold on Sam, not able to let her go, as he waited for POTUS to announce the truth to the world. It was Owen's idea, and if it failed . . .

"Ten years ago, a Ukrainian militant, acting on his own and without government knowledge, kidnapped a Russian scientist, Tatyana Kozak."

Gasps blew through the room. Owen looked straight at Laszlo.

The man's shoulders sagged forward at the president's words, and he turned away from the screen and began scanning the room. He was searching for someone, and the look on his face—

"He's surprised," Sam whispered over her shoulder, echoing Owen's thoughts.

The president continued to explain the events that had taken place, but Owen could barely hear him as he tried to make sense of the situation at hand.

The look in Laszlo's eyes now. The flirting with the blonde. "I don't think Laszlo planned this," he whispered into Sam's ear.

"I'm here before you today asking for your forgiveness," President Rydell said. "Please do not let the wrongful actions of the past eclipse what you are trying to do here today." He paused, and Owen looked back at the screen. "The United States has every intention of rectifying the mistakes made, and I am asking for all three countries to work together for peace."

"I have to find Alexander," Owen said as the president finished his words, the room surprisingly silent, as if trying to work through their shock.

Sam faced him. "Did Laszlo really not know what his son was planning?"

"I don't know, but the fire alarms are about to go off to clear the building," he said softly, so no one would hear. "Stay with your dad's Secret Service. The second the alarm goes off, get the hell out of here. Got it?" He gripped her shoulders, staring deep into her eyes.

This would be the hard part, the part of the plan where he'd have to leave her.

"What about Laszlo?" she asked, a frantic tone to her voice now that everything was actually happening.

He peeked at Laszlo rubbing the skin on his forehead as if reliving the loss of his wife. "If he's guilty, he'll stay behind."

"Okay. Be safe," she said as the alarms started to screech, and the howling sound created the intended panic among the guests.

Owen wished he could escort Sam out himself, but he might not be able to get back into the building, and he couldn't leave, not with his men inside. He'd have to trust the Secret Service agents to keep her safe.

"I'll be okay," she said, reading his thoughts as people began bumping into them.

Her father reached for her arm and looked Owen's way, perhaps recognizing Owen was behind the sudden commotion.

He didn't know what to say at that moment, so he nodded and turned toward the kitchen, fighting against the storm of people.

Outside the banquet hall, he retrieved his pistol, maneuvered through the kitchen, and then took the flight of stairs below.

Two dimly lit tunnels.

Two directions.

He turned left and rushed down the basement hall.

No doors in sight, and the damn tunnel felt never-ending, but if Alexander Kozak was planning to escape, one of the tunnels would be his exit strategy.

"We're . . . bah—on . . . comms." Jess's voice, with pops of static, sounded in his ear a few minutes later.

"Bravo Three deactivated the weapon?"

Static and muffled words.

Shit. He needed to get out of the tunnel to hear her, to make sure everything was okay.

He'd have to give up his hunt for Alexander and hope to hell one of his teammates had already gotten to him.

He hurried up the stairs and into the kitchen.

Flames were crawling up the walls and leaping from stoves to counters.

That sure as hell wasn't part of the plan.

"Do you copy?" He covered his face with his shirt and made his way back to the banquet hall, finding that room up in flames as well. "What the fuck is going on?"

"Bravo Two, the device has been deactivated, but the place is burning," Jess announced.

Owen glanced around at the flames now climbing all of the red floor-to-ceiling drapes. He lowered his shirt from his mouth to answer, "Yeah, I'm still inside."

"We have a problem," Jess announced, and it had him slowing near the double doors that led to the exit. "I did a deep dive into the metadata tonight while I was waiting, and—"

Her words had him halting altogether. "Just tell me. What is it?"

"It wasn't Laszlo Kozak who paid Cheng."

"Bravo Two, you copy?" It was Luke's voice on the line now, interrupting Jess.

"Copy," he sputtered, trying to process Jess's news. He began to cough from the smoke, and he caught sight of firefighters heading through the doors, motioning for him to come toward them.

But his feet were stuck to the fucking ground.

A crackling sound. Static. And then Luke's low voice came over the line. "Samantha never exited the building."

CHAPTER TWENTY

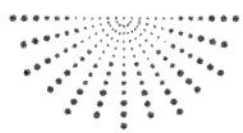

Ten Minutes Earlier . . .

The fire alarms wailed in her ears, and she could practically feel the pulse of the noise moving through her veins. Men and women frantically gathered, pushing and shoving to get toward the exit.

"Come on." One of her father's guards urged her along.

Her dad peeked at her from over his shoulder, making sure she was okay before he began moving with the crowd.

Sam did the same, glancing back to spy Owen on his way out. Their eyes connected, he gave a hard nod, and then he disappeared through the side door that led to the kitchen area.

Please be safe. She started to walk, only to stop seconds later at the feel of something hard pressing into her back.

Before she could pivot to see who or what was behind her, a voice whispered, "Come with me, or you die."

Her body stilled, and her mind went blank.

"Come, or I start shooting at the crowd." The command in her ear had her lids nearly dropping.

She slowly slipped her hand to the chain at her neck, hoping to draw strength from Owen's necklace. "Okay," she said over her shoulder.

Walking backward as a hand tugged at her hip, she spotted her dad and bodyguard near the doors. Her dad glanced back and threw his hand in the air, motioning for her to hurry. But then he was pushed and shoved out of sight by the herd of desperate people, fleeing as if the room were actually on fire.

Suddenly, the smell of something burning caught her nostrils. She whirled around to see the overhead screen, with POTUS's face, up in flames.

"Now," the voice raged in her ear, and she spun to face the man. Viktor Frigging Gromov.

"You," she whispered.

He yanked her arm in the direction of the flames eating at the screen. The gun poked into her side as they exited the room.

Once in the kitchen, a cloud of smoke slammed into her. She began to gasp for air. Her legs moved slower, and she coughed into her fist. The fire roared to new life, the flames licking the ceiling with purposeful intent.

"Hurry!" His fingers dug painfully into her arm as he dragged her out of the kitchen.

Away from the fire, she sucked in a breath of air through her burning lungs. "Where are we going?"

Gromov yanked open a door that led to a stairwell and then pointed to the steps with his gun. "Go down."

When she didn't move, he grabbed hold of her arm and drew her closer, pointing the gun at her forehead. All she could see was the black metal.

His fist connected with her abdomen a moment later, and a cry of pain tore from her mouth. Her lips twisted in rage;

she didn't want to give him the satisfaction of knowing he'd hurt her.

"Go. Now. Or I'll throw you down the stairs." His dark eyes leered at her, and he stepped closer, as if ready to hit her in the face with the butt of the gun.

She surrendered with upheld palms and rushed past him as fast as she could without tripping in her heels.

Another hacking cough broke from her lips when she found herself in a basement.

"You've ruined everything," he snarled as he shoved at her back.

She stumbled forward and fell to her knees.

He grabbed hold of her hair, a sharp pain at her scalp as he pulled her upright to her feet. He nudged her in the back again with the gun. "Which way?" she asked, looking left and right. The two halls looked more like tunnels that led to a black nothingness.

"Right," he rasped.

She slowly moved, trying to dodge the few low-hanging bulbs that dangled from thin cords. "So, you *are* working with the Kozaks. How'd they convince you to get on board?"

"You think a weak man like Laszlo could've planned this?" He sniggered. "I invited him here tonight, but he does not know what is going on." His Russian tongue swept through his words, and the hairs on the back of her neck stood.

"You care to enlighten me?" she boldly asked, hoping to keep herself alive for as long as possible to give Owen a chance to get to her.

"Laszlo told me about some hacker approaching him—offering him evidence that his wife did not die in Iraq." The words ripped from his mouth like a blast from a rifle, hot anger spilling hard into the air. "But he didn't want to do anything about it. He wanted to let the past stay in the past. Not even tell his son."

She spun to face him, nearly bumping into his tall frame. "I-I don't understand."

"I went to this hacker and made the purchase when Laszlo refused." He looked heavenward for a moment. "There is no place in Russia for weakness."

"Not even for your friend?" Her arms trembled at her sides. "You were never in support of border peace, were you? The day we met, you were lying to me—but why?" She thought back to Brussels, trying to wrap her head around everything.

He lowered his gun to the side, and she considered making a move for the weapon, but she had zero hand-to-hand combat skills, and so she stood frozen in place.

"There can never be peace. Ukraine belongs to Russia."

"So, you were always planning an attack, but you were going to blame Ukraine, right? Have both the U.S. and Russia turn on them. That way, they'd never get into NATO." She gathered a breath. "And then you realized you didn't have to find someone to blame when you learned about Teteruk and the U.S. cover-up."

"At first I thought this couldn't possibly be a coincidence. Our lives being connected as such. But when I had the photo of your fiancé delivered to you . . . I realized you didn't know the truth. Your father—he did, but you were a victim." He let out a heavy sigh.

"What?" She lightly shook her head.

"I had liked you, you know. When we met in July, you had balls. Bigger balls than your father, and I can appreciate that. But your plans for peace and to help Ukraine are absurd. Do you really think the people here tonight from Russia expect to bow down to your country or Ukraine?" He *tsked.*

"I had hoped you'd do the right thing when I gave you the evidence, and then maybe I'd spare your life tonight. But you didn't. You sided with the Ukrainians, just like your father, even knowing they killed your fiancé."

"That's not why—" She cut herself off, realizing the asshole didn't deserve an explanation from her. "So, you've been using me since the moment we met." She swallowed the lump in her throat as she edged down the hall.

"Better you work with me than find some weak man to try and get your agenda passed."

"It sounds like you were confident I'd succeed," she snapped.

"I guess fate kisses the hands of the worthy. And clearly, my friendship with Laszlo was meant to be, so I could discover the harsh truth of what that Ukrainian militant did—and how your country hid it from the world. The U.S. chose to pay off a murderer—and for what?"

She slowly turned, a bone-chilling fear creeping up the back of her neck. "Are you sure you care about your country so much? Or do you love the money your defense company would make if there were war?" She took slow steps, not anxious to go wherever the hell he wanted to take her, knowing it'd be the end of the road.

His hand curved around her bicep, stopping her, and he yanked her back around.

She sneered at him. "There are other ways to go about finding justice, you know. Killing a crowd of a hundred and fifty people and turning nations against each other? That only makes you a terrorist and a psycho."

"It makes me smart." He leaned forward. "My company relies on war and violence. There will never be peace as long as greed exists."

"So, we're back to money?"

He pointed toward the ground, an angry scowl marring his lips. "Tatyana Kozak deserves justice."

"Right. Love of country is a distant second to money. And justice is a far third. You just wanted to use what happened to Tatyana to get you closer to your goals."

He forced her back around. Before moving forward, she kicked off her heels.

"How do the Kozaks fit into all of this?" she asked a minute later when she found herself facing a closed door at the end of the tunnel. "Are you setting them up? Are they your fall guys? Is that how much your friendship is worth?" She faced him, her stomach wrenching, disbelief an echo in her mind as he remained quiet. "You hired someone from Alexander's company, making it look like he smuggled in the weapon earlier as an A/C guy." She thought back to everything Owen's team had discovered, everything that had led them to pin the crime on the Kozaks.

"You think you're so smart, but you're down here with me, are you not?"

She ignored him, trying to buy herself more time. She just needed a little more time.

"That's why you demanded a change in the date for the event, huh? You wanted it around the time of the ten-year anniversary to really shove the idea that this was about revenge down everyone's throats." The veins in her blood boiled as she thought about how he'd pulled her strings and manipulated everything—and she had the distinct feeling this wasn't the first time.

A man like him had probably pulled off similar events to create tension and produce a greater need for the weapons and technology his company produced.

It was sickening.

"If you really cared about Russia, you wouldn't sacrifice

Russian lives tonight. How do you think your government would feel about that?"

"My government will never know. The truth will die with you." He maneuvered around her and shoved the door open, and her heart leaped into her throat at the sight on the other side.

A dead body lay sprawled on the floor, and a man was gagged and tied to a chair at the center of the room.

She gathered up the images Owen and his team had shown her before heading to Russia in her mind.

Young. Tall. Blond. The corpse was Alexander Kozak.

But the man in the chair . . . Pavlo Teteruk.

Gromov closed the door behind them and waved her toward Teteruk with his gun.

She tried to fight the acid rising in the back of her throat as she walked around Alexander, trying not to step in his blood.

The room was small, and the walls lined with lead. Probably an old Soviet bunker. But there was another door on the other side of the room; it might be how he'd brought Teteruk into the room.

Teteruk's dark brown eyes met hers, and he cocked his head, his eyes pleading for her to help him.

How could she possibly help him? *You! The reason we're in this mess to begin with.*

She pressed her fingers to her mouth, fighting the urge to crouch and close Alexander's eyes. "So, you were going to have the world learn about what the U.S. did and then set off your device once you were safely down in the tunnels . . . *and* you were going to kill Teteruk yourself on the way out." She tipped her chin toward the Ukrainian tied to the chair. "Guess we screwed up your plans."

Gromov rubbed the butt of his gun against his temple, a

flash of irritation crossing his face. "Kill Teteruk, and I may let your friends live after all of this is over."

She staggered back a step in disbelief.

"Untie him." He retrieved a second gun from the back of his pants. "Or I will execute you right in front of your friend, Owen York."

One gun in each hand, he tipped his chin Teteruk's direction, and she finally crouched before the murdering son of a bitch who had killed Brad and Jason. Her fingers trembled as she worked at the ropes.

"You sit behind your desk making decisions, but you don't see yourself as a killer, even though the men who put on the uniform murder in the name of your country—at your government's orders. Why not? Do you not think you are just as much a killer as your military? As the sailors you came here with tonight?"

With one gun pointed her way, and the other extended toward Teteruk, Gromov strode a few steps closer to her.

Then, he surprised her by flipping the gun to its side and holding it out to her in his palm.

"It's time you get blood on your hands." He glanced at Teteruk then back at her as she stood upright. "Kill him, or I'll kill you right now."

Her hand trembled as she slowly took the gun and lifted it into the air.

"Good girl," Gromov hissed, and Teteruk held up his palms, blood staining nearly every inch of his body. He'd probably been battered and beaten for days.

This is a test. He wouldn't give me a loaded gun. "You killed my fiancé." Her finger touched the trigger. "You started all of this," she whisper-cried, her voice laced with the obvious fear of death.

"Let him feel your anger." Gromov was at her side now.

She pinched her eyes closed and fired the weapon, hoping to hell it was empty and she hadn't just committed murder.

Click.

Empty.

"I didn't think you'd have the guts to go through with it." Gromov snatched the gun from her hand, and her stomach turned as he loaded a bullet into the chamber. "Now, do it for real this time."

As he started to hand her back the gun, Teteruk charged their way, and Gromov's other weapon fell to the ground at the contact.

With her back to the wall, she observed the two men wrestle, blocking her path to the other gun.

The second door—maybe she could get to it.

Grunts and groans.

Fists connecting with flesh.

She couldn't look at the men; she couldn't lose her nerve, her chance at freedom.

Her hand steadied on the rusty door handle, but at the sound of a bullet piercing a target—she halted.

"Back away from the door and don't fucking move."

Hands in the air, she turned to find Gromov's lifeless body close to her feet.

"I'm leaving this place." He circled the bodies. "If you don't want to die, I suggest you get away from the door."

The escape route. She couldn't let him leave.

Her gaze darted to the black metal peeking out from the side of Gromov—the second gun.

One was empty. One was loaded.

But she had no idea which one Teteruk had . . . if she went for the firearm, and she was wrong—it'd be game over.

And so, she watched as the murderous son of a bitch

disappeared out the door, and only then did she drop to the ground to grab the gun.

In a rush, she jerked the exit door back open, unable to see anything but darkness . . . and she fired.

An empty click like before. And now Teteruk was gone.

Her shoulders slumped in disappointment, but at the sound of the other door opening behind her, she spun around, the adrenaline coursing hard and fast through her veins.

"Easy. It's me."

She let out a broken sob and fell to her knees at the sight of Owen. He holstered his weapon and ran toward her, and she dropped her empty gun to the ground.

"Are you okay?" He gathered her in his arms, holding her tight.

"I let him get away."

His fingers threaded through her hair, and he cupped her head. "What are you talking about?"

"Teteruk," she cried. "He's gone." But before she could say more, the room flooded with Russians with guns.

Angry shouts were flung in their direction, and rifles were aimed their way.

"It's okay." He reached for her hand, but a booted foot stepped between them, kicking his hand away from her.

"Stop!" a voice called out, a familiar voice she was damn grateful to hear. She lifted her eyes to see Jessica standing with two armed FSB officers—Russian FBI agents. "They're with me." Jessica patted the air, motioning for the men to lower their weapons.

Owen helped Sam up a moment later, and she watched as the FSB agents crouched to check Alexander's pulse, and then Gromov's.

"Teteruk killed Gromov, but before that, Gromov killed Alexander. He was going to set up the Kozaks for everything to turn everyone against each other. He was doing it for money, but under the guise of justice," Sam said in a daze. She noticed that Owen's face was covered in ash as if he'd gone through hell and back to get to her.

"I'm sorry I didn't figure it out sooner," Jessica said apologetically.

"Sooner?" Sam asked, confused.

"Something was bothering me about the hack, so while you guys were inside, I took a deeper look and discovered the money trail leading from the Kozaks to Cheng was too on the nose," Jessica explained, and it had Sam taking a deep breath.

"Gromov was the one who paid him off." Sam looked back at Owen. "I tried to stop Teteruk, but I couldn't."

"Everyone's okay. That's all that matters." Jessica gave a reassuring nod. "Your dad told security he lost you in the crowd, and once the device was deactivated, I turned comms back on and let Owen know what'd happened."

"I should've gone right instead of left," Owen said under his breath as they began walking down the hall.

"Did you get all the bad guys?" She sniffled.

"Yeah," Owen replied.

Except Teteruk. "Are the Russians mad?" Sam whispered her question from behind the agents.

"You mean about what the president said tonight?" Owen asked. "Too early to tell."

But they had a plan for that, and God, she hoped the plan worked.

"You could've died back there," Owen said once they'd climbed the stairs and were in the charred hallway. "I shouldn't have left you."

"It's not your fault." She tried to stop walking and face him, but the agents behind her nudged her along, anxious to get her out of the building, apparently.

"I'm sorry," Owen said once they were outside. "I'm so goddamn sorry."

Before she could respond, her dad whisked her into his arms, clutching her tightly, and she squeezed her eyes closed.

"Are you okay?" he cried into her ear, showing emotion for the first time in years. "I'm so sorry."

She tried to find the words to say, but then she spotted Laszlo Kozak in the crowd, falling to his knees at the sight of his son's body being carried out.

Alexander Kozak may have been the Grim Reaper in the military, but he hadn't been responsible for the night's events.

Laszlo Kozak had lost his wife, and now he had lost his son to his traitorous best friend. Sometimes the world just wasn't fair.

"I love you," she said to her dad, even though she still clung to a fraction of anger about his lie. But he was a good man, despite his faults, and she could've died tonight without letting him know she still loved him.

"I love you, too," he said into her ear.

She pulled back to scan the crowd once more, noticing Owen was nowhere in sight.

When her gaze fell upon Asher alongside Jessica, she hurried toward them, only one thought in mind. "Asher. Jessica!"

"Hey." Asher wrapped a hand over her shoulder. "You okay? You were pretty damn brave back there." His dark eyes thinned. "What's wrong?"

She skimmed the crowd of guests mixed with police and firefighters, searching for Owen one last time. "It's Owen." She exhaled a deep breath. "I think he's gone."

"Gone?" Jessica asked.

"Yeah." A hard knot fisted in her stomach. "I think he went after Teteruk."

CHAPTER TWENTY-ONE

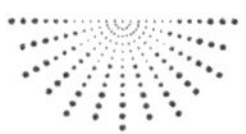

EMILY EXTENDED A CUP OF COFFEE HER WAY, AND HER EYES followed the swirl of steam drifting lazily above it. "I bet you've barely eaten since you've been home. Am I right?"

"I only got here an hour ago." Sam rolled her eyes, but her stomach grew angrier by the minute with each passing hour without food—because Emily was right, only she'd barely eaten since Owen had disappeared.

Where the hell are you? She toyed with the chain around her neck, smoothing her thumb over the cross.

Thirty-six hours without a word from him.

Emily shifted her gaze toward Sam's front door, where two bodyguards—two guys from Owen's team she hadn't met before today—were stationed outside. Luke and Jessica, as well as her father, had insisted she remain protected until the dust settled.

She'd invited them in, but they'd said they'd prefer to stay visible outside as a deterrent to any possible enemies.

Two Navy SEALs on guard should've made her feel safe, but nothing would ease what felt like a bullet wound to the chest until she saw Owen again.

"I still can't believe everything that happened," Emily said with a shake of the head.

"That my desire to bring peace between Ukraine and Russia nearly led to war?" She faked a laugh. "Just a normal day at the office."

"Funny. You can't hide behind humor." Emily's espresso browns narrowed. "Not with me."

She decided to finally take the cup of coffee from Emily, and a triumphant smile touched her friend's lips. "How bad was the Russian inquisition? They didn't strap you to a chair and interrogate you, right?"

"Just barely." She'd spent twelve hours at the Russian FSB office, answering the same questions over and over again.

Thank God for Jessica and her ridiculous number of contacts—contacts she'd worked with before under the guise of the Scott & Scott alias—or they'd probably never have gotten out of there.

"I guess we shouldn't assume the worst about people." The Kozaks hadn't been bad people—they were victims, the same as Brad and Jason.

"Well, you can't assume the best about so-called good people, either," Emily pointed out.

"No more assumptions, period, I guess."

Emily took a sip of her coffee. "I can't believe the Sven Group has been behind similar attacks in the past."

"Creating conflict and chaos to drive up weapons demand and stock prices."

Emily tucked her long legs beneath her and shifted to better face Sam on the couch. "It's crazy, though, right?"

"Hm?" Sam looked at her, still in a bit of a daze.

"If Viktor Gromov hadn't been friends with the Kozaks,

and you hadn't had a connection to them, it's possible the attack would've been successful."

"Doesn't that make it worse?" She blinked, trying to understand.

"Gromov could've just planted a bomb at the event and blamed some Ukrainian militant, but instead, he went through this elaborate plot to set up the Kozaks, which led you to Owen and his people."

"So, you're saying this isn't my fault?" She placed her free hand over her chest.

Emily leaned forward, her browns sharp on her. "Is that what you think?"

Sam nodded.

"You helped put a stop to this. Your desire for the truth—and thank God, you didn't listen to me—is the reason why a bunch of people didn't die," Emily said softly. "Gromov's plan backfired because he didn't expect for you to be so strong and brave."

"No, Owen's team . . . they're the brave ones."

Emily wrapped a hand around her forearm.

"And you're not supposed to know most of this, by the way." Sam forced a smile, but it quickly dissolved. "I'm sorry again you got dragged into this with Blane."

"I'm used to tragedy in my dating life." She faked a shrug as if it was no big deal, but Sam knew her best friend was simply sporting a mask. She was pretty good at that, too.

"If only I had shot Teteruk Owen would be here now," she said a moment later.

"You tried."

She frowned. "I should've tried harder."

"He'll come back to you." Emily set her coffee down.

"He has to. I can't lose him." Before she could say more, the outside doorbell buzzed.

"It won't be Owen," Emily said softly as Sam approached her security camera. "He'd call the second he could to let you know he's okay."

Her heart pounded in her ears as anticipation built, and then her lungs quickly deflated at the sight of Luke and Jessica outside her building. Only them.

She flung open her door, waiting for them to come upstairs, hoping to hell they had news.

But the second her eyes connected with Jessica's dark look from down the hall, she stumbled back into her apartment. "No." *No. No. He has to be okay.*

She flashed back to the day the Navy SEAL stood outside her college dorm room and told her Brad had died, and she started to tremble.

"Where's Owen?" Emily asked from over her shoulder when Sam couldn't get her voice to work.

Jessica and Luke nodded hello to their teammates in the hall, but they didn't come inside.

"We think he's alive," Jess began, "but—"

Sam took an immediate step toward the doorway, her eyes widening. "You *think*?" She stared into Luke's eyes, searching for answers.

"Can we talk in private?" Luke looked at Emily, who instantly sidestepped Sam.

"I'll be out in the hall." Emily waited for Luke and Jessica to enter before she left.

Sam's mind raced, panic creeping into every crevice of her mind.

Luke closed the door behind him, and Jessica bit into her lip—something Sam had never seen her do.

"What's going on?" She shook her arms out at her sides, trying to regain feeling in them.

Luke dragged a palm down his face, and his shoulders arched forward a hair. “We think the Russians have him.”

“I don’t understand.” She clutched her stomach as it tucked in.

“We don’t have any specifics, I’m afraid. Owen didn’t contact us after he disappeared,” Jessica explained, and her blues drifted to the floor as if she couldn’t make eye contact.

“But you think the Russians got to him? Will they keep him to retaliate against us for what they learned?” Sam took quick shallow breaths, trying to wrap her head around it all.

Owen being held captive.

Tortured in some old Soviet cell.

Her hands went to her knees as she struggled to breathe.

“The good thing is, we think he’s still alive.” Jessica’s words had her lifting her chin to find her eyes. “My contacts in Russia informed me this morning that someone matching Owen’s description was brought to the president at zero six hundred.”

“The president?” She stood upright and swallowed, her hand sweeping to her chest. “Like, the president of Russia?”

Jessica nodded. “The problem is that our group doesn’t technically exist, and in this situation if one of our people is ever captured . . .”

“No.” She shook her head. “Don’t tell me that you can’t try and get him back.” She spun away, on the brink of losing it as she looked for her cell phone. “I’ll call President Rydell. He has to do something.”

Jessica gently grabbed her arm. “The president’s working on the deal with the Russians as planned—as Owen suggested.”

“But does that deal now involve getting Owen back?” she asked, desperation in her tone.

"You know we'll do everything in our power to save him," Luke said in a low voice. "Regardless of the rules."

"You promise?" She rubbed her arms, trying to kill the goose bumps, to not crumple to the floor and totally break down.

Jessica looked her square in the eyes. "Knowing Owen, he'll get himself out of there before we have a chance to try and look like heroes." She smiled. It was the same kind of D.C. smile Sam plastered on at work. "Trust me. Owen has a way of always landing on his feet."

Sam touched the chain around her neck. "But he's not wearing his necklace."

CHAPTER TWENTY-TWO

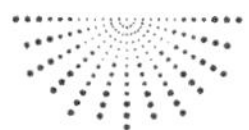

"In a surprising turn of events," the reporter began, and Sam turned up the volume on the TV, "President Rydell has decided to drastically reduce the tariff rates for China. We're not sure what led to his decision, but we're still investigating the sudden change in his policy."

"It worked," Sam said under her breath. She rubbed her hands up and down her thighs.

"In other news, the video President Rydell released seven nights ago, which exposed the truth about a joint CIA and Navy SEAL operation over ten years ago, continues to spark controversy and public outcry from leading officials. They want to know how many times the U.S. has interjected themselves into foreign affairs. We reached out to the Kremlin, but they've yet to offer any kind of statement . . ."

The rest of the reporter's words became white noise at the sound of her buzzer.

Owen? But Emily's words came back to mind. Owen would call her the second he could, right?

She crossed the room with slow steps, hating herself for

clinging to the idea that it could be him, even if, as the rational part of her brain told her, he was still missing.

She dropped her head and closed her eyes as she pressed down on the intercom. “Hello?”

There was a pause and then, “It’s me.”

Quick breaths had her clutching her chest.

Seven agonizing days since she’d seen him.

Owen York.

Alive.

Outside my building.

Tears filled her eyes as she buzzed him in, unable to speak. Unable to do anything but run to the door.

“Wait,” the guard outside called after her, but she pulled free of his grasp and went to the stairs—knowing Owen would take the stairs to get to her faster.

She rushed down the steps.

“Miss McCarthy!” one of the guys—Wyatt, maybe—called after her as she shoved open the door to the lobby.

The area was empty, though, and the elevator was on her floor.

Shit. “He’s upstairs,” she sputtered, bumping into Wyatt as she headed back into the stairwell.

Once on her floor, she captured a breath of air at the sight of Owen outside her door, talking to his other teammate.

He turned, his arms at his sides as if anchored to the ground.

Forgetting Wyatt trailed behind her, she ran toward Owen.

There was a limp as he moved, but it didn’t seem to stop him from grabbing her, from gathering her into his arms, from pulling her off her feet and tight against him.

She looped her arms around his neck, clinging to him for dear life, never wanting to let go.

"You're alive," she cried. "But you look hurt."

"Nothing I can't handle," he said, and she could tell he was hiding a wince. He lowered her to the ground a moment later, and he brushed his thumb over her cheek and found her eyes. "I would've called first, but no one would let me near a goddamn phone."

She wrapped her arm around his waist and peeked at Wyatt still behind them. She needed to be alone with Owen, damn it.

"You okay, man?" Wyatt asked Owen, his gray eyes narrowing, worry crossing his face.

"Yeah. Thanks for keeping an eye on her." He shifted his gaze toward the other guy now heading their way. "You can go. Thanks again."

"Be in touch, brother," Wyatt said, and the guys exchanged a few more words before Owen and Sam headed toward her place.

She took purposefully slow steps, knowing Owen wouldn't want to fess up to whatever pain he was in.

"The second the president let me leave the White House, I rushed straight here." Once they entered her place, he stood with his hand perched atop her breakfast bar, his eyes on hers.

Just how severe was his injury?

"I'm okay," he said as if reading her thoughts.

"Why don't you sit?" She swiped at the tears on her cheek and gestured to the couch.

"What I have to say . . . I think I need to stay standing if you don't mind?" His eyes fell to the floor, and her shoulders shook from a sudden chill.

"What happened?"

"I got Teteruk."

His words were like a hard blow to the spine. "Is he

dead?" she whispered, not sure if she wanted to hear the answer.

"I tried to pull the trigger." His brow creased. "I tried damn hard to kill him." He tapped at his temple. "But then Jason was in my head." His voice cracked, and his eyes became a glossy greenish brown. "I wanted to murder the son of a bitch so bad, but . . ." Both hands fisted at his sides now. "I couldn't do it. I knew Jason wouldn't want me to, and I couldn't let him down, you know?" A tear slowly rolled down his cheek.

She stepped forward, touched his forearm, and looked up into his eyes. "You're not a killer."

He was quiet for a moment, his forehead creased, his body tense. "I thought maybe Teteruk had my ring." His eyes lowered to the chain around her neck. "Your rosary beads, too. I thought if I got them back, it'd somehow make things right." He shook his head. "I couldn't find them, though. I'm so damn sorry."

Tears brimmed in her eyes, and she wasn't sure how long she could hold them back. "No, it's okay," she whisper-cried.

His nostrils flared, and he wiped at his face as if embarrassed by the show of emotion. His lower lip trembled, and he touched his chest. "It's over, so why the hell does it still hurt so much?"

She shook her head, trying to stay strong. "Because nothing will bring them back."

He sucked in a sharp breath. "I can't bring them back." He hissed the words as if coming to the realization for the first time. Then, he slowly fell to his knees, and she went with him.

She held on to his face, touching her forehead to his, and she cried with him.

For their loss.

For everything they'd been through.

"You're so strong, Owen." A heaviness filled her chest, moving through her lungs and sweeping down her arms. "But it's time you let someone in." She edged back to catch his eyes, still holding his face. "Let me in."

CHAPTER TWENTY-THREE

"You act like you've never seen the color purple before." He flicked his wrist, motioning for her to come closer to his nearly naked body sprawled out atop her bed.

She clutched a bottle of oil tight in her hands, staring at the bruises that wrapped around his torso and cut straight up his neck.

The only untouched area of his body was beneath his boxers—thank God for that.

"What the hell did they do to you?" Tears built up in her eyes again as she sat next to him and poured some of the oil onto her palms.

He tried to hide a wince when he shifted in the bed to sit up higher. It'd been a couple of hours since he'd shown up at her door, so he supposed it was time to share the truth with her about what had gone down in Russia.

"Since I couldn't kill Teteruk, I decided to leave Ukraine and hand him over to the Russians, hoping it could help pave the way for them to accept the president's apology."

She began to massage the oil near his hip bone, and the smell of peppermint flooded his nose.

He gathered a breath, hoping to hide his discomfort, before speaking again. "When we crossed into Russia, we were both arrested." He closed his eyes, and another grimace touched his lips.

She lifted her hands from his body. "And the bruises?"

"Ironically, it was the Russian version of the Navy SEALs who beat the shit out of me." He slowly peeled his eyes open. "They wanted me to admit who I really was, but I kept with my story. I was hired as protection for the event, and then I went after Teteruk when I saw him flee."

"And they did this to you to try and get you to talk?" Her fingers trembled as they rested upon his abdomen.

"I think they also took their anger out on me after having learned about what had happened ten years ago." He tried to shrug it off, but the movement of his shoulders caused a sharp throb of pain in his ribs. A pulse of agony shot down his spine when he took in a breath a moment later. "They'd never be able to break me, though. I'm trained for situations like these."

"How'd you get free? I thought the president wouldn't be able to save you. Luke and Jessica mentioned—"

"Yeah, well, after they finished treating my body like a piñata, they let me go since we did help save a bunch of Russian bigwigs from dying that night. And actually, the official deal between our countries was only wrapped up on my plane ride back."

"I saw on the news this morning about the tariffs in China." Her fingers slowly caressed his sides, tracing his bruises. "I assume they handed Cheng over to Rydell?"

He nodded. "Yeah, the president briefed me about it. Everything fell into place like we planned."

"Except for you getting taken and tortured."

"You nearly dying in Russia—that was unplanned. Anything happening to me is part of the job."

She was silent for a moment. "What did Cheng tell the president?"

"Apparently, when he hacked Russia a few months back, he downloaded files that helped us ID three Russian spies within U.S. agencies."

Her mouth rounded in surprise. "Really?"

"If they let go of the past, in return, they'd get their agents back."

"Deals," she whispered, probably remembering the deal her father had been ordered to make, the one that had started this all. "I think I'm going to quit."

"What are you talking about?" Owen cocked his head and held on to her wrist.

"Gromov said something to me, and—"

"Don't begin a sentence with Gromov and expect me to want to hear any more." He tried to slide his legs over the side of the bed, but a hard gasp left his lips, and he clutched at his side.

She gestured for him to relax, her eyes scolding him for the movement. "The decisions we make in Washington have such hard-hitting consequences around the world," she began, her tone somber. "It's not fair we put guys like you on the line, while blood never touches our hands."

He shook his head. "You can't quit."

"How can I not? Look at what Gromov did because of the choices made in D.C."

"You can't quit because I need to know someone like you has our backs. Someone sophisticated and caring. Someone who understands loss and uses emotions to make informed decisions."

"How is that a good thing? It's made me weak and—"

"No, it hasn't." His palms rested at his sides. "You're anything but weak. Losing Brad, knowing what it's like to lose someone you love—it's made you more cautious with the power you wield." His lips gathered into a slight smile. "And I know it's you, not so much your father, who has been breaking political ground."

His fingertips touched her cheek and swept to her lips as she stared down at him.

"Okay," she conceded after a minute in thought. And he knew that, in her heart, she didn't want to give up her work.

She started to stand, but he held onto her wrist, never wanting to let go.

"I have a question, and I want you to take your time and really think about it."

Her brown eyes, lighter in the middle and wrapped in a dark chocolate rim, sucked him in; he nearly forgot his words. "Yeah?"

He released a breath. "Pancakes or waffles?"

The dimple in her cheek appeared at her smile. "You came all the way from Russia to ask me that?"

"No, I came all the way from Russia to see you smile."

CHAPTER TWENTY-FOUR

"THAT'S GOOD TO HEAR. I'M GLAD HANDLIN'S FEELING better. Too bad he'll need to be replaced, but as long as he's healthy that's what's important," Owen said over the phone. "How are the boys holding up?"

"Canton, Shaw, and Robins are doing good. Pretty much recovered," Luke answered.

Owen scratched at his cheek in thought. "Mentally, though, how are they?" Physical wounds tended to heal a lot faster than the internal ones.

"I think they're angrier someone got the drop on them than anything else."

"I'm glad we managed to keep their names out of the media. The last thing they needed were microphones shoved down their throats."

"Thank God for that."

"Everything else good?" Owen asked, sensing there was another reason for Luke's call during Owen's mandatory time off.

"Yeah, actually. I managed to convince Eva to have a

gender reveal party, and before she can change her mind, I'm organizing it for this weekend. Virginia Beach."

Owen smiled. "But the baby is due next month." He pinched the bridge of his nose, hiding a laugh.

"Yeah, but that still gives me a few weeks to plan," Luke said. "You think you're up for meeting a bunch of Hollywood bigshots?"

"Of course I'll be there." Owen looked over his shoulder at Sam exiting her bedroom. Then he stood and went to the window, catching sight of the Washington Monument in the distance.

"It's only been two weeks since you got home."

"I'm good. Besides, I have to be there when you hear you're having a girl."

Luke cursed under his breath. "Be sure to bring Samantha. Eva's dying to meet her. She's excited about having another woman amongst us all." Luke was quiet for a moment. "You two are still good, right? You haven't fucked it up?"

Owen laughed and faced the room. "Trying not to."

"Good. See you Saturday." Luke ended the call, and Owen tossed his cell onto the couch.

"Luke?" Sam tightened the knot of her silk robe and peered at him beneath long lashes.

"Yeah. Baby shower this weekend. You want to come?" He looped his thumbs in the front pockets of his jeans, unable to take his eyes off the beautiful woman before him who smelled like a damn breath of fresh air.

"I would love to." She pulled her bottom lip between her teeth and dragged her gaze south of his face and down his body.

She took a tentative step toward him as if there was

something she wanted to say, but she couldn't bring herself to do it.

"What's wrong?" He cocked his head to the side, trying to get a read on her.

"Just losing my mind, waiting for the doctor to clear you." Her eyes landed on his pants, and his cock immediately stirred at the idea of being balls deep inside of her.

"I've rather enjoyed tasting every inch of you," he said while closing the distance between them, "over the last two weeks." He touched his stomach. "I feel fine." The bruises were nearly gone, and the fractured rib healing. "I don't think we need to wait three more days."

His finger swept down the V of her robe, and he palmed her breast, the feel of her hard nipple beneath his touch making his dick even more painfully hard.

"I don't want you getting hurt." Her breath quickened when he reached beneath the robe and parted her thighs.

"You're the one who has been hell-bent on making me wait. I don't give a damn about my injuries. I never did." He nipped at her bottom lip when her eyes fell closed at his touch. "I've wanted to be inside of you the moment I came home."

"We should wait." A throaty moan followed when he slipped a finger inside of her.

"So, I should stop touching you right now?"

Her hands landed on his shoulders, and she stared deep into his eyes, worried. "Are you sure you feel okay?"

She had wrapped her gorgeous mouth around his cock and gotten him off plenty of times in the last week, and he'd given her more orgasms than he could count . . . But damn, he needed to be inside of her.

He brought his lips to her ear as he stroked her clit. "I think the pain of waiting three more days will be a hell of a lot worse." He breathed in her beachy scent, like rolling waves and a coconut breeze—a new perfume.

"I wouldn't want to be responsible for hurting you."

His hard-on strained against his jeans, and he stepped back to unzip them, never taking his eyes off her. Her cheeks blushed, lust warming her, and she unfastened her robe, allowing it to drop, so she stood naked before him.

He kicked off his jeans and boxers and tore off his shirt. His hand glided up and down his throbbing length as he observed her standing naked with the light coming through the window, splashing onto her body.

He lunged for her, ready to lift her into his arms, ignoring any last drops of pain, but she turned, squealed and took off toward her room.

He laughed and chased after her. "You're going to give me a heart attack."

She positioned herself on the bed, her arms resting above her head, and her knees bent, hiding her sweet spot. She was a decadent display of soft femininity, and right now, she was all his.

Two weeks had gone by, and they hadn't discussed the future . . . or the past. But they'd spent their mandatory vacation time getting to know everything about each other, and he'd loved every damn second of it.

The heavy conversations could wait; they deserved a little bit of fun after what they'd been through.

"How much do you want me?" She sank her teeth into her lip, her gaze skirting down as he stood at the side of the bed, simply watching her, amazed to be here with her.

The only thing she had on was his necklace—his brother's necklace. He hadn't let her remove it; he wasn't sure if he ever wanted it back.

He'd figure out what that meant later, though.

"I'm going to show you just how much." He slowly crawled on top of the bed and braced himself above her. "I have a feeling I might not last as long as normal." He was ready to explode just at the idea of filling her.

He bent forward and pressed his lips to hers and groaned against her full mouth when she captured his cock between her palms. "I don't want to wait," she said between quick kisses. "After two weeks of foreplay, I want you inside of me right now." She guided his tip to her center.

"Then, by all means . . ." He filled her in one hard thrust, and his head fell forward at the connection, the emotion thickening in the back of his throat.

"Don't stop," she whispered, holding his eyes. "Don't ever stop."

* * *

"WHY DON'T YOU WANT TO GO TO CHARLESTON?" SAM rolled to her side and propped her head up with her hand to face him. "Are you afraid I can't handle going to your bar?"

"Where is this coming from?" His gaze dropped to the white tank top she wore, her nipples pressing hard against the fabric. It was probably a bad time to have lust gathering inside of him, considering the conversation he knew they were about to have.

"We haven't talked about Brad or Jason since the day you came home."

His eyes fell closed, and his mind went back to Russia, back to the waterboarding—to his hands being tied above his head while a guy took a bat to his ribs.

"If you think I can't handle going there because I'll remember Brad and—"

"No." He shook his head and forced his eyes open. "I

want you to remember Brad. Don't ever think I'd want you to forget him." He tensed, not sure how to handle the conversation since he'd never been very good at dealing with emotions. "I'm afraid being there will make you regret being with me," he said at last, fighting to get the truth out between them.

She fell back onto her pillow, and her eyes went to the ceiling. It had his heart slamming in his chest, worry stripping his thoughts down to only one—*am I right?*

He sat upright, dropped his legs to the other side of the bed, and stood.

"Owen." She quickly came to his side as he pulled on his boxers, and she reached for his forearm.

He stilled beneath her touch, wondering if he'd be going to Luke and Eva's party solo tonight. "I'm worried you'll decide it's a mistake to be with me . . . just as much as I'm scared you'll want to be with me."

"I don't understand."

His eyes followed her fingertips on his forearm as they maneuvered up his bicep. "When I was being held," he slowly began, "my number one concern was making it back to you because I couldn't handle the idea of you losing someone else." He let out a hard sigh. "We barely knew each other at the time, but I knew it'd still gut you if I didn't make it back."

She reached for his cheek, and his eyes met hers.

"Even if we both get over the past, I'm terrified of hurting you, of someday not coming home, like Brad." He looked over her shoulder toward the light splintering through the partially closed blinds. "That's why I didn't want to go to the tavern. I didn't want to have this conversation." He turned away, and she released her hold of him. He dragged his palms down his face. "I wasn't ready to have this chat."

"Owen, I—"

"We should get going," he interrupted, unable to face the music. "That is if you still want to go to the party with me." He slowly faced her again.

She nodded. "Of course I want to go."

He was screwing this up, wasn't he? *Damn it.* "We can, uh, talk about this later, okay?"

"I should get ready, then." She fidgeted with the hem of her tank top and chewed on her bottom lip.

"Sam," he nearly breathed out her name, and she lifted her eyes, her lashes now wet.

"Yeah?" she choked out.

"Fuck it." He squeezed his hands at his sides, his body wrapped tight with tension.

"Fuck what?"

"Let's not do this. Let's not wait until later," he said in a rush, surprising himself.

Her arms fell lifelessly to her sides.

"I want you. I don't know how not to." He lightly shook his head. "I don't want to do the dumbass thing most men do." He squinted, as if she were this bright light, making it hard to see—but she *was* so damn bright, and it was one reason he was inexplicably drawn to her.

"What thing?"

He swirled a finger in a circle in the air. "The stupid thing where men run out of fear—only to come back later, with their tail between their legs, after realizing their stupidity." He half-smiled. "Could we skip that part? Could I just tell you now that I'll probably make mistakes in the future, but I don't want one of them to be pushing you away?" He dropped his head, his heart pounding like a jackhammer. "I could die tomorrow, or I could live until I'm a hundred and my abs could become flabby and my skin wrinkly and—"

She grabbed hold of his face and kissed him, cutting off his words. He pulled her tight against him, wrapping his arms around her body to lock her in place.

A touch of laughter left her lips a moment later, brushing against his mouth, and he damn near buckled at the sound.

Her hands pressed to his chest, and she pushed back a little to view his eyes. "This thing between us is messy and complicated," she said with a nod, "but it's ours." She let out a breath and then kissed him again. "It's ours."

CHAPTER TWENTY-FIVE

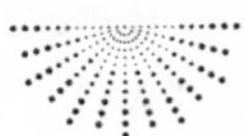

"IT'S BEEN LESS THAN FIVE WEEKS SINCE I MET HIM." SAM pressed her palms to her cheeks and eyed Emily in the reflection of the bathroom mirror. "Am I crazy?"

Emily smiled. "First of all, you fell in love with Owen, like, the second you bumped into him in the lobby in Mexico; otherwise, you would've told him your name that day." She pointed a scolding finger in the air. "And second of all, you're not crazy because you love him; you're crazy because you're in a bathroom right now, at a party, talking to me."

I love him. She had wanted to tell him this morning, but she hadn't been able to get the words out.

She pursed her lips together and turned to check her dress in the mirror, trying to deflect her thoughts so she could focus on the party. "The mix of Navy SEALs and Hollywood hotshots here today . . . it's pretty damn awkward."

Emily's palms landed on the counter. "Yeah, but interesting, right? And Luke's fiancée's brother, Harrison"—she fanned her face—"is so hot."

Sam folded her arms, a smirk on her face. "I know who you actually like; don't even pretend."

"And, on that note, I'm going back to the party before we miss the big gender reveal." She swirled her index finger in the air and turned away.

"When do I tell him?" she rushed out before Emily opened the door.

She pivoted to face her. "You'll know when the time is right."

After their conversation this morning, she was still terrified of one thing. "I don't want him to think he's replacing Brad or he's my second choice."

Emily released the door handle and faced Sam. "Brad will always be in your heart, and I think Owen might be the only man who won't be jealous of that fact."

"And if something happens to him, too?" She thought back to the agonizing seven days Owen had been in Russia, and then her mind circled to Owen's words to her that morning. He'd practically warned her he could die any day.

"Sweetie." Emily wrapped a hand around her forearm and gently squeezed. "There are no guarantees in life, and you know that. But don't give up a good thing because you're afraid." She smiled. "Now get your ass out there so I can go flirt with some hotties."

A laugh broke through, stifling her tears. She knew in her heart Emily was right—she couldn't lose Owen.

"Thank you." Sam swiped at her face, ensuring she was tear-free, then followed her friend out to the party where throngs of people were gathered.

She was grateful Owen had asked her if she wanted to bring Emily so she wouldn't feel so overwhelmed.

Sam scanned the crowd, spotting Owen chatting with Eva and her brother, Harrison. He tipped his head back and laughed at something Harrison said before his eyes caught hers from across the room.

He raised his Corona to his lips and held her eyes, and it had her pulse jumping. He motioned for her to approach, and she nudged Emily in the back, encouraging her to come with her.

As far as she could gather, Eva and Luke weren't married on paper, but they both wore rings, and she was pretty sure they were married in their hearts.

"There you are." Owen winked and then pulled her to his side and wrapped his arm around her waist.

Her sense of security heightened about a thousand times. "Are you nervous to find out?" Sam asked Eva, and she rolled her eyes in the direction of Luke standing a few feet away, talking to some of the guys from Echo Team.

Apparently, there were ten guys plus Jessica in their black ops group, but retired Navy SEALs also worked with them at Scott & Scott Securities. Pretty much everyone who worked with Owen was crowded into the restaurant they'd rented out, but she could barely keep track of all of the names, except for one couple she quickly adored: Grace and Noah Dalton. She'd learned Grace was a die-hard *Rocky* fan, like her.

"I'm not nervous," Eva finally answered.

Her brother elbowed her in the side and raised his tumbler to his lips. "Sure you are," Harrison said and smirked.

Eva shook her head. "Okay, maybe I'm nervous that if we find out we're having a girl, Luke will go into cardiac arrest."

"Better now than in the delivery room next month," Owen pointed out.

"Touché." Harrison clinked his glass to Owen's bottle.

"Excuse me one second." Emily left their sides and joined Liam, Knox, and one of the Echo guys.

"My money is on Liam," Owen said, following Sam's gaze.

"What?" She smiled.

"No, no," Eva said. "Knox all the way. Both from the D.C. background." She chuckled. "I could write their story in my sleep."

Sam laughed. "Nah, that Echo guy, Wyatt, from what I can tell . . . he's the exact opposite of her type, which is why he'd be perfect."

"We placing bets?" Harrison reached for his wallet, his steely grays catching Sam's eyes.

Owen flicked his hand through the air. "Like we can match yours." He polished off his drink and announced, "And here's the man of the hour."

"You ready to get this over with?" Luke pointed to the large present in blue and pink wrapping on a table at the center of the room.

Eva rested her hand beneath her belly. "You sure you don't want to wait until the delivery?"

"No damn way." Luke tapped his watch. "By my calculations, I still have three weeks and four days to make preparations. Give or take a week if you're early or late."

"Speaking of which, you going to take some paternity leave?" Harrison asked, and Luke looked to Owen.

Normally, Owen took over whenever Luke wasn't around, but honestly, he didn't know if he wanted to be in charge, and based on the way Luke was looking at him, he had already figured as much.

"My last day was yesterday, in case Eva delivers early. I'll be taking an additional two months off once the baby is here." Luke jerked his thumb toward Asher. "I just told Jessica she'll be co-leading the team with Asher."

Sam chuckled as she saw Jessica waving an angry finger Asher's way while he casually bit into a celery stick and shrugged.

"Guessing she's not too keen on the idea," Harrison said with a laugh.

"They're fire and ice." Eva shot Sam a knowing look; clearly, she had more insight into the two than Sam, but it didn't take a genius to figure out there was more between them beneath the surface.

"Don't let them kill each other while I'm gone." Luke nodded Owen's way.

"I'll do my best, man." He glanced at Sam and winked.

A few minutes later, the entire Hollywood Reed family from Eva's side, as well as Luke's buddies, gathered around the present.

Eva stood on one side of the gift and Luke on the other, and then they slowly cut the center of the box open. When pink balloons flew into the air, Sam cupped her hand to her mouth as a grin stretched her lips.

She'd swear Luke had tears in his eyes.

Luke slowly moved around the table and cupped his fiancée's face. Then he kissed her like there was no tomorrow.

Owen squeezed Sam's hand and whispered into her ear, "Want to get out of here? There's somewhere I'd like to take you."

* * *

"I CAN'T BELIEVE YOU HAVE ME STRAPPED IN THE COCKPIT OF a plane." Sam eyed all of the instruments around her.

"Not just any plane: it's a Lear 60XR with less than a thousand landings clocked in, which is pretty decent for a '14 model."

She studied his hands, moving deftly over the buttons and controls, none of which she knew anything about. She hated being in the back seat, let alone in the front—where, she now realized, everything looked that much more complicated. "How did you pull this off?"

"I made a few calls before the party and arranged some flying time." He smoothed his hand over the wheel, which he'd informed her was called a yoke. "It belongs to a friend of mine who has a lot more money than me."

"I still don't know how you talked me into flying." Her hand fell to her lap, and she double-checked that her belt was secure, even though they were already at cruising altitude.

"The fingernail marks in my right arm might take a while to disappear, but . . ."

He wasn't exaggerating. "Shit, I'm sorry." Her fingers stroked his arm.

He released the yoke and pivoted to face her.

"Wait! Don't let go of that thingy!"

"The thingy will be just fine for a second. Planes have autopilot, like cars." His lips stretched even more, and she touched his clean-shaven jaw. This was her first time ever seeing him sans beard, and she loved both looks equally.

"I know flying is a big part of your life, and I'm grateful you wanted me to experience it with you." She lowered her hand to touch his arm again. "But if you try and get me to jump out of a plane, we'll have some problems."

His rich laughter met her ears and heated her body, but then he grew quiet for a moment, and his warm hazel eyes shifted back out the front window. "Flying always makes me feel closer to my brother." His voice was throatier this time. "I'm not sure if heaven is really above the clouds, but either way, I feel more connected to him when I'm up here."

She gently squeezed his arm, trying to calm her fears enough to feel how Owen did—at peace, maybe?

"Sam, you make me feel like it's okay to live my life and be happy."

Liquid gathered in her eyes faster than she'd thought possible, and her chest tightened.

"I've felt guilty," he said, facing her again, "for surviving when others in the past haven't. But meeting you has changed me." His jaw muscle tightened. "Changed everything, actually."

He reached for her hand and laced their fingers together before releasing a breath.

"You changed me, too."

His eyelids tightened for a brief second before his hazel irises found hers, and then he reached for the chain around her neck with his free hand and smiled. "And I'll fight like hell to always come back to you. I promise."

He sat back in his seat but kept his right hand with hers. They both peered toward the clouds, toward their second chance at life.

EPILOGUE

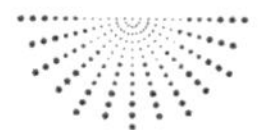

Three Weeks Later - Los Cabos

Sam's fingers traced over the initials R.M.H., and a smile skirted her lips.

"Ride me hard, maybe?" A voice like rough velvet blew over her bare shoulder, and her palms flattened onto the bar.

"If you'd like to," Sam whispered, goose bumps spreading over every inch of her skin when his hand slipped to her hip.

Owen spun her around in one quick movement, and she looped her arms around his neck. "You're back."

"I'm back." He edged closer and captured her mouth, kissing her with a ferocity that she'd missed over the seven days he'd been gone.

Everything sizzled inside of her, a warmth spreading through her limbs now that he was safe and with her. When their kiss ended, and he pulled back, her brows drew together at the sight of a new cut along his right temple, disappearing into his hair. "You got hurt."

"Just a scratch." Lightly shaking his head, he motioned for her to have a seat at the bar. Once she complied, he rested a hand on her jean-covered thigh.

"I have to admit," she said with a smile, "getting a text to meet you here . . . you surprised me."

"You opposed to a weekend getaway?" He ordered a round of drinks and looked back at her.

"Of course not. This past week has been hell. I buried myself in work so I didn't think about what could be happening." She cleared her throat. "And what did happen?"

"How is working with your father, by the way?"

Eerily normal, given what happened. "Don't change the subject." A smile teased her lips.

He reached for her hand on her lap and squeezed it. "I'm here, and I'm fine. The bad guys—not so much." Owen winked, but then went quiet for a moment. He smoothed the back of his free hand over her cheek. "Do you want me to quit?"

Her eyes stretched at his words. "No." She shook her head, no doubt in her mind as to her answer. "I would never ask you to do that."

"I don't want you to be a nervous wreck every time I'm gone." His hand dropped from her cheek. "I could take a position at BUD/S. Be a teacher."

She almost laughed. "Funny."

"I'm serious."

She pivoted on her stool to better face him. "I love who you are, and I don't want to change you. It may never get easy waiting for you, but I want you to be happy."

"I am happy. Finally."

"We can revisit this conversation when you're in your forties." She smiled. "That was when you originally planned to retire, right?" She thought back to what he'd told her about running the bar with his brother.

He released a lungful of air. "Deal." Their arms fell between them, and he leaned forward to kiss her.

"But why are we here, at this exact spot?"

He sat up straight and took a sip of his drink. "Because the night I met you here changed my life."

"But I lied to you; doesn't that taint the memories?"

"That's why we're here. To make new memories." His brows lifted and fell quickly and he tilted his head toward the DJ who played the song *"Something Just Like This,"* by the Chainsmokers and Coldplay.

"Perfect song, huh?"

He stood and extended his palm. "I'm Owen York. I love flying, chasing down bad guys, and hot fudge sundaes." He shook her hand, and she chuckled. "And I love you so damn much."

She rose, allowing his warm hand to continue to envelop hers. "I'm Samantha McCarthy, and I'm starting to hate flying a little less, and I'm beginning to believe in fairy tales and superheroes. And I'm never opposed to ice cream."

He gently yanked her against him, her body colliding with his.

"Oh!" She smiled. "And I love you, too."

* * *

Two Weeks Later - Charleston

"You have to wear the blindfold. I don't trust you won't look." Sam folded her arms and glared at Owen.

"Fine. Fine." He surrendered his palms, and she wrapped

a red tie around his eyes and knotted it. "But I'm telling you, I'll pass your test."

"Sure, you can identify every smell. Blah blah. Heard it before." She went over to grab her prepared bottles from behind the bar.

The tavern was closed down for the winter, and so she and Owen had the place to themselves for the weekend.

Her gaze swung to the spot where Brad had proposed, but guilt didn't claw at her; in fact, she was pretty sure Brad and Jason would want nothing more than for them to be happy. Even her dad had told her last week, *"Brad would approve. Owen York is one hell of a man."* She didn't need her father to convince her of that, though.

"Okay." She came back in front of him and held an open bottle out.

He leaned forward and breathed in the scent. "Eucalyptus." He shook his head as if unimpressed by her attempt to outsmart his super-nose.

She waved the tin of coffee beans in front of him before offering the second scent. "Next one."

"Funny," he said. "You added basil to the aniseed. Nice try."

"Oh my God, you're ridiculous." She chuckled.

He shrugged and his smile stretched.

"Okay. Give me a second. I have something you won't guess."

She hurried around to the side of the bar, where she'd asked Owen's neighbor from the townhouse next door to wait for her.

"Thank you," she said in a hushed voice, and the old man saluted her before she tentatively walked back inside.

Before she had a chance to test Owen's nose, a howl erupted at her side, and Owen quickly shoved off the tie and stood. His eyes fell to the dog on the leash, and she lifted her shoulders.

"What's going on?" He crouched to pet the dog. "Why do you have a Siberian Husky?"

She squatted along the other side of the black and white dog and found Owen's eyes, but the dog lifted his nose and bumped her in the face.

"When we were in Mexico, it got me to thinking about what you said about having a dog."

"Okay." He cocked his head, still petting the dog.

She stood upright and pressed her palms to her hips. "When I was grabbing us breakfast in town yesterday morning, I saw this handsome guy at a rescue shelter. His blue eyes roped me in."

"That's why you were gone so long?" He arched a brow.

She nodded. "I have to bring him back later for the rest of the papers and stuff, but they let me bring him here to meet you first."

"You're adopting him?" He rose and cupped the back of his neck.

"We work a lot, but maybe between the two of us—we could take care of him?" Nerves tangled in her throat. "He needed a home, and I thought who better to—"

Owen sidestepped the dog, grabbed hold of her, and kissed her, seizing her words and her train of thought. But at the feel of the dog's paws at their sides, he released her and laughed.

"I think he's letting me know you're his," he said with a smile.

"There's enough of me for the both of you." She swallowed and reached down to pet him again. "His name is Ollie, and he's ten. Old, I know. But, I mean, he was born the year that . . ." She let her words trail off, knowing Owen would connect the dots.

"I love him." He dropped to one knee to get closer to Ollie, but extended a hand to her, only to surprise her by pulling her to the ground next to him.

He fell all the way back, and Ollie climbed up on top of his chest as if to make the claim that he'd be the alpha of the house.

Good luck with that. "I really like him."

"Yeah, as long as he doesn't try and kick me out of bed at night, we'll be good." Owen sat upright and reached out to scratch the back of Ollie's ear. "She's all mine in the bedroom, you got it? No compromising on that."

Ollie got up on his hind legs and began to howl.

"Thank you," he said, and she could hear the emotion catching in his throat.

"For the dog?"

"For everything." Water started to pool in his eyes, and her lip trembled at the sight. "For making me so damn happy." He reached for her and pulled her onto his lap.

"Then I should be thanking you, too." A flutter of quick kisses met her lips, and her heart tripled in size. "There's no place in the world I'd rather be than with you."

*

If you missed the first bonus scene for the Stealth Ops Series - be sure to download your free copy - see my website: brittneysahin.com.

New Bonus Scenes: *A Stealth Ops Christmas* features mini-stories for Owen & Sam, Luke & Eva, and Asher & Jessica. *It's recommended you read the prologue for *Finding the Fight* before reading *A Stealth Ops Christmas.*

A Stealth Ops World Guide is now available on my website, which features more information about the team, character muses, and SEAL lingo.

ALSO BY BRITTNEY SAHIN

A Stealth Ops World Guide is now available on my website, which features more information about the team, character muses, and SEAL lingo.

Hidden Truths

The Safe Bet – Begin the series with the Man-of-Steel lookalike Michael Maddox.

Beyond the Chase - Fall for the sexy Irishman, Aiden O'Connor, in this romantic suspense.

The Hard Truth – Read Connor Matthews' story in this second-chance romantic suspense novel.

Surviving the Fall – Jake Summers loses the last 12 years of his life in this action-packed romantic thriller.

The Final Goodbye - Friends-to-lovers romantic mystery

Stealth Ops Series: Bravo Team

Finding His Mark - Luke & Eva

Finding the Fight - Asher & Jessica

Finding Her Chance - Liam & Emily

Becoming Us

Someone Like You - A former Navy SEAL. A father. And off-limits. (Noah Dalton)

My Every Breath - A sizzling and suspenseful romance. Businessman Cade King has fallen for the wrong woman. She's the daughter of a hitman - and he's the target.

Dublin Nights

On the Edge - Travel to Dublin and get swept up in this romantic suspense starring an Irish businessman by day…and fighter by night.

On the Line - novella

Stand-alone (with a connection to *On the Edge*):

The Story of Us– Sports columnist Maggie Lane has 1 rule: never fall for a player. One mistaken kiss with Italian soccer star Marco Valenti changes everything…

PLAYLIST

Something Just Like This - The Chainsmokers/Coldplay
Body - Loud Luxury, Brando
Youngblood - Marshmello, Bastille
Two Souls - Joseph Gallo
Despacito, Remix - Luis Fonsi, Daddy Yankee (Feat. Bieber)
Whatever It Takes - Imagine Dragons
Shape of You - Ed Sheeran
Get Low - Zedd, Liam Payne

Check out the playlist on Spotify

CONNECT

Thank you for reading Owen and Samantha's story. If you don't mind taking a minute to leave a short review, I would greatly appreciate it. Reviews are incredibly helpful to us authors! Thank you!

www.brittneysahin.com
brittneysahin@emkomedia.net
FB Reader Group - Brittney's Book Babes
Stealth Ops Spoiler Room

Made in the USA
Coppell, TX
11 July 2021

58842831R10184